ADVANCE PRAISE FOR *SLEEP OVER*

"A book that gains momentum as it unfolds, taking a truly panoramic approach to a worldwide apocalypse that's both unexpected and unsettling to read. Highly original and recommended."

—Cat Sparks, author of *Lotus Blue*

"Prepare for many sleepless nights. *Sleep Over* is richly realized, and I fully admit: reading the dozens of accounts of what would be personal hell was instead an absolute pleasure."

—Andrew Post, author of *Aftertaste*

"Bells creates some truly memorable, haunting images and vivid scenes that stay with you long after your eyelids are closed. Whether or not you get any sleep is another matter entirely."

—Mike Bockoven, author of *FantasticLand* and *Pack*

"H.G. Bells is brilliant in this chilling, down-to-earth tale that illustrates with frightening ease just how close to disaster our society really is."

—Bennett R. Coles, author of *March of War*

AN ORAL HISTORY OF THE APOCALYPSE

SLEEP OVER

H. G. BELLS

TALOS PRESS
NEW YORK

Talos Press books may be purchased in bulk at special discounts for sales promotion, corporate gifts, fund-raising, or educational purposes. Special editions can also be created to specifications. For details, contact the Special Sales Department, Talos Press, 307 West 36th Street, 11th Floor, New York, NY 10018 or info@skyhorsepublishing.com.

Talos Press® is a registered trademark of Skyhorse Publishing, Inc.®, a Delaware corporation.

Visit our website at www.talospress.com.

10 9 8 7 6 5 4 3 2 1

Library of Congress Cataloging-in-Publication Data

Names: Bells, H. G., author.
Title: Sleep over : an oral history of the apocalypse / H. G. Bells.
Description: New York : Talos, 2017.
Identifiers: LCCN 2016018136 | ISBN 9781940456690 (paperback)
Subjects: LCSH: Insomnia--Fiction. | BISAC: FICTION / Horror. | FICTION / Science Fiction / General. | FICTION / Suspense. | GSAFD: Horror fiction. | Suspense fiction.
Classification: LCC PR9199.4.B4577 S54 2017 | DDC 813/.6--dc23
LC record available at https://lccn.loc.gov/2016018136

eISBN: 9781940456720

Cover design by Jason Snair

Printed in the United States of America

This book is for my friends and family. Your support over the years has been amazing. At last, here's that thing I've been working towards my whole life. Thanks for coming along for the ride, and for all the help along the way.

Love,
H. G.

PART 1
THE FIRST DAYS

Foreword from the editor

If there had been a great bolt of lightning or a thunderclap, if the earth had shaken, if a blood moon had risen and cast a hellish pall over the whole world, we would have had some event to point to and say "There, there is where the end of the world began." No dogs howled, no wave of prickling goosebumps swept over our skin, no measurable occurrence registered in any of the things we love to measure. The end of the world began not with something happening, but with something *not* happening. And because we don't do well with understanding danger from absence, and most people didn't know that going without sleep is fatal, the whole world began to die.

Every person on earth and in orbit around the earth ceased to be able to sleep. It was instantaneous.

Each one of the survivors that contributed to this collection managed to crawl through the seemingly never-ending gamut of the insomnia and emerge on the other side. It's with many shards of story, each one a window into that time, that we can begin to see a whole picture of what nearly wiped us off the face of the earth.

At times I almost dream
—Graffiti on the roof of The O2, London, England

Did you know that, without sleep, human beings die? Because no one told me. I mean sure, us projectionist types, people that work in the night, we have messed up sleeping schedules. People in our lives are always telling us we need to get more sleep, get *better* sleep, sleep between the optimal hours of 10:00 p.m. and 2:00 a.m. (*thanks mom*), but no one ever talks about what happens when people *stop* sleeping.

We die.

And not like, in a few years we die. In a month. In weeks. In *days*.

In those early nights though, on that first day, hardly anyone knew that.

I went to work as normal, pretty groggy, but able to drag my feet up through the fire exit stairwell into my projection booth, able to thread up the first set. Digital cinema was taking over the world, but little places like us were last on the list for conversion. People in Lima didn't seem to mind watching 35 millimeter *film* films, or at least, when given the choice between the more expensive digital ticket price and our price, we could at least hold our own against our larger competitors. I certainly didn't mind projecting it; it was fun, and I got quite good at it.

Well, when I wasn't sleep deprived I was good at it. That first day, after one missed night of sleep, I made three mistakes, but they were injuries to my skin, and not damage to the film prints, thank god.

Most everyone has missed a night of sleep at some point in their life. Staying up all night studying, worrying, working. So the morning after night number one, everyone was pretty sour, but it's not like we knew the end of the world was beginning.

Social media had exploded in the night. #whycantisleep #massinsomnia #fuck4AM and a myriad of other hashtags spoke to the collective frustration and confusion over the lack of sleep. I didn't use social media a ton, but that's how overwhelming the response was—it still made its way back to me, even without a Twitter account, even without much of anything. Print news didn't have anything on it in the morning, it was too slow for that; but all the TVs in the Tube and at the coffee kiosks had crawls of every sort of headline pulled from the internet. I made it to work okay and continued on, hoping to learn what had caused the night of sleeplessness after my shift.

As usual, I went up to the booth to be alone without speaking to a single other employee.

I threaded up for the day, feet dragging, head groggy, eyes sore.

I took my break by the freight elevator that we used for film deliveries. It was the only place my phone got any reception, and the best place to catch the news while I took my break for dinner, between the first evening set and the last, while most people were already in bed.

The news had an expert on to say something about how solar radiation can mess with our brain function, but we normally don't notice it. *Well we sure noticed it this time*, joked the anchor.

At some point in all our lives, we learn what our threshold for detecting patterns is. For most of us, it's three instances of something. Someone comes to a film three Tuesdays in a row, I expect them on the fourth. My bus driver every Friday is Julio, and he's wearing a pink knitted hat and has a strangely spiced coffee scent wafting around his driver's seat; after I'd seen his setup for the third time it was no longer remarkable. I expected it.

But flip a coin three times, and it comes up heads each time? Gotta be tails next, right? Even though the odds of it landing heads is exactly the same as it was for all three previous flips: 50 percent.

Which is why we didn't get it right away. One night without sleep was still huge, don't get me wrong, but like I said, no one had ever talked about a sleep apocalypse before. It wasn't in the public consciousness that this would be our undoing. It was just something to excite the news media, to speculate over the water cooler about, to use as an excuse to say those terse words you've been holding back.

"Sorry, I'm just so goddamn *tired*," must have been the phrase of the second day. Everywhere you went, people were grumpy and short tempered, sour and mean.

But that's not what you asked me to write about, so I'll talk about that first day, the day after the first night. Or maybe the first night bears a mention? I think there were two types of people that first night, like every night before that. Those who would lay in bed awake, wondering if they should just get up and do something until they felt sleepy, until they gave in and got up. The other type of person lay in bed and tried to will themselves to fall asleep. Some people have breathing exercises. Some people go to a happy place that their mind can wander around in until it transitions to a dream.

In both cases there's a lot of glancing at the clock. Calculating. *If I fall asleep right now, I'll still get . . .* —fingers tapping out the number of hours while the mind advances the clock—*four and a half hours of sleep.*

I was fond of the getting up method, just doing stuff to occupy me until my mind could get it together to fall asleep. The first sleepless night, I watched a show I was binge-watching, played a bit of Hearts, and had a go at fixing the HD antenna I had made from a two-by-four and coat hangers. I liked to stay away from screens, as in the past I'd found that it only hindered my ability to fall back asleep. In between each of these, I went back to bed, and lay there for an hour. Giving it a good try, of falling asleep. An hour was long enough to really give it a shot, but tolerable enough if it still wasn't happening.

That night, it wasn't like my mind was racing, or doing anything really. It just *wasn't sleeping*.

I think people like me, we understood something was way more wrong, right from the get-go. Though you're not really, really sure. . . . Until you see something.

Like I said, I bumbled around the projection booth that first day. I had six projectors to keep track of and run at the same time. The start times were offset so I could go from one to the next and do my dance, threading the film through their rollers and clamping them into the teeth that fit in the sprocket holes to pull the acetate through the aperture at twenty four frames a second. You only have to do it a few hundred times to get the hang of it, and then maybe another few thousand to really get the feel for those beasts. I'd been there seven years. Six projectors, twice each on a shift, five shifts a week: I'd threaded up somewhere around the neighborhood of twenty-one thousand times. More because of rentals and special showings, but also less because of the rare sick day.

So yeah, I was good at the dance. Got good at fixing things on the fly, too. On normal days, my hands knew what to do, and they did it without me having to tell them.

The first time I hurt myself was at number three. I was pulling the head of the leader (that's the junk film I can get my grimy fingerprints all over as I'm getting it threaded into the projector). Down around the foil sensor, loopdy-loop around the soundtrack reader. Down over the big toothed roller that held it steady in front of the apert—clamping my finger between the intermittent pad and the toothed sprocket. I snatched my finger out from between the teeth and roller and snapped it back and forth a few times. No one was up there with me to hear if I swore, but I was never one to lose my cool, even bitten by a roller like that. It hurt, but there was no blood drawn. I'd done it before.

I was grumbling about it to no one but myself as I rounded the corner of the garbage chute room when I clipped my arm against the key, sticking out of the round doorknob. I did swear this time, but could hardly be mad at it.

It was just a door into a little recessed closet, with a hatch to the garbage chute. One of my favorite things was throwing old projector bulbs, secured in their boxes with foam padding, down that chute and hearing them explode at the bottom. Compressed xenon gas glass hand grenades. Usually touching that key was enough to make me smile with memories of hearing the echo of a spent bulb bursting, a shocking death knell from a faithful piece of equipment. So when instead I clipped my arm on the key and swore, it wasn't long before I composed myself and forgave the key. I threw some paper tape over the jagged scrape that had left about an inch of my skin bleeding.

And like I said, I didn't do anything that had hurt the film. But that third mistake was the one that told me something was really wrong.

"Projection?" came the call over my radio. They always said *Projection*, even though it was always me, on a weekday, always me.

I froze in my tracks. I had a network of hallways that led from projector to projector, and I paced them while I made sure everything was running fine, but until I knew where I needed to be running, I stopped; no sense heading in any direction until I knew it was the right one. I unclipped the radio from my belt, and pressed down its button harder than was strictly necessary.

"Projection here, what's up?" I asked.

"Number two is—" I started running "—uh, there's like, squiggly lines all over the left side of the screen," said the theatre checker. "And it's all out of focus. And there's no sound."

"Oh is *that* all?" I said, my voice bouncing with each step of my sprint down the number two hallway.

Indeed, it was as bad as all that. The squiggly lines were actually the soundtrack, and *seeing* them instead of hearing them meant that I had threaded the film in the gate inside-out. Worse, I'd missed the startup of the print. I should have been there right as those sprockets started pulling acetate through the gate at twenty-four frames a second. Why hadn't I?

"Tell them I'll be three minutes," I said, then tossed the radio indelicately onto the bottom of the three film platters, unused and still. It echoed a metal clang from the radio skittering across it as I worked to unclamp the projector and set it right.

It only took two minutes to fix (hey, I did mention that I was a damn *good* projectionist), and I got it back on screen while it was still in the trailers. No harm, no foul. In hindsight, I don't think the audience was going to be too harsh with me—not that I ever heard their complaints, but I could feel them, through the port glass that their films shot through onto their screen, I could feel them.

So those were my three mistakes. The two little physical injuries on their own were not remarkable. Even threading inside-out had happened to me once before. But put them all together in the space of an hour, and I knew something was wrong.

I went down to the office.

Prit, my manager, sat in front of one of the two office computers. She held a take-out coffee cup in one hand, up near her cheek, like she might be drawing warmth from it. She didn't seem to hear me come in. I cleared my throat, and she sat up a little straighter, but didn't turn around.

"I uh, I messed up threading number two. Everything's fine now, but, sorry. Threading error, audience interruption," I said. "Under two minutes, caught it in trailers." She turned and nodded. I could see she was tired too.

"No one slept last night," she said, matter-of-factly. "I'm following the news. I thought it was just me. But then Allesandro tried to call in 'sick' and Maria has burned two batches of popcorn tonight, and they told me—they haven't slept either. So now I ask you, with this threading mistake not even rookie-you would have made: did you sleep last night?" Prit was always eloquent. Even as the realization of her revelation was dawning on me, I found myself thinking that she was always clear and precise with her speech.

"So *no* one slept last night?" I answered her with my own question. She shook her head tiredly. But to me, no one at the theatre looked any different from how they'd look after we'd had a big opening. After the Marvel/DC crossover, when we'd had the busiest weekend of our existence, everyone looked like this. Tired, grumpy, slow.

"But this is different," I said to Prit. She nodded. Once I was aware of it, the smell of burnt popcorn enveloped us. It's something you get a little used to, working in a theatre.

"No one slept, here, but we'll see about back home soon enough," she said, *back home* being Jodhpur, India.

"Well goddamn," was all I could say. "What a weird thing." She nodded and turned back to the computer.

"Be careful with the rest of the night," she said. "Our damage deposit's never been lower thanks to you." Rare praise. I was hardly ever even out of the projection booth, and most of my communications with the other staff were about problems. Never about my prowess. So I puffed up a bit at this tidbit of flattery.

"And get a good sleep tonight," she added with a sideways glance.

I took my leave and wondered about the oddity that was a night without sleep. It was something to gripe about, something to shoot the shit with the boss about, something that was a curiosity.

I went back out into the lobby, which I had to cross to get to my preferred fire escape. Maria was at the bar, but her back was to me, as well as a line of people as she frantically scooped burnt popcorn off of the batch of good stuff that sat in the popper. Another burnt batch. My god. The lobby smelled bad. I crinkled my nose and hurried to get to my fire escape stairs, back up to solitary safety and the hum of my projectors. If everyone was bumbling around making mistakes, even me, then I'd have to put all my efforts into making sure the rest of the night went all right. They were here for the films after all.

An older gentleman came out of cinema one and was walking slowly across the lobby when our paths intersected near the front doors. I stopped out of politeness, but also curiosity.

"You're not staying?" I asked, knowing that number one was only forty-seven minutes into the feature, and that there was no reason for him to find it boring. Or too violent. Or crude. He was number one's target demographic and he should be sitting there glued to his seat.

"No, I feel like going for a walk," he said simply. We exchanged tired smiles and I acquiesced. There's no accounting for taste, as the saying goes. He walked out our front doors and I watched him go. I don't know why I watched him. Usually I would have been in a hurry to escape back to the safety of my booth. Usually I wouldn't have even said anything to anybody. But something was different. Maybe I was just slow from the fatigue. Or maybe I'd seen something in him.

So I watched him go. I watched as he made his way to the curb to cross the street. He didn't wait for the light to change though, and stepped out onto one of downtown's busiest streets. A bus shot through the intersection and hit him. It didn't stop right away, either. I heard the screech of tires half a block away.

Evolution Revolution? So much time for activities! Call if you still want to do stuff!

—Printout, with detachable phone number tags, on a cork board, Tamaulipas, Mexico

At first it was kind of fun.

It was all anyone could talk about, and we never got tired of talking about it. It was new. It was a small-talker's dream. At the office, people actually seemed to enjoy coming in, just to share whatever new tidbit they'd learned. The omnipresent hum of the lights was perhaps a little louder and more annoying, but I felt comfortable in the familiar arrangement of desk islands in the open plan office. Comfort in routine, comfort in the familiar faces that had become my second family.

It felt like a sleepover; a weird thing to equate it to, but it was that same feeling of quiet, punctuated by "Hey Jenny, are you awake?" "Yeah. You?" "Did you know that we used to be diurnal?" and then suddenly everyone in the surrounding desk islands were listening. Ginny in sales spoke to Fan, manning the secretary desk. Fan was a young man quite adept in sales himself, but he was filling in for the usual guy, who hadn't shown up that morning. He looked up with his huge brown eyes and I could see the whites all the way around them as he seemed jolted out of whatever he was doing. But then his lids dropped and he relaxed, and Ginny went on.

"Yeah, I was reading that we used to actually have two sleeps every night—at dusk was the first. Then we'd wake up and do stuff for a few hours. There's records of people like going and hanging out in the middle of the night, like leaving the house and doing stuff, because everyone was awake. And then we had what they call the Second Sleep, and get the rest of the night's sleep until dawn."

"Well what the heck, man," said Hackie, our IT guy, clearly able to hear just fine from beneath the desk he was working under.

His name was Hakimoto (sorry if I butcher the spelling—even on his commendation plaque his name is Hackie) but I guess it was too perfectly like a "hacker" to not earn him the nickname. His sleek attire was a departure from the expected garb of "one who works in IT," and I was constantly trying to steal fashion tips from his style.

"So what, people would like, go to a movie?" asked Fan, clearly more interested in Ginny than about what she was saying.

"No, silly—" ah, it was reciprocal perhaps, for how long I wondered "—it was before electricity." Fan made some hand-waving gesture.

"So a play, then," he supposed.

"No, no, nothing big like that. It was just for a few hours, and it was a quiet time. An In-Between-Time, some called it. I mean, most people stayed home and read or did quiet things in the candlelight. The ones that went out are more interesting because they left more of a record. Two sides of the story recorded then, corroboration," said Ginny. Fan nodded and Hackie stood from his wire adjusting under the desk and stretched out his back. Shirt tail deliberately untucked? Or an oversight in dressing due to fatigue? Didn't matter, looked casual and good on him.

"I had a prof," he started, and it was like a sleepover again—this was the conspiratorial call to garner a listening audience, even though Ginny had already set one up for him. "He wanted to see how little sleep he could get away with having, so he started chopping fifteen minutes off of his nights. Each month he'd take it down another fifteen minutes. He'd been at it more than a year when he told us about it, and by then he was down to under four hours a night."

"Jesus and they let him teach? Was he a mess or what?" asked Fan.

"Seemed fine," said Hackie with a shrug. "Said he had a lot of extra time for things." This was directed over Ginny's table to Walt, who'd abandoned any pretense of work for the last several hours, and was methodically painting a miniature game figurine. "What do you think Walt, more time for painting?" said Hackie, trying to draw him in.

"More time, but more mistakes." He sighed, tiny paintbrush hovering over his work, a slight shake in his hand translating to a huge jitter at the tip of the brush. "I'd rather sleep and get it right in two hours instead of effing it up and taking three to do a shitty job in the end anyway." He held up the piece he was working on, inspected it dramatically, for our benefit, sighed, put it down, and leaned back in his chair.

"Quality, not quantity for you then," said Hackie. "For my prof anyway, he seemed to learn how to live with it. Said he would drop right into delta wave sleep as soon as his head hit the pillow."

"Did you ever try it?" I asked.

"Hell no, I need my full seven hours or I'm a mess," he said.

"Seven!" said Fan, eyebrows up and making his broad forehead into a canvass of wrinkled valleys and rolling hills. "I need at least eight or I end up biting someone's head off the next day," he said, frowning at Ginny in what I guessed was an apology for some past digression, explained by a night of less-than-eight.

"Why is it so different for everyone . . . why do we all need different amounts?" asked Ginny to no one in particular.

"Did you ever stay up a whole night?" asked Walt after a pause in the conversation, abandoning his painting in earnest now.

"I guess kind of, but I went to sleep in the morning."

"What?" said Hackie. "You didn't have stuff to do the next day?"

"Well, no, it was during a vacation," he said.

"And did you wake up in the afternoon and then sleep normally the next night?" continued Hackie, intrigued with Fan's seemingly alien experience.

"No actually, I slept straight through to the next morning."

"You slept for twenty-four hours?!" said Hackie.

"What? I had to reset myself and I was tired. Have you guys never—" he asked, seeing all of us aghast at his anecdote.

"No man, god no, how on earth can someone sleep for twenty-four hours?" said Walt. "You stay up the whole night, you make it through the next day and just go to bed a little earlier the next night to fix it."

"Yeah man," said Hackie, "unless you have to stay up that night too."

Hackie upping the ante. He was not usually one to play the one-up game, so we took him at his word when he told us this.

"Two nights?" said Fan. "Wouldn't you get some kind of kernel panic?" Ooh, throwing out a computer term at the IT guy; bold move, Fan-from-sales-masquerading-as-a-secretary . . . Hackie shook his head.

"And the day after too. Day, night, day, night, day— then sleep. Ten hours that night, I'll admit, but after that I was fine." We were quiet for a while after, mulling over these new tidbits, formulating the next part of the conversation.

It was a practiced repartee between us. Sometimes the conversation would begin in the morning, we'd be quiet and diligent workers almost until the clock was up, and then we'd resume like no gap had occurred between part one and part two of our discussion.

Sometimes we did this deliberately around our boss, and he joked that we'd developed some sort of group telepathy from being in the same room for so long. We enjoyed the notion and even went so far as to plan little bits of conversation ahead of time, to play into his rather charming idea. He would sometimes pretend that he was in on it too, and make some response with a wink, as if it were all part of the arrangement. I think sometimes he got lonely in his office. The rest of us out here, having our sleepover moments, and he, alone, doing—what could he possibly be doing on day three? What were any of us really doing?

Comforting each other.

I caught a glimpse of the boss man, peering at us through the venetian blinds of his office. He caught my eye, gave me a slight nod, and withdrew back into invisibility.

I think he knew that he would break the spell by joining in. It just wasn't the same with him around. He was a nice guy and all, but the mood just sort of changes when the boss is around, no matter how personable they are. What he was doing in the office though, *was* part of the spell. He was the one casting it.

Other office managers told people they didn't have to come in any more. Most didn't want to be there themselves, so it was their ticket out, during *the time*. But not ours. Danie Greyston was the reason why it was fun for us. He let it happen, let us keep coming in.

Those first few days were a riot.

Fan cooked some phở for us in the break room on the second night, and we sat around and told stories of great food we'd eaten. Ginny brought out some cupcakes she'd made for desert, and they had had spirals of icing on them.

"What is this supposed to be?" asked Hackie, turning a cupcake over for inspection.

"Like a hypnotist's thing," she said, waving one up in front of Fan's face. "You are getting sleepy, sleeeepy," she said. Fan lurched forwards and chomped into the cupcake. Ginny looked shocked, then laughed and smushed the rest of it against his lips. He recoiled and caught it as it tumbled away from him.

"It's delicious," he said though chewing. And they were. Gentle orange flavors with a hint of cinnamon in the spiral icing.

On our way out that night, we saw the sway of the blinds in Danie's office, a giveaway of his hasty retreat, perhaps from watching across the open office into the break room window. We exchanged some guilty glances, knowing we were having a good time while he was alone, in there.

"Here," said Ginny, handing Fan one of the leftover cupcakes. "Go," she said, gently prodding him towards our boss's office. Fan hesitated, then strode forwards and knocked boldly on the door.

Danie called from within, and Fan stepped in, leaving the door open. Danie was behind his desk, some stacks of papers on either side of him, an important looking notepad splayed out across his keyboard.

"Gettin' it done?" asked Fan.

"Lots," said our boss. "Loads. Oh, is that for me?" he asked. Fan leaned in and presented him with the cupcake. Danie leaned aside so he could see us through his doorway. We were getting ready to head out, hats and coats and all that, but watching him nonetheless. He waved the cupcake at us.

"You are all getting sleepy, sleeeeepy," he said.

"See!?" said Ginny. We smiled at him.

"Have a good night everyone," he said. "See you tomorrow." We nodded and left.

He always stayed until we were ready to go. Even on the nights when it started to get bad and we didn't even leave—he stayed with us. Near us. He was never invited to our sleepovers, but without him we wouldn't have had them.

"Move fast and break things. Unless you are breaking stuff, you are not moving fast enough." —Mark Zuckerberg #movefast #breakstuff #DayofIdeas

—Front page of Facebook on their "Day of Ideas"

Can you even imagine being the marketing firm that had just launched the "Tired of sleeping?" campaign? The aerosolized spray meant to keep you awake? Can you imagine getting that email forward? The one with only the work "**FUCK**" in the subject line. The email that linked to the most popular clickbait site that had a list of *Top Ten Most Likely Causes the World Can't Sleep*. Clicking it. Seeing your product at the bottom as Suspect Number One. Seeing the "*We're not saying this is a marketing stunt, but if it is holy fuck you made your point!*" at the bottom of the page.

Of course we had nothing to do with it. No, we didn't somehow disperse it in the atmosphere with those Falcon 12 rockets tests; no, we didn't somehow fuck up and accidentally release a contagious form of our compound; no, it wasn't a marketing stunt. I mean for christsakes it's a goddamn energy drink, only in aerosol form. But because we were different and we were new, and we launched right before the insomnia hit, of course we were responsible.

My social media team was on it. But all it took was one goddamned wrong-footed tweet and we went up in flames like a moth over a campfire.

"@TiredofSleeping Looks like it works!"

What. The. Absolute. Fuck. Were they thinking? There's no such thing as bad publicity? Do you know how many people died because of that tweet? I don't, and I never want to. Some stupid ass intern thinking they were helping us out fucking threw a goddamn water balloon full of gasoline on the campfire. All us moths warming ourselves near the gentle and lucrative flames of energy products had our wings melted off in a fireball and plummeted into the inferno.

The ensuing Twitter war dwarfed any online spectacle that had come before it. It transitioned from digital to meatspace impressively quick. The reaction videos, the videos of people burning our product, of people trying our product, of that corner store clerk getting held down and sprayed with it . . . The doxing, the DDOSing, the office printer getting hacked and printing death threats and pictures of beheadings. The explosion at the Redbull factory was related, I'm sure. As was the mobbing of that research lab.

The talk shows that had experts on to talk in our defense couldn't save us, nor could the hourly tweets we put out to educate the public about our product in an attempt to acquit ourselves in the court of public opinion.

We tried releasing the test results that showed that our product was actually pretty ineffective, we tried tweeting the videos of people trying our product and falling asleep (from before, of course).

Fake.

Liars.

Die in a fire.

I wonder if your canisters can fit into an eye socket; I am going to find out.

Tweets of the addresses of our employees, our distributors, the artists that designed the label, the freaking timetable of our release schedule.

After that, I packed as many supplies as I could and went to my friend's cabin in the mountains.

For the record, we didn't cause it. We were just the first easy scapegoat, and we were a sign of things to come.

Survive and try again; the world needs parents like you.

—Handwritten note in a "Congratulations, It's a Boy!" card, Jackson Memorial Hospital, Miami, Florida, United States

People in the medical profession, especially in a high-volume hospital like Jackson Memorial, are no strangers to sleep deprivation. The morning after, I mean the first morning after that first night, everyone was just overtaxed. I think everyone had gone through that before; been up all night studying, or had to take a late shift or something. Us nurses especially.

And yet it was worse than that. Before, it was just you, just the one in a group wherever you went that had missed out on a night's sleep. We were all used to having to cover for someone at the end of a huge shift, when they got sloppy, or when they were at the end of their rotation and were exhausted.

But that first morning, it was everyone. And no one was understanding, no one was accommodating. Everyone was off in their own little hells, sullen and angry and grumpy and just trying to function.

We were trying to keep up with a night shift that should have been quiet but instead was full of people who, when not asleep, had nothing better to do than worry why they weren't asleep. So the people getting off night shift were not happy. And the people getting on in the morning were equally unhappy, having been up all night.

I sulked in the break room off of obstetrics. People were guzzling coffee. I dug out the old coffee machine that we had replaced a while back. The new one was nicer, but the old one still worked, so I put it to use, so there was even more java to be had by the constant trickle of people, all bleary eyed, all desperate to focus and attend to the day. I got out my sticky note pad and drew a smiley face on it and stuck it to the old coffee pot. It was a sad attempt at a peace offering, but I liked to think that a smile was usually helpful. A smile *and* a fresh pot of coffee? Well, no one wants to work with a sourpuss, so maybe it was more self-serving than I realized at the time. I stared at the sticky-smiley as the coffee began pouring out of the filter and into the carafe, and tried to heed my own advice. I managed a meagre smile.

Things were pretty standard at first. The tiredness was there, sure, but I mean the workload was much the same. We went about the business of doing our jobs, if not well, then at least adequately. Until around noon, when a woman was bussed to Emerg. in early labor. She was a patient here before, and her due date wasn't for another three months. Her doctor was miraculously on shift, and I and several others assisted him in such a task as he hoped to never have to face.

It was all hands on deck trying to save a preemie and her mother. Dangerous, but not unsalvageable. Modern medicine has become so advanced, compared to our past methods, that we sometimes forget how dangerous childbirth is. You don't expect a woman to die in childbirth, not in one of the best hospitals, with the best doctors, in a first world country. Well maybe the public doesn't expect it, but when you are in the business of handling births, you know it's a possibility. I'd lost one mother before, the only patient I'd ever lost, and it was as horrible as I'd feared it would be. She had gone into labor three months early too, which is why, when this patient came in to us after a night when none of us had slept, I felt the pang of terror and guilt and sadness hit me in the guts. Every patient is different. I needed to not have some weird PTSD trigger; I needed to be able to deal with women who were in labor three months early. I sucked it up and put on a happy face and talked to her.

When I asked if anything had been wrong recently, she said that she couldn't sleep. The obvious was everywhere, with every conversation we heard that no one had slept, with every glance we could see it etched into people's faces. And yet there's something so powerful about **denial** . . . and also about childbirth. We got her through it, and that overshadowed what was actually the larger symptom of all encompassing, inexplicable insomnia. We didn't understand the scope of it yet, even if it was plastered all over social media and digital news outlets.

Our second early labor came in at two, our third half an hour after that. Within six hours, every available space in obstetrics and emergency was taken up by mothers going into premature labor. Every length of gestation. Not all were early labor; many expectant mothers rushed to us with the feeling that "something was wrong," which they were usually right about; it was a flip of the coin whether an expectant mother went into early labor or whether examination revealed an intrauterine fetal death.

We set up a triage for all the women coming to us for help. The ones in early labor were sent straight into delivery so we could try and save the mother's life. After a few of those deliveries, we realized that we weren't going to save any of the babies. I couldn't yet tell you why they were going into early labor, but my guess was that it was a combination of the stress on the mother and the disruption of the neonatal REM sleep cycle. Or there was something else at work, something that we still do not understand . . . it couldn't have been insomnia alone that killed all of humanity's unborn, could it?

The ones who had in-utero deaths were shuttled to psychiatric, where we called in every available councilor, social worker, psychiatrist, or otherwise remotely qualified person that we could to help them cope with having their baby die inside them, and have to wait to have anything done about it.

The ones who were coming to us in distress, the ones at or near term, were sent for further assessment. Many of those, I am pleased to say, ended up giving birth to healthy babies. They were robust enough that the early days of insomnia were distressing, but not fatal. At least not until after they were born.

For hours, it was chaos. Running from one mother to the next, trying your best to do your specific task or pick up the slack when someone wasn't there for theirs; god, it was a frantic, awful mess. And yet we functioned like a well-oiled machine, even with all that; we did our jobs and did them well, though sometimes maybe our sterilization practices weren't quite up to code. When the seemingly never-ending stream of women finally abated, we were exhausted, shell-shocked, numb, devastated . . .

I was shaking. A support staff came by and handed me a Danish.

"Eat this honey," she said. "When did you get on?" she asked.

"Ten," I answered.

"Ten . . . three hours ago?" she asked, perplexed.

"What time is it?" I said incredulously.

"Honey it's one o'clock in the afternoon."

"Tuesday?" I asked.

"Wednesday," she answered. She fished into her support bag and handed me a protein bar.

"You eat this right this minute," she commanded. I did. I'd been on for twenty-seven hours, and twenty-three of them had been filled with the most death and sadness that a person could experience.

Twenty-three hours of the city losing its next generation. Even with the few newborns that had been successfully delivered at term being swaddled and warmed in the incubators, I couldn't shake the feeling that they would soon face the terrible consequences that lack of sleep wreaked on a developing brain.

The grief was there, but it was overpowered by denial. Bewilderment and denial. It couldn't have possibly just happened like that. Perhaps it just didn't hit me right away.

I had a cry. The support sat there with her hand on my back as I clutched the protein bar and cried. It was brutal, but it was quick. A few wracking sobs that made my face feel like I would break all the capillaries in it. As it was, it just forced out a stream of tears from both eyes. I indulged for a moment, then took some gasping breaths which transitioned to quivering, deliberate deeper breathing. I wiped my eyes.

"Eyeliner check?" I asked the support staff, as part of *pulling it together*. She nodded. "Then we've got more work to do," I said, standing. She held onto the fabric of my scrubs and didn't let me leave.

"Finish it," she said. I took a big bite out of the bar, chewed it enough, and popped the last of it into my mouth. She let me go.

I got on the phone to my friend over at St. Joseph's.

"Angie?" I said. There was a tremor in her voice as she answered. "You too?"

"All those babies," I said, covering my mouth with my hand.

"Oh Maddie, what is happening?" she said, her voice cracking.

"I'll see if anyone's called the CDC," I said.

I hurried to the head administrator's office. He was already on a call; it was on speaker phone. He paced back and forth, with a cell phone pressed against his ear, on a second call.

The speaker phone line was busy. He slammed a finger on the receiver and redialed, keeping the other phone pressed to his ear. He hadn't noticed me yet, but I took a step inside, towards one of the chairs across from his desk. I caught his eye and I gestured at the phone. He nodded. It connected as I sat, and we were put on hold. I ate a sandwich I'd remembered I'd thrown together before my shift. We were in a hold cue for *two hours. Please do not hang up and call back; your call will be answered more quickly if you stay on the line.*

While I waited, I went in and out of the office to help with other things as they needed me. I made more coffee, three times, sending grounds spilling into the sink on my first try. After I put on the third pot, I turned the chair in the office to face out the window in the corner and watched as doctors and nurses came and went without seeing me. But eventually people noticed and word got out that we were in queue at the CDC, and people trickled in to hear the call. When we finally got through, the administrator's office was packed with people waiting.

As it rang, he turned to us, all his gathered staff.

"What do I even tell them?" he asked, exhausted. Someone picked up on the other end.

"CDC, hello this is Gwenevive, please report your location and situation," she said hastily. I jumped right in.

"My name is Maddie Hopkins, and I work in the obstetrics department of Jackson Memorial Hospital, and today, all of our expectant mothers came in and either went into premature labor, or presented with intrauterine fetal demise."

The operator was so matter-of-fact, so cold, almost dismissive, that it felt like a slap to the face: "What percentage of each, how many babies did you lose, how many mothers did you lose, and how many did you manage to deliver?" came the voice on the other end. Such a blasé reaction to the most horrible thing everyone present had ever witnessed.

"Um," I started. What percentage? What kind of reaction is that? The kind where they were gathering data. No shock. This was not news to her. I was one of an unending number of calls exactly like this for her today.

"Um, we lost . . ." I tried to count the numbers in my head.

A doctor, the attending doctor who had dealt with the first death of the night, stepped in to answer, referring to a chart on which he'd done up some math.

"Twenty percent of the mothers. We lost perhaps 90 percent of the babies; the other 10 percent were at or over term. We delivered seven successfully, all of the mothers survived." That felt good to hear.

"And they are healthy?" she asked again, cold, calculating, dry.

"As far as we can tell. But if they don't sleep . . ." The attending physician's shoulders tensed. Another nurse put her hand on his back to comfort him. I could feel an edge of desperation and righteous anger creeping its way into my gut, into my voice, uncontainable in my exhaustion. And certainly unquenchable.

"What's going on? What do we do?"

"We don't know yet. Monitor the newborns, and the other infants in your neonatal unit. We're starting to lose them."

"What? What do you mean, lose them? Is it a flu? Is it a virus?" I asked, desperate for her to elaborate on the one piece of information she offered us, so it was not just a one-way transference of mortality statistics.

"Turn on your news, there will be a CDC press conference on all stations in one half hour. It will answer some questions." Then the line went dead.

The attending physician spoke to the administrator, his cell still pressed to his ear, waiting on another call to god knows who. The rest of us who were just beginning to experience the true nature of the tragedy listened to the exchange, hoping to glean some hope, some sense of the shape of things.

"They need sleep to form their neural connections. The extreme stress of it is going to affect the youngest first," he said, without elaborating on what that would mean. *Affect*.

"If that's all that's going on," said the attending.

"To your stations. We will save who we can," said the administrator. He put his cell phone down and I could see that it wasn't even turned on. That whole time, a dead phone pressed to his ear. Jesus.

We dispersed, and many people rushed with me to the incubation room. Doctors were already crowded around one of the newborns, trying to save its life. A nurse called out from another infant's incubator. I hurried to help her. The infant's eyes bugged out, wide, searching left and right, scanning randomly.

"He's having a heart attack," said the nurse. "I need the baby de-fib!" she shouted over her shoulder at the others attending to another infant. Another baby's alarm went off.

Today's Specials:
Insomnia Bomber: Four shots espresso &
5 mg of amphetamine—$45
Blaze of Glory: Six shots espresso &
800 mg THC drops—$23
—Sandwich board outside Confeitaria Colombo, Rio de Janeiro, Brazil

No one was buying my coffee, but that was okay. I was just glad that they were stopping by. I had a sign by the till that read CDC PRESS CONFERENCE: 5:00 P.M., and the crowd gathering were those that couldn't be home in time to catch it. So I turned up the volume and passed out some cups of water. This was day two, after two nights of sleeplessness. The world was worried, but not panicked—not yet. Not when the internet gave us unending venting capacity, where we could let waves of commiseration wash over us from every angle now that the Eastern hemisphere had had their first night of insomnia.

Funny how the timing of it cost us a day. Because it happened during the day for China, for India, and early in the morning for Europe, they didn't really see what was happening until they had their first night. Even though the Americas knew that something was terribly wrong, for everyone else all over the globe it was just something that was happening to someone else. Because more than half of the world didn't have it happen right away, it didn't really seem real.

But after everyone on the planet, and in orbit if I recall correctly, had missed sleep, then it was real. Then we were all in it together. Only the Americas were one night down, at the front lines of the sleep apocalypse.

And my coffee shop was transitioning into an upper café.

A Centers for Disease Control splash screen was up with a timer counting down until the press conference. The crowd shuffled nervously, a few muttered "sorry" and "no worries" as people bumped elbows while they jockeyed for a better view.

The timer ran out and we waited tensely while it began to count backwards into the negative for a solid minute before it cut to their podium, where a man in a suit stood before the camera. He had silver patches at his temples and grey flecked in his stubble, which he rubbed absentmindedly before he put his hand hurriedly at his side, perhaps getting the signal a second late that they had gone to air. He straightened up and took a deep breath.

"The CDC is aware that there is a situation occurring," he started lamely. He coughed, glancing off-camera nervously. After a second's pause, he mustered his courage and straightened up, spiked the camera, and spoke directly to us all in a confident and convincing tone. "This is a new one. We are doing everything in our power to learn what is causing this mass-sleeplessness. Please have faith in your government, and the scientists around the world who are sharing their work. We will unlock this puzzle box. In the meantime, please remain calm. Do not leave your house if you do not have to. Right now the biggest danger to us all is the clumsiness that comes from not getting a good night's rest. If you have a nonessential job, do everyone around you a favor and stay inside, safe and sound, and do your part to keep order during this health concern." He was handed a piece of paper from off screen, and he took it and held it up. The camera zoomed in. Apparently, control room technical capabilities were already slipping, and they couldn't get text up on-screen in time; they made do with a printed sheet of paper with a phone number on it.

"If you have any information you think urgent and pertinent, please call this number. Do not call to report that you are not sleeping—no one is sleeping. Only call if something other than that is occurring.

"We are not alone in this. This is happening to every country.

"We have very good people working on this. Very tired, but very good people," he said, with a half smile on his tired face in an attempt at disarming humor. "So we ask that everyone be patient, be safe, and please, do not operate heavy machinery or drive while you are too sleep-impaired to be doing so.

"We will have another update for you tomorrow, unless we all get the best sleep of our lives tonight," he said. The CDC splash screen logo came back up.

I thought that was good of them, to mention not driving. They knew what happened every year, after daylight savings time. When people even lost a single hour of sleep, there was a noticeable increase in traffic accidents. Hurry up already with the self-driving cars. I wouldn't have been surprised if a curfew was the next step in trying to keep things under control.

"That's it?" asked one of those gathered. "No questions? No answers? What the hell is going on?" he said.

There was a loud honk and a piercing crash as two cars collided in the intersection outside my café.

"Jesus," said a woman, rushing out to help. We filed out and hurried to the scene: a head-on collision in the intersection. It was a stupid intersection to begin with; a hill leading right up to it in one direction, and at ninety degrees, a hill leading down to it. I'd seen many accidents there before, during the course of pulling espresso and grilling paninis.

I went to a smashed green Volvo, where one of the men who'd been watching the press conference with me was trying to keep the driver's head straight, keep him from moving too much, while we began to free him from the twisted wreck of his car. I marveled then at the wonder of engineering, that these two metal hulks could smash into each other at such speed, and yet both the drivers were not only *not* splatters on the windshield, but also looked like they could very nearly walk away from it.

I was pulled backwards by someone as the world became a jumble of screeching and crumpling metal; the green Volvo lurched away from me as it took another hit. It scraped along the asphalt until the momentum of the added collision had been spent. We were just regrouping to help again when another car hit, and the one behind it swerved and avoided the wreck, but smashed into the streetlight pole on the corner by my café.

"Get back, everyone get back!" I shouted. "Get off the street!" We did, retreating to safety as yet another set of screeching tires sounded out in the intersection.

Just One-a-Day'll Keep the Insomnia Away! Shake & Take AntiWake™!
—Hand-painted billboard in Karachi, Pakistan

Traffic was a mess, everywhere a mess. People were anxious to keep from driving, so the need for rides in an already taxi-poor Vancouver was well beyond any sane capacity. Strange that they thought we could drive when they couldn't; but then, we were supposed to be professionals. I fixed my cab up with a sign on the roof that read I'LL GET YOU THERE, FOR A FAIR FARE. Other cabs had outrageous and garish signs or even paint jobs to lend credence to the idea that somehow we were okay to drive even when the general public was not.

And when people saw an available cab, they were fighting for them. Things were getting downright rowdy on the sidewalk of Kitsilano, where whole blocks consisted of nothing but coffee shops, yoga studios, and extremely niche specialty stores, like All Alpaca Yarns, and Button Button, which sold, as you may be able to guess, alpaca yarn, and nothing but buttons, respectively.

I had a degree in business, but I was having trouble finding work. My English wasn't so good yet, and perhaps my degree being from Delhi worked against me, I'm not sure. The bottom line was that I couldn't find work in my field, and I was waiting on the mind-numbingly slow process of getting my family into Canada to join me. So I drove cab, and in my free time, I lined up interviews and searched for something better. Perhaps I wouldn't have seen what I saw without driving cab though, so maybe it was for the best.

I worked alongside these monstrosities of specialty stores and played a game called "How long will it be there?" I had pretty deep analysis going on of Kitsilano especially, because the business models there were so fascinating in how much they were able to fly in the face of reason. . . . For a few months, anyway. And then the fickle public would find some new extravagant craft or hobby, some new *fair trade organic emu plumes* or what have you. It was at once fascinating and sickening.

It didn't take my degree to viscerally understand what supply and demand would mean for cab drivers. I hung back as things got more dangerous, trying to see where my fellow drivers were succeeding, and where they were going wrong. Fatally wrong, in one case. But mostly it was just difficult, dealing with desperate and exhausted people, just difficult. Profitable enough to make it worth it, though.

Even in the time before the riots, I watched my fellow cabbies get mobbed by suit-dressed yuppies and pretty working mothers, several pedestrians rushing to a cab when it tried to stop and pick up one single fare. I took note of their failures and tried a different approach, getting out of my cab and addressing an orderly line of people waiting down the block from the ruckus.

"Look, now stay there, and we'll figure this out," I said, my hands up to try and keep them from surging forward to my cab. "Let's do this with some civility. Please raise your hand if you are going downtown." Every person in the line put their hand up.

"I mean, not just downtown." They put their hands sort of half down, but still ready to reach back up at a word. "Let's say, to Burrard and Georgia. I'm going to Burrard and Georgia," I said. Six people's hands shot back up.

I took the first four of them from the line, with what I hoped would be taken as a somberly apologetic look at the others still waiting, and beckoned my fares to my cab. I made sure to watch as they buckled up.

"Two nights without sleep and the cabbies have to come to the rescue," I said, smiling as I helped a slender woman in a business suit get her strap adjusted. She smiled back, obviously weary, but looking pretty enough. The facade of mascara did wonders to maintain a sense of order. Her drooping eyelids showed off her colorful eye shadow, twinkling blue and purple in the light of the sunrise. The care and attention she had taken in making sure to keep up that part of her routine was even more attractive than the look it afforded.

"Turn on the news, would you?" asked the man in the front seat, bringing me out of my hazy revelry. He was dressed smartly and had a sleek briefcase on his lap, but he'd forgotten to shave. The appearance of appearance wasn't as important to him, and, while it was endearing to see how expensive his suit was and yet how unshaven his face, he was not nearly as attractive as the woman with the eye shadow. His was a hasty mask, hers was something deeper.

"Sure," I said, "but first I must ask you all the million-dollar question. Anyone get any sleep last night?" Their silence was my answer. I turned on the news and drove them downtown. There was coverage of Russia beginning to push troops around, and just the first hint of trouble between India and Pakistan with that fight at the border crossing. I tried to keep my attention on the road; I drove us by three different accidents. My passengers kept their eyes deliberately dead ahead as we drove by the flashing lights. This was when there were still flashing lights to be had.

We drove over the bridge and into the financial district. Everywhere people shuffled to and fro, dragging their feet to whatever destination they felt needed them so badly in such a dire time. Busses and cabs crowded the streets, but also cars, still, also cars. All vehicles were dangerous, but none more so than the human-driven weapons we had built our cities to accommodate. And planes still in the air—they were a later danger though; I looked on as a gentle seaplane approached Coal Harbor. As we waited at a red light, my passengers and I watched it touch down gracefully in the harbor at the end of Burrard Street. The light changed and I took us forward once more, checking the intersection, left and right, several times while inching forwards until it was safe to go onward.

I pulled up in front of the bus stop to deliver my quadruple fare. They paid me and thanked me and got out to go to their office jobs. This was while people still went to office jobs. I sat for a moment, hands on the steering wheel, engine off (in an idle-free city, of course the engine was off). I watched another seaplane come in for a landing, touching down in the still waters, silent and smooth. Where were they coming from? And what was in downtown Vancouver that they were risking flights on two nights of insomnia? One of the many things being repeated in the vast cloud of social media and talk radio is that missing a single night's sleep was equivalent to having a blood alcohol content of over .1 percent, which was over the legal limit to drive. But two nights? We were all driving impaired.

A van pulled up to the curb just ahead of me and the driver got out and went to the back doors. I watched as he opened them in a way that radiated excitement. He moved quickly and deftly, all his gestures perhaps 10 percent larger than they needed to be. Though, as he turned, I caught a glimpse of his face, and thereupon was not the look of happiness, but one that I had seen time and again in business, the look that transcended cultures and languages: the look of greed.

I continued to watch as he pulled things out of the back of the van to create an elaborate tent. He put a sandwich board on the sidewalk.

THINGS TO MAKE YOU FEEL BETTER! ALSO: BE PREPARED! was the name of his jalopy shop. Incredible: he appealed to the need to feel any sort of reprieve from the awful insomnia but also preyed upon that most effectively manipulated emotion, fear. On the board were prices for things such as FACE AND GAS MASKS: $28, $78. WATER PURIFYING DROPS: $30. MULTIVITAMINS: $18. and so on.

Then, at the bottom, was simply a smiley face, with an innocuously tiny price tag next to it, spelled out so there could be no confusion, reading $100 (ONE HUNDRED DOLLARS).

I watched as he started to get customers. People walking by first disregarded him, but then I could see them slow, pause, and consider whether it just might be the best thing they could buy, for who can say they have water purifying drops at home? And with that missile being launched at Jiddah, who can say what will happen? People were scared, and a thing like that can really make people think about how well-supplied they are. The mere suggestion that they might be needed, and that things had become so dire that they were being sold out of a van in the financial district of downtown Vancouver—well, that man probably made quite a tidy profit.

People like that had stocked up well before the Panic hit. He probably had his house stuffed to the gills with supplies to sell, if a house has gills to be stuffed to. Stacked to the rafters perhaps? In any case, people like that . . .

I watched as he unsuccessfully tried to mask his greed with an air of helpfulness.

I saw whispered transactions as people forked over one hundred dollar bills for the "smiley face," which, through brief glimpses, was revealed to be a phial of some dark brown liquid.

Who knew that we could revert back to buying snake oil from the backs of street-side wagons in mere days.

And when I realized that, when I saw that this would be the most exciting time for someone with a degree in business and who loved analyzing markets, well, those four people I'd just let out of my cab were the last four fares I ever drove.

I didn't even make a ton of money. I'm not one of the ones that has to be in hiding, that preyed upon fear, that sold snake oil. Well I suppose technically . . . If my logo is still on a whole line of sleep aides, well. I never made false claims. I simply tried to see what I could do to get myself as deep into the market as possible, and, well, what fun I had! My brother in Delhi, he's one of the ones in hiding. Sure, I did the North American marketing, but he's the one that got rich off it. Quite a nice bit of serendipity that he had just the right product at just the right time. While the infrastructure was still up to make shipments, he shipped.

And when it wasn't the right product anymore, when it was my label going on something completely different, he didn't even tell *me*. He still shipped. I was putting that now infamous brand name on a product that *was* snake oil. But I believed at the time, along with the rest of them. Ignorance is seldom an excuse, but I can at least take comfort that I was unaware of my deception, and that there was no malice in my actions.

No, I don't know where he is. He used me just like he used everyone else.

At least I had the time of my life on that brief roller coaster. I got to play big, and I'll be damned if I'm going to apologize for putting my talents to good use.

Everything feels cold. Like, I know it's cold out, but it's, just, more so. I feel the cold deep inside, to my bones. Oh Christ and my eyes hurt. Like I blink some times and it feels like my eyelids are sandpaper. I'm trying to drink water enough to stay hydrermated but my tummy feels all full of pinecones and sticks.

And I didn't even eat any pinecones adn sticks today

My eyes track all on their own. Like this one time I had vertigo—the room spins even though I know it's just my eyes. I've gotten used to it a little, and it's not that bad, now, in this sleepless hell, but it's sitll aweful. I I think this is what kills us. I knwo there're probablly people doing better than me, people with drugs, and maybe that AntiWake stuff works for some fof them, but it didn't work for me.

My fingers feel like globs of butter. They're hitting keys and theysort of stick to them, and it's really hard to get them to lift off again.

My mouth tastes like old coffee and maybe dirt. Sort of like iron I think, though I can't say I've ever full on eaten iron. Maybe it's blood I taste. And smell.

If all that they find of us, of our civilisation I mean, the record of how we went out, is these notes from people dying of no-sleep, whatever that word is, then we're going to look like a bunch of idiots. Please don't judge us from these notes from our end-time, oh alien visitors. We were once great, or at least, we were ok.

At least once I didn't have fingers that felt like butter and sandpaper for eyelids.

Please body, just let's get through this. I swear I'll take better care of you. I knew you needed sleep, but now, now you get to call the shots. No more staying up late against your will. If you help me through this we can both

PART 2
PANIC

You come to the shit holes, looking for drugs, when before you condemned us to die for the same thing that's now saving your lives! Fuck you!
—Graffiti on a building in Somerset, Ottawa, Canada

Now you gotta understand the panic. Once that third night turned into the third day, and we really caught on that something was up, like, nothing was stopping it, we started to get our collective freakout on. People were finding all kinds of crazy stuff on the internet. That damned *Russian Sleep Experiment* bullshit was scaring the crap out of people, even though it was fake (*Creepypasta* I believe the kids called it). *Fatal Familial Insomnia* was suddenly a term everyone knew. It was the Bay of Pigs, or maybe for my younger patients, Y2K, only worse, way worse. We were all going to die of lack of sleep, and soon.

It was a prion disease, a solar flare, a chemical warfare mistake. It was an epigenetic shift, a mutation, the beginning of a new species. It was aliens. It was the government. Unending theories.

And people were flocking to medical clinics, doctors, nurses, anyone that had any sort of idea of neurology or the ability to prescribe drugs. Ottawa had mandated all doctors to work, trying to quell the rising panic in the country, and itself; the fourth largest city in Canada was brimming over with the chaos. It was everywhere, underlying the attempts at politeness, the clinging to civility in the face of societal breakdown. Sure, having a doctor to go see may have seemed like a comforting idea, but we had nothing to offer them. We had the official pomp of medical know-how to placate them perhaps, to try and lend some sort of comfort to them, but it was a Band-Aid on an axe wound.

"Did you know about those dogs that were kept awake to see what would happen?" asked one of my patients. That was when I was still taking patients. Day three, the day the riots started, yes, so early, so little idea of what we were in for.

"Yes, and she kept them awake and they died," I answered, having answered variations on that anecdote all morning.

"The puppies died after five days. Five days, doctor! And the other dogs lasted like what, eleven to nineteen days? And they died!" I did not tell him, or any of my other other patients, that the lack of sleep was affecting human infants even sooner than they had the puppies in that particular experiment. The death was creeping up the ranks, and had already wiped out most of the newborns. It hadn't gone fully public yet, but doctors knew. We knew. And we could both do nothing and say nothing, the first of our agency being stripped from us as the plague wiped away every trace of our humanity.

"Well Mr. Kobb, it's been three nights. The official world record is eleven nights, and I have no doubt that you can make it that far too. No one is in d**anger** of dying from this lack of sleep, in and of itself. The car crashes, sure, and tons of other accidents, have taken their toll, but the lack of sleep itself is nothing to worry about just yet. You just keep from driving and try and wait it out." I talked a bit faster than normal; the Ritalin I had taken an hour before was in full effect.

"Please doc, you gotta help me. I'm goin' nuts here, I can barely see straight. Isn't there something you can give me?"

I knew other doctors were giving their patients things, trying to either help the individual patients, or help in the efforts to diagnose the larger issue at hand by prescribing various remedies, coming at the insomnia a dozen different ways, trying to see if anything worked. I would not be a part of it. We didn't know what was causing it, and I certainly didn't know how to cure it. It was one thing for me to take things, mild doses at first, just to continue to try and help, but entirely another to start down that road of experimenting on people or caving into their desire to take a pill to make it better.

"Mr. Kobb, I'm afraid we're going to have to wait this out. Until I know the cause, I simply cannot prescribe anything to you. We just don't know what would help and what would harm."

"Please, anything, I'll try anything."

Jesus, three days without sleep and people become the biggest pussies. I was drop-dead tired and barely keeping my head screwed on, but there I was, seeing patients. Starting to slur my words once the Ritalin wore off, but seeing them none-the-less.

"You'll have to muddle through it like the rest of us are doing. I'll not experiment on you," I said tersely, writing a note on his chart. They at least felt like I had done *something* when I wrote on their chart. He sighed.

"Yeah, well, when this is all over you'll be getting an earful, but for now, I'm too tired." He sighed and looked up from the exam table apologetically. "No, forget that, sorry Dan, I'm just so damn tired!"

"I know John, I know. Me, too," I said, putting my hand on his shoulder. He sighed and stood, walking to the door with a defeated hunch in his shoulders. He paused with his hand on the doorknob, usually the time when patients would get to the point of their visit, the real reason they'd come seeking help. If it was something psychological or something to do with sex, it was always when their hand was on the doorknob that they finally got to the crux of their problem. Not with Mr. Kobb, though—it was just a simple addition.

"Doc, I've been eating more fish like you said. It's been making me feel like I have more energy, so, thanks," he said. Then he left.

I picked up the phone and punched in to reception.

"Jen?" I said. "Anyone that's here about the insomnia can cram it," I said. "I mean, send them away. I have nothing for them. We should put up a sign."

"Doctor, I don't think they'd like to hear that," she said. There was a fear in her tone; something was wrong. Jen was the kind of person that could be telling me there was someone bleeding out in the waiting room but sound cheerful when doing it. She had a permanent smile, the perfect person to welcome people to a doctors' office when they're feeling anything but happy. Just as important as the doctors were their staff; Jen coming in to work as she did made my job possible. If she could put up with a waiting room full of my patients, I could grin and bear it to see them one at a time.

"Jen, is something wrong?" I asked flat out.

"Well Doctor, that's lovely to hear," she responded. Shit.

"Jen, I'll be right there. Say Tuesday if you think I need to call the cops, or say Wednesday if you think I can handle it."

"Oh yes, it's on Tuesday," she answered. Goddamnit.

"Ok Jen hang in there, I'll call them, and then I'll come and help. Just stay calm."

I pressed the receiver down long enough to reset the line, then dialed 9-1-1.

"9-1-1, what's your emergency?" asked a man who answered.

"I'm, I'm not entirely sure. My receptionist asked me to call the police; I think one of my patients is giving her trouble."

"Sir, have you *seen* the trouble?"

"No," I said tersely, "I wanted to call you before I went out there and got involved. Can you please send someone to help?"

"Sir, we have no units to spare unless we have a better idea that there is some danger involved. Are you able to go assess the situation?"

"Goddamn it, are you kidding me?" I spat.

"Sir, please call us back if you cannot deal with the situation on your own," said the man. He hung up. Jesus, 9-1-1 hung up on me. I never thought I'd see the day.

I put the phone in its cradle and leaned on the door of the examination room. Jesus.

I straightened up, put on a stern face, and strode out and down the hall, towards the waiting room and my secretary. I went straight for her, looking to her to give me some indication as to the problem. Her eyes darted to a man sitting in the corner.

His right leg was bouncing up and down rapidly. His hands were fists bouncing along in his lap, knuckles white from clenching so hard. His wide eyes stared out the window, focused on a spot of nothing, seeing nothing. His brow was beading sweat. All the other patients waiting were well away from him, looking up at me uneasily. The only one whose gaze was elsewhere was a boy who sat motionless on the chair beside his mother.

That was one of the strangest things I think I saw during a time when every day was filled with strange things; that little boy sitting there in my waiting room, motionless, not looking at me. His little feet were hanging off the chair well above the floor, the toes of his superhero-print sneakers drooping slightly down. His hands were clasped, palms up, in his lap, and completely still. I suppose you don't even notice that children are in constant motion until you see one that isn't, and it sent a chill down my spine.

"So who's next?" I said, looking back at my secretary. Her eyes darted from me, to the man in the corner, to the list, where her finger tapped urgently at a name scribbled messily across the sign-in sheet.

"Mr. Glendale," I said loudly, looking directly at the man in the corner. The name was not familiar, and I'd never seen him before. It was a time of random drop-ins, people of every sort filtering in to any doctor that was hanging the ol' leaches'n'cane outside their practice.

The man's leg bounced up and down, and he continued to stare out the window.

"Mr. Glendale?" I repeated, louder. He blinked and was shocked out of his stupor. He leapt from his chair and strode quickly towards me. The other waiting patients recoiled as one, each pressing back into their seats to avoid getting any closer to the man as he passed by them on his jittery way across the waiting room. When he arrived in front of me, all eyes were on us to glimpse the first hint of how it would play out.

"Doc, doc, you gotta get me some more of this," he said with barely a pause between each word. He fished into his pocket. "It's great. Some more of this, more of this," he said, thrusting an empty bottle into my face. "More, more, it works, it really works-it-works," he said in a continuous stream of run-on words.

Over his shoulder, I saw more than a few of the waiting patients perk up at this testimony. *Something that worked* was the holy grail in those first few scattered days. Their eyes turned from *fearful* to the much more dangerous *fearful and greedy, and desperate*.

"Well now," I said, turning my full attention to the frazzled man, "come into an examination room, and we'll have a little chat," I said, casually beckoning him to go ahead of me down the hallway.

"No need. Just get me more of this. Now. More." He shook the bottle up and down, and it was conspicuously silent.

"I can't do anything out here in the waiting room," I said, but he didn't want to hear it.

"Look man," he said, louder, "these things are helping keep my brain focused, let me think, think, more, awake," he said quickly. His foot started to tap up and down rapidly, making his whole body shudder. I noticed that his shirt was soaked with sweat, a detail that had escaped me at first because it was so soaked that I thought the dark grey was just the color of it. A trickle of sweat ran down his forehead and dripped off the end of his nose. One of the closer waiting patients saw it too; her eyes went wide.

"Sir, you are not well," I said urgently, hoping I could bring him away from the others before examining him, but he wouldn't have it. He pulled away from my attempt to usher him down the hall, and he shouted.

"Just get me more of these!" he yelled. I growled in frustration and dropped him down onto the chair. I thrust my fingers against his neck. While he was dripping sweat, he was cold to the touch. He lurched away from me but I followed and kept my fingers pressed against his neck to feel his pulse. It was racing. He tried to get up.

"Mr. Glendale, you need to stay sitting down, you're going to hurt yourself," I said.

"More of these," he said simply, his arm jerking up and down ungracefully, like a toy with karate-chop-action. I stepped back and spoke to Jen, though I kept my eyes on the man about to go into tachychardia before my very eyes. He stood up and began blinking rapidly.

"Jen, we're going to have a Code 1 here in a moment," I said, hoping it would be enough to rouse her from the inaction the frightening man had imposed on her. She hurried away to get the paddles for me. Outside, somewhere down the street, I heard smashing glass.

"No, look here," said the man, his arm chopping up and down, up and down, while his foot tapped and tapped, his whole body jittering, his eyes blinking. "More of these, more, of, these," he said, the words halting and difficult. His face started shaking up and down, and I caught him as he seized and collapsed.

"Jen!" I shouted. The other patients waiting were at last spurred into action, and had one of three reactions.

Immediately, several of them fled, rushing out of the waiting room and into the burgeoning chaos of the world. The first one to leave had the bright idea to push the wheelchair button, and the door stayed open long enough for the stream of panicked people to make their scrambling exit with at least a semblance of grace.

A second and much smaller subset of them rushed to help me with the man having a heart attack.

And lastly were those too out of it to even realize what was going on. They stared at the wall or at the floor. How did they even get to my office? What was driving them when it looked like nobody was home? I focused back on the man seizing on my floor.

His saliva was frothing at the corners of his mouth.

"Jen!" I shouted. I needed the defib machine. We had a little portable one just in the back, she should have been back, it wasn't far. I stood and rushed to see what was keeping her and was met with a tall woman holding a kitchen paring knife to Jen's throat. The woman's eyes were wide and wild, desperate and deadly serious.

"Write me a prescription for Adderall, right now, or I kill her," she said.

Goddamn Canadians; why couldn't they just rob a drug store like any sane American would do? Like this woman: still so attached to the medical system that it hadn't occurred to her to bypass the middleman. Well no one was thinking clearly I suppose, and using the systems in place must have seemed more approachable than striking out into new territory. She was tall, but she had thin fingers and a slight build; her eyes were wild but also frightened. She looked like a knitting instructor or something; definitely not versed in the art of crime. Her hand was trembling as she moved the kitchen knife closer to Jen's throat.

"Ok now, you don't have to do that. Let me just get my pad," I said, reaching slowly into my pocket. Behind me, I heard thumping as the man's limbs bashed the floor, his muscles contracting violently as his seizure intensified.

“Doctor!” shouted one of the other patients who had rushed to help. “What do we do!?”

“Name?” I asked the woman with the knife to Jen’s throat.

“Barb Higgins,” she said. I scribbled out a prescription and thrust it towards her.

“Now get out!” I shouted. She nodded and edged along the wall to the door.

“I’m sorry,” she said, looking at Jen. She fled. I turned to Jen.

“Jen, paddles,” I said. No time to parse what had just happened; I’d hoped the shock would be enough to at least get her through the next trauma, namely the man dying in our waiting room.

To her credit and my relief, Jen rushed to the back and reemerged to set the portable defib machine up next to where I resumed helping with the man. His mouth was frothing and all the tendons in his neck were taught as he shook, arms slamming down when they managed to pull free of my impromptu assistants.

I pulled the scissors from the machine and cut his shirt open. I attached the leads and the machine read his vitals, preparing to shock him.

“Stand clear,” said the device in a calm monotone.

“Nobody touch him,” I ordered. My helpers removed their hands and the man slapped his arms and legs against the ground, until the defib machine shocked him and he tensed in electrified rigor. It showed his heartbeat, which was fast and irregular, and it shocked him again. His heart stopped.

“Oh lord,” said the woman whose child was still sitting, eerily still, superhero shoes dangling limply off the chair, sitting, staring at nothing.

The machine jolted the man again, but he was gone. I turned it off and sighed.

"I'm sorry you had to witness that," I said to those who'd stayed in the waiting room. As awful as it was, I took it as a teaching moment. Maybe it was good that they'd seen it. "He was on uppers, stimulants, trying to feel energized. That's not the way, and I'm afraid I don't have any help for you. I will *not* give uppers like this to people, you can see why," I said with a nod at the dead man, final beads of sweat trickling down his slick skin and onto the hard carpet. "And none of the medications are working to make people sleep, so I won't do those either." I looked from face to face, each with their own brand of resignation and frustration.

Over the years, I'd seen the look of "about to break" more than a few times. The psychological stresses of the rat race necessitated some to seek my medical advice (which was usually a referral to a therapist), and had provided me with a pretty good blueprint for the face of someone right on the cusp of losing it. As I looked from face to face, my patients waiting for something, anything more, I saw that look on more than half of them. It was all in the eyes. You can't hide that kind of panic.

"Thank you for your help. I think we're done for the day here. Unless anyone has anything non-insomnia related?" I asked, casting my gaze at each of them. All eyes averted, some despondent, some perhaps ashamed—for who in those first days didn't think of doing something unthinkable to get that holy grail, *something that worked*? They filed out of my waiting room one by one, the first ones at a pretty good clip, rushing back out into the world to try their plan Bs. As the door shut behind them, I realized that there was the constant wail of faraway sirens. None of them were for a single doctor's office which may or may not have had a problem, but constant all the same.

Everyone had left, all but one; the little boy in the super-hero print shoes was still there, and he sat still, staring, staring. I ran to the door after the people who'd just hurried back into the world.

"Someone's forgotten a boy!" I called after them. A woman doubled back, a hand over her mouth in alarm. She couldn't hide her panicked eyes, and maybe she'd hope I'd see them—she fixed me with a desperate glance as she passed me while I held the door for her.

"Oh god, I'm sorry, Ricky, come on now," she said. She took his hand but didn't lead him out of the waiting room. "You don't have anything, doctor?" she asked, lifting up the boy's hand. She let it go and his hand sunk slowly back into his lap, his eyes still fixed on nothing, no response, no sign of awareness. I shook my head. Fascinating, horrifying.

"I'm sorry," I said simply.

"Ricky, come on now," she said, shaking him by his shoulders.

"Mom?" he asked, blinking languidly. "Mom, why are there fish everywhere?" She looked up at me, desperate for something, anything, to help her. I shook my head again.

"Sleep deprivation causes hallucinations," was all I could offer.

She led the boy out of the waiting room, and he stared down at the dead man on the floor. He paused at the door though, eyes coming to momentarily focus on my face with a soft sympathy that seemed to come naturally to his tiny face.

"It's okay, Doctor, you couldn't have saved him. We're all going to die soon anyway."

They left, but stood just outside while I locked the door to my practice after them, quiet except for Jen's soft crying coming from behind the reception desk, and the sound of constant sirens. I sunk to the floor and stared at the dead man on my carpet.

But then, when I finally got back up, I saw that the woman and her boy were still outside, and something in me shifted.

"Jen," I said, "we're going to try something new. Now's the time to leave if you don't want to be part of blurring the line of medical ethics." I looked at her. She sat up straighter, smoothed a hand down her shirt, and nodded.

I unlocked the doors.

"Ma'am," I said loudly, "why don't you bring him back in here." She led the boy back into my waiting room. "Let's see what we can do," I said, starting down the road of desperate, but necessary, experimentation.

The memory lapses are the worst. Everyone knows that feeling of walking into a room and forgetting why you're there, but every moment of every day is turning into that feeling. People are forgetting to eat, forgetting to take medication, forgetting where their babies are, that they even have *babies. Take away our memory and we are becoming golems, only we have no masters to give us orders. Remember! Remember! Remember!*
—Transcript from an unknown HAM radio operator, Stephen, Minnesota, United States

In some places, parents still brought their children to school. It's amazing to see which parts of our daily routine were clung to until the bitter end. My class dropped by several students each day, but still we did our best. It wasn't about education being essential, it was about no one else being there for those children. Kids would be kept home at the drop of a hat those days; it was amazing to see how useful routine started to become. So we had kids at my school. And from what I've heard, we were the exception, not the rule. Not that we stuck to the curriculum. And even though perhaps it was already more of our function than I'd be willing to admit, we truly became a glorified day care.

I didn't want to ignore what was going on, so we talked about it. The students asked questions, so many questions. I tried to lead them to discover their own answers, because I had none. If it hadn't been so dire, it would have been a marvelous teaching opportunity. I mean, it still was, but it's rather grim to be talking about it when there's yet another empty seat in the story circle, and often we were given no reason for the absence.

As the attendance dwindled, we conglomerated the kids from different classes.

I had been married once, but had no children of my own. I enjoyed the rolling stock, each year a new class to meet and care for. Some years I would go up in grade with them, just to hold onto a special group, or to foster something that hadn't quite reached its full potential. Children are potential personified, and they never cease to amaze me. They were all my children. And for those last few days, I was, while not quite their mother, at least the person who stepped in when their mothers weren't there.

My class was sixth grade; just on the precipice of puberty, jogging their minds into more advanced thought. They were more hungry for the truth, and more able to understand it, than the younger grades. So we talked about it.

We went over all the options. We watched videos on Fatal Familial Insomnia, videos on Bovine Spongiform Encephalopathy, and several videos about sleep and the circadian cycle. We watched the news and looked at social media to help develop a critical eye; what were the facts, what was conjecture?

We spent time talking about their own sleep cycles, from before, and made a chart of bedtimes. We learned all about sleep, charting the ups and downs of people's sleep cycles as they went from alpha to delta wave sleep. We looked at the history of sleep, and how we even used to be diurnal, waking in the middle of the night for a few hours before returning to bed for the *second sleep*.

When the panic hit, about half of the kids in my class didn't get picked up from school. The riots, and yes even Small Town USA had them, swept us up in hysteria. I kept the children at the school, as did the other teachers. We decided upon a good course of action, and we gathered together a dinner and some blankets so we could stay the night with the children at the school.

It would have been cruel to call it a sleepover.

But I made popcorn, and we watched movies all night, with breaks in between each to get up and move around.

The different archetypes of no-sleepers manifested themselves quite dramatically in the children. It was through them that we got a sort of early warning system as to what we, the adults, would go through. A cruel warning of things to come—to have the symptoms manifest themselves in the children first was enraging.

Children's brains are all soupy. Their neural pathways are not fixed; they're undeveloped. They can't even see all the colors yet; not until we're around eighteen do we have access to the full spectrum. Their brains are in a constant state of flux, trying to fit things together into who they are going to be. Habits are formed, people are solidified. That is why they were affected sooner. The stress of fighting against it, coupled with the devastating lack of sleep that would allow them to reinforce neural connections and repair damage, was just too much for a developing brain to handle.

The first archetype I noticed was well into the panic, I think it was Day 5, when we were still managing to keep children at the school.

I was watching a classroom full, half of the kids that hadn't been picked up that day, and another teacher, Mrs. Miles, was watching the other half of them in the grade four classroom across the hall.

We had just finished up watching *Tangled*, and most of the kids were okay, going through cycles of being grumpy and exhausted and sometimes inexplicably exuberantly awake and energetic as only children seem to be able to be. I poured glasses of juice for everyone while we took our break from the cartoons. A quick scan over their activities revealed that all was well, except for one of the youngest, Jarred, a grade two student. To be frank, Jarred had been a rambunctious little brat. But of course he was in grade *two*, and that whole mess must have been such a terrifying nightmare for him, for all of them of course, but Jarred got quiet pretty much from the get-go.

It was partially a blessing though, that some of the children sort of lost themselves. It was much easier to move them around, get them to do things, to stay put if need be. Easier to take care of them. So when Jarred started to be quiet and still, I'm sure his teacher didn't mind. I didn't either, but it started to get strange.

Like I said, we had just watched *Tangled*, and I did a scan over the class as I poured juice. Some of the kids were coloring, some were playing with pipe cleaners (already, a scale model replica of

Rapunzel's tower was emerging atop one of their desks). But little Jarred was still watching the TV, the TV which was now off, silent and black. I handed a cup of juice to Hannah, one of the older kids, and whispered to her.

"Hannah dear, could you please go invite little Jarred there to come get a cup of juice?" She nodded and did what I asked. I watched while I continued pouring juice. Hannah crouched down next to him and spoke in a soft voice. Jarred didn't move. Hannah put her hand on his back and spoke again. Still nothing. She turned to look back at me, frowning. I nodded and beckoned her to come back.

"It's all right, thank you," I said. Still she frowned. Hannah was never one to accept failure though; I diverted her attention to the juice.

"You take over here for me, would you?" She didn't smile, but I could see a look of satisfaction at having a task to do. God, it was so nice to have children eager to help. I ducked out from behind the desk, letting Hannah take over, and went to Jarred.

He sat on a cushion, one of the ones we had taken from the old blue couch in the teacher's lounge. He sat on his hands, legs crossed, back straight, eyes wide, fixed on the screen we had been watching the movie on.

"Jarred dear?" I asked. He was absolutely statue still. I had to watch him for a moment to see his chest rising and falling, which it did slowly and regularly. I snapped my fingers next to his face. He didn't twitch, didn't so much as blink. I put my hand on his shoulder and rose to find every eye in the room on me.

"Oh goodness, maybe he's day-dreaming of riding Maximo!" I said jovially. Some of the others smiled and one of the boys did their best impression of the horse from the movie. I used the distraction to find a flashlight, and went back to investigate Jarred. I sat in front of him. He still stared; he didn't move, even when I was right in front of him, eyes directly in his line of sight.

I brought the flashlight up to his face and shone it in one of his eyes. The pupil contracted in the light. I moved the beam away, and the pupil reacted. I did the other eye, and it was the same.

"Jarred darling," I said, "can you hear me?" I felt his neck and counted his pulse; it was slow, but steady.

The other children were back to looking at me examining him. I stood.

"Hannah, you're in charge for just a minute. Would you hand out the granola bars? I think it's just about time for a story!"

"What about Jarred?" she asked. One of Jarred's grade two classmates came to his side. She studied his face and looked up at me with alarm.

"He's not there!" she said. "Where did he go, Mrs. Teller?" I smiled gently at her.

"He'll be all right," I said. "I'm going to take him to lay down and he can be in a quiet place."

"But he's not even there," she said again, stooping down to put her face in front of his, moving it back and forth, running her own brand of diagnostics. She prodded him on the cheek.

"Now now, let's not be bothering him," I said. I stood and freed one of Jarred's hands from underneath him.

"Jarred, we're going to go for a walk. Can you get up, sweetie?" I asked. No response. I pulled on his hand and he leaned forward to follow the motion. I took his other hand and pulled, and he unfolded from his cross-legged sit and got to his feet. His eyes still stared into nothingness.

"There we go. Let's get you somewhere to lie down," I said. I led him by his hands, and he took halting steps after me. The children watched us go.

"Thank you, Hannah," I said. She didn't acknowledge me. "Please save me one of the chocolate chip bars," I said with a wink.

"Chocolate chip bars!" said one of the children, rushing to Hannah. I led Jarred out into the hall and over to the classroom where Mrs. Miles had the other half of the bunch. I let go of his hand and it sunk slowly to his side. I walked around him, to see what he'd do. Nothing. He stared at a blank patch on the wall underneath a cork board covered in handprints cut out of construction paper with glitter and googley eyes glued all over them.

I peeked my head into the classroom and found Mrs. Miles and the children engrossed in *Minions*. She saw me and rose to join me at the door.

"Are any of your children, um, staring?" I asked. She looked puzzled. I stepped aside, out into the hallway, to show her Jarred. She scrutinized him, stooping down in front of him to look him in the eyes.

Unlike me, Mrs. Miles had children. They were grown up and off in other cities for university or work.

"Jarred honey?" she asked. "Hey Jarred?"

"His eyes react to light. His pulse is normal. And he'll move if I move him," I said, taking his hand and leading him down the hall, then in a tight loop, and back to Mrs. Miles.

"Oh dear," she said.

"What do you think I should do?" I asked.

"Put him in the coat hall?" she suggested. "Lay him down, and keep him away from the others. This is terrifying enough for us, imagine what they . . ."

I nodded.

"Let me know if any of yours . . ." She nodded grimly.

I led Jarred back into our classroom and all eyes snapped to us.

"Jarred's not feeling well, and going to lay down for a while," I said to them. "Does anyone want to come and wish him a Get Well Soon?" I said. It had long been a tradition of mine to have the class make get well soon cards for any of their classmates that had fallen ill. They crowded around and offered hands on his shoulders or small hugs and various versions of "feel better."

"Good, good. See Jarred? Isn't it nice to have such wonderful schoolmates?" I asked, squeezing his hand.

He blinked, slowly, but never moved his eyes. I led him away to the little coat hall at the side of the classroom. I left him standing there and went to retrieve one of the couch cushions for him to lay on. When I returned, Hannah was standing in front of Jarred with his hand in hers. I thought it was sweet at first, until I saw the terror on her face. I rushed to her and found Jarred's limp wrist in one hand, a stapler in the other. There was a staple in his hand, sticking in near the back of his wrist.

I snatched the stapler away from Hannah and hurried to take the staple out of Jarred's hand. He didn't flinch, didn't move.

"Is this what's going to happen to us all?" she asked. It was half question, half statement. Even then, some of them knew. Just as they knew that Jarred *wasn't there* any more, they knew that it might happen to them too.

"Hannah, what are you thinking? Go back to the class," I said, trying to keep my voice down in both volume and horror. She remained in front of Jarred, demanding an answer. I sighed and watched as Jarred's hand sunk slowly back to his side.

"I don't know," I said sadly. "I hope not," I added. "All we can do is take care of each other," I said. "No more staples," I said. She nodded, placated by my honest answer.

"I'm sorry, but I had to know," she said.

"Don't tell *me* you're sorry, tell Jarred."

"It doesn't matter; he's not there," she said as she turned and left the coat hall.

I got Jarred to lay down on the cushion. He stared up at the ceiling, unmoving, blinking occasionally. I went back to the other children, not certain I could hide the terror that was roiling away in my gut.

He was the only one that night to get the Stares, to become one of "the away people," but the next night there were two more, and it only got worse from there.

That was of course only one of several responses to the insomnia plague. It was one of the more forgiving; at least we could move children around, put them in safe places, feed them, take care of them. They'd use the toilet if we put them on it. They would drink water if we held a glass up to their lips.

The other reactions . . .

Some of the children were hallucinating, which was pretty obvious. At first it was confusing, them asking about things that weren't there, trying to interact with imagined people, animals, monsters. It was pretty harmless, but some of them started basically dreaming nightmares while they were wide awake. And walking around. Or running.

Some people thought the Screamers were a separate archetype, but I am pretty sure they were just Dreamers who weren't moving around as much. Still in the grip of waking dreams, but only able to react verbally to them.

When it was just a few, we could handle the Dreamers. We put them in closets and empty hallways, or, if they were prone to at least sitting still, we could keep them in the classrooms with us. Early in the symptoms, they would snap out of it and join the real world in brief moments of lucidity, but mostly, once they slipped into the waking dreams, they were there permanently.

One morning when I was outside with some of the kids, waiting to see if anyone would show up to collect them, or drop off any others for the day, Hannah jumped off the roof of the gymnasium and landed right in front of the school. She died instantly. We rushed to cover her up and shield the children from the gruesome sight. Some didn't react at all, and I wondered what they had seen already.

The suicides were not intentional, I don't think. Sure a lot of them were I suppose, but not Hannah. She was one of the Dreamers.

"'You miss 100% of the shots you don't take.
—Wayne Gretzky'
—Michael Scott"
—Jake Wellington
—Graffiti on the steps of the Washington Monument

We couldn't report on kids jumping off of roofs, we just couldn't. We had to find adults, and sort of mash their stories together.

My journalistic integrity took a hit during the Panic, sure, but god, I was trying my best to get the information out there as fast as possible, and as delicately as possible. We knew we were on the verge of a panic, and, despite how it might look in hindsight, we were trying our damnedest to prevent it.

Once the Dreamers started jumping, and they were all fuckin' *kids*? Jesus Christ, how do you report that? So we took their symptoms and used adult jumpers, the ones that were just jumping to get away from it all, to try and spread the word.

Is someone in your household hallucinating? Ensure they are in a safe place, and do not have access to high places. We didn't say it was children. We couldn't. Maybe we could have, I don't know. We have a lot to second guess, the media especially, but I mean come on. We only got one shot at it, and yeah, maybe there's some stuff we'd change, but I don't think that was one of them.

The Panic? No, we didn't cause it. It would have happened without TV or radio or the newspapers. God that was one of the funniest things I think I saw in the whole mess—a Newsie standing on the corner, selling papers and actually calling out headlines like it was 1850. Even funnier? People were crowded around him, listening. Jesus. We were all traveling back in time.

"Two weeks to live? How long can society keep it together? First man dies of insomnia plague!"

OK *maybe* we incited the panic, a little. But I mean, come on, that was the way of it. Any newsworthy event got the full nine yards, and the insomnia was no different. We gave options, nothing more. We explored what it could be, and what people were doing to try and cope.

You get two birds with one stone here, right? Along with my brilliant on-the-street reporting during the London riot, you get my expertise on the whole Fatal Familial Insomnia bent, right? Practically no one had heard about FFI before. But after my piece on it, well. And since it was the closest analogue to what we were going through, people ate it up even though it made everything just that much more terrifying.

Realize that FFI had only ever occurred spontaneously in eight people before. *Eight*.

All the other cases were genetically inherited, hence the *Familial* part of Fatal Familial Insomnia. And then it was only present in about forty families, affecting only a hundred people worldwide. It is a prion disease. Certainly once gene therapy gets better, we'll be able to repair the mutated protein on chromosome 20; where codon 129 should be aspartic acid (D), there is instead asparagine (N).

Basically, you're fucked in your DNA and there's shit all to be done about it.

In about three-quarters of cases of FFI where the patients were administered barbiturates or sedatives, it actually accelerated their symptoms drastically. Once people present with symptoms, it is an inexorable decline through four stages into death.

Stage one is a bummer; light insomnia, coupled with the panic attacks, paranoia, and phobias that develop as a result.

Stage two is shit; basically escalation as the insomnia becomes more pronounced, and hallucinations get added to the increasing panic attacks as the body starts to realize just how hooped it truly is.

Stage three: you're fucked. It begins when sleep becomes completely impossible. Accompanied by rapid weight loss.

Finally, in stage four (completely, ultra-mega-fucked), people exhibit what is essentially severe dementia. They become completely mute and unresponsive. If no one was taking care of people at this stage, they would die (as if they could even make it to this stage without being cared for).

Death arrived from seven to thirty-six months after the *onset* of symptoms.

After the Panic hit, I could only speculate that everyone in the world had, essentially, jumped straight into stage four.

We went from zero to completely, ultra-mega-fucked overnight.

And while it was a good blueprint for some sort of semblance of a timeline, it wasn't exactly what was happening to the world. I mean, with FFI, it was a gradual introduction of all these symptoms as sleep became progressively interrupted and sporadic. We had very little data to suggest what we should expect with the sudden and absolute cessation of sleep. Though as I said, it was as if we'd jumped straight into stage four, completely ultra-mega-fucked.

So yes, the FFI article was mine. Everyone picked it up and ran with it. Gene therapy got a huge boost, both in attention from the public, as well as in the medical community. It was all hands on deck as they honed in on it to see if that was the cause.

So am I the devil for giving them a possible cause? With a timeline?

At least my report wasn't so sensationalist. It was the shitstorm that came after it, all those panic-inducing headlines, that really got the ball rolling.

Aside from FFI though, reporting on what was happening was difficult enough.

The Arab states were starting up with that blockade and it wasn't getting meaningful coverage—some real shit was about to go down in the Red Sea and all I could do was hope to find out about it after the fact. You can bet there will be some spectacular drone footage if anyone had the sense to automate monitoring that clusterfuck. But for me, I could only document my immediate situation. So I did.

How do you report suicide as a side effect when there's a standing ban on reporting suicides? The copy-effect was too costly. We knew this from the past, before all this mess. Report a suicide, and more would follow, as a direct result. But *not* saying things would have allowed more people, more children, to wander up to rooftops and jump, fleeing demons, chasing angels. We don't know how many were from the copy-effect and how many were Dreamers. I think we saved more than we killed.

I hope so, anyway. Not that it did much good, in the end.

But once the information was out there, that was the first step toward panic. The next, I think, was when we started looking at studies of sleep deprivation. Aside from FFI, human-caused sleep deprivation was our best window into what we were experiencing. And my god, it was well documented. It never ceases to amaze me the capacity we have to inflict suffering on our own. The CIA torture techniques got blown way out of proportion, I'll admit that. But goddamn, two hundred and sixty-four hours resulting in three deaths? Those were the only human studies really, that resulted in death I mean.

And two hundred and sixty-four hours is eleven days, just to do the math for you. Same as the voluntary world record.

There were the Nazi experiments too, but people didn't really want that as part of the dataset. Some things are just too awful. Of course we couldn't help ourselves; we, the media, looked them up. But there was a silent agreement that somehow *that* was too far, that the Nazi horror experiments were off-limits. And the Japanese stuff. Awful.

The animal studies though, people ate that shit up. Puppies died after five days, rats after two weeks, give or take a few days, and dogs got seventeen to thirty-three days. And that's in a laboratory setting, where they're getting all their nutrition and welfare taken care of (you know, other than not letting them sleep).

People could relate to dogs the most. Seventeen to thirty-three days.

I think maybe that's what set it off, when people realized just how short a ticking clock we were on.

It's not like there was an enemy to fight. All our firepower, our armies, all our contingency plans, and the closest thing we had to help us were plans in place for influenza outbreaks. But how to you counter a disease (and we didn't even know if it *was* a disease) which already had one hundred percent saturation? How do you enact plans when our collective competency was dipping past the point of klutziness and into danger?

We panic. We do the only thing to combat it that we can, which, for a lot of people, turned out to be rioting. Those with the energy to do so took to the streets, and those without the get-up-and-go took drugs to join them. A lot of the deaths in the riots were from ODs. People who'd maybe not taken anything that exciting for a decade or two or three, and didn't know what they were taking or how much. People wanting to kick themselves into gear to join the mass protests, the marches, the parties, all of which inevitably turned into riots.

I was covering the march in London. I saw the danger, but goddamn what a story. A million people in the streets cannot be ignored, not by a reporter with a camera crew and speed pumping through his veins. Yeah yeah, but what do you expect. *Someone* had to document it, and it at least gave me some clarity, some goddamn energy to keep up with it all. Find me a reporter with a clean urine test during the panic and you'll have found a needle in a haystack the size of the sun.

About 15, maybe 20, percent of the marchers were hopped up on something-or-other.

And if you want sources for anything during that madness, all you'll get is someone's observations. It's not like we have blood work or an exit survey or anything. So when I say that maybe 20 percent of the people there were on drugs, it was because to me it looked like one in five of them was strung out on something. This is just personal opinion. Terrible journalism, but it's all we got from that time, as far as a record goes. I have footage I suppose, so we could go through and try and attribute behavior to symptoms of insomnia, versus symptoms of drugs, versus the adrenaline of *being in a riot*, but really, how would you tell?

I was there to try and show the world that it was okay. We, the media I mean, knew that we needed to calm the fuck down. We saw we were on the edge of the panic, and we didn't want to be the ones to tip it over the edge into madness, not for the sake of viewership or advertising or whatever bullshit like that. So we went there all quiet like, not even interviewing people; we just watched and recorded, and tried to capture a sense of calm while the place still felt sane. Ordinary people standing in solidarity. Marching peacefully. Holding funny signs.

It was pretty nice at first, a show of support, a gathering together to try and feel some sense of *we're not alone*. And then came our one fuckup. Or at least the first, biggest fuckup. We were so set in our ways that we couldn't ignore a celebrity story; Alec Crips, actor extraordinaire and BBC honorary mascot, died of an OD from taking things to stave off the effects of the insomnia, the very thing the general public was trying to do. Christ for some reason it wasn't real enough, but if the *celebrities* weren't able to save themselves, what hope did the common man have? That was the tipping point for London. In other cities it was a different trigger, but in London, that was when the *great big tired* turned into Panic with a capital P.

The madness in London was enough to spur the rest of them on. They got huge, pulling people in as riots do, even if many of them had no original intent of joining. These mindless, barely functioning madmen, sleep deprived and feeling the first pangs of desperation, felt the pull of the crowd, and found their adrenaline kick in, felt their pulse race, and found that they felt alive again.

I saw men in suits wield crowbars, smashing anything in their way like they had been born to do it. I saw a gang of older women, all with identical perms, beating the shit out of a car with a selection of canes and golf clubs. Always there was the youth leading the pack. They had the fuck-the-man ingenuity closer to the forefront of them anyway, not having stomped it back to participate fully in *polite society* yet, and boy did they let their urges fly. They were goddamned creative about their destruction.

Homemade explosives went off all around us on the outskirts of the crowd (thank Christ it was just on the outskirts—not like in a lot of other cities whose rioters hadn't perfected the goddamn art of making a proper fuse). Molotov cocktails were being thrown like confetti. If London wasn't so grey and concrete it might have burned down, but nothing greatly flammable was hit, in the city proper anyway. Some of the Molotovs I'd actually call *cute*. Little single-serving bottles full of cool-burning rubbing alcohol made for a flash-in-the-pan effect rather than an ignition source. Someone in the crowd had a sense of flair I guess, to go with some thread of sanity they were still clinging to.

Glass everywhere. Any window on ground level was smashed as we passed. Then there was that unfortunate building where the crowd got in and went up up up—when they broke that huge plate glass window on the fourth floor and it fell away and down onto the crowd below—just terrible. I got some good shots of that though; that guy with one of his arms sheared clear off—maybe you know it, was one of mine.

It was bloody and angry and terrible, but of course it was temporary; each person only had to participate for a few hours to keep the whole thing going. I stayed with it from beginning to end; we went through the downtown, out into the 'burbs, the rich houses taking quite a bitter beating (some larger and more serious Molotovs were let loose there—another layer of anger, one at the growing class divide, rearing its head with a satisfying outlet for expression at last).

So the riots were fueled by pulling in people wherever they went, even as others dropped out from exhaustion or injury, there were always more in their paths to join in.

I knew we were fucked when we went back towards downtown; it was a lost cause. I took more speed and tried to keep up, hoping it wouldn't be too much longer—how many hours of that could I take, goddamnit. It was worth it though . . .

I suppose it's to my credit that I at least paused after I got the footage. After it was safe in my camera I took it back to the studio to have a look, privately. And when I knew what I had captured, I did pause. I didn't just turn it over. I sat a good long while, wondering if I should destroy it. Even if I handed it over, I wasn't sure they'd air it. There were many decisions that had to happen to get those shots on the air in front of the whole world, and I had already made the first one, by keeping my camera rolling as it happened. The second decision, to hand it over to my producers, I thought about, then agonized over, head bowed in the blue light of the monitor in the tiny screening room.

In the end, wouldn't there be other footage of it? Or of something similar enough? Eventually the world was going to see it or something like it. And I knew it wouldn't be as good as my footage.

Yes, the footage of the mass of jumpers off the top of Tower Bridge was mine. It was the most iconic of the locations where such horror took place. All over the city there were dozens of people jumping to their deaths, spurred on by the crowd around them or even in some cases pushing at their backs. Some of the mass jumps were not entirely voluntary, I'm sure. I had filmed murder, or at least manslaughter. I could have scrapped it.

But the shots of Tower Bridge were too perfect, the golden light of sunrise too beautiful, the way they sailed past the shouting crowd leaning on that blue railing over the Thames too amazing.

I was covering it as best I could. I know it triggered others, but that was the reality of it. It would have happened eventually. People had a right to know. So sue me.

Boomsticks beat petitions any day of the apocalypse; WE TAKE; WE TAKE; WE TAKE

—Sticky notes on the windows of the Phoenix Water Supply Building, Phoenix, Arizona, United States

Report: Alive in Phoenix, Arizona. Saw massive governmental/military power abuse. City remains in the control of the Reformed Arizona State Protectorate Militia. Suspect they have a nuclear weapon; don't come unless you know what you're doing.

Day 4. Plane crash.

Nearly concurrent bombing at the Greater Phoenix Chamber of Commerce.

Plane crash likely accidental, bombing likely intentional to capitalize on the chaos.

Militia took over the city, using both the plane crash and the bombing as lures to attack the city's first responders. Police killed, fire fighters killed, but paramedics rounded up and taken hostage. Anyone with medical background plucked up out of their jobs, tossed into vans.

Military rolled in on Day 5. Killed bulk of militia in the course of three hours, recovered the hostage paramedics, abducted entire staff of all hospitals and medical clinics. Took city's medical professionals to work on cure? Rolled out approx. six hours after arrival.

Central city fire was between 7th Ave and the 10; South as far as E. Baseline Road, North and spread just past Washington. Military started the fire? Or remaining militia?

Managed to flee to desert bunker.

Writing to propose an addendum to the Constitution; will be willing to testify in court as to the nature of the "well-regulated militia" that destroyed Phoenix.

Say again: they have a nuclear weapon, use extreme caution if attempting to liberate Phoenix.

I was either a god or public enemy number one. People wanted answers and were willing to beg, bribe, or beat them out of me. Not that I had any answers. We didn't exactly have a huge budget. Well I mean now, sure, but before . . .
—Notes from Dr. Jayasurena, Sleep Lab, Columbo National Hospital, Sri Lanka

As requested, I've sent you a redux of this chapter with some of the terms defined. I knew we had our own language, but I guess I didn't realize how strange it must look to someone not from the internet.

That's right, *from* the internet. It seems so natural for me to say, because it's how we, denizens of the internet, actually say it. We're from the internet. There's no borders there. Sure, we still show our loyalty to our own countries; 'MURICA has a big part of the online culture, Canada is sorry, of course Australia is upside-down, and don't even get me started on Madagascar. Those fuckers, always closing their goddamn ports. **(In reference to *Pandemic II*, an online game where you engineer a plague in an attempt to wipe out the entire human race. Madagascar is notoriously hard to infect.)**

But there we were, already all together, already sharing in-jokes and this amazing culture that differed depending on what sites you frequented. When it hit, we were already one step ahead.

Denizens of the internet were right at home with all that. Staying awake and trouble sleeping. The boards **(message boards, where users can have back and forth conversations, using text, links, images, videos, whatever they want to use to contribute to the topic at hand)** were the funnest they'd ever been. Reaction threads went on for ages. Whole memes sprang up and were beat to death within *hours*, as opposed to the usual *days*. **(Memes: image macros with text superimposed over them.)**

No Sleep Suzie and No Sleep Stuart, Insomnia Wolf **(instead of Insanity Wolf)**, all sorts of new ones. And all the old ones got a good ol' shoop **(shoop: shop, short for "photoshop" [Adobe: dealwithit.gif])** to make them look tired. Condescending Wonka **(an image macro of Willy Wonka with his chin on his fist, looking quite hoity-toity and condescending, usually used to belittle someone for their unjustified complaints)** got a shoop and was all over the front page.

"*Tell me again how tired you are*" and "*Oh you didn't sleep last night? / Let me accommodate you in all things.*" and variations on that were soon overused, and we switched to less on-the-nose stuff. Where Insanity Wolf used to be things like "*Plays paintball / Uses knife to conserve ammo*" now it was Insomnia Wolf, and told tales like "*Played on my Hardcore Deathban server* **(gaming slang for a multi-player server where you are banned if you die, even once)** / *Naked* **(without armor)**" which could have actually been an original Insanity Wolf; insomnia or no, those servers are brutal.

As usual, the boards went on the hunt. The witch hunt. The bad guy hunt. Conspiracy theories were everywhere and people were quick to jump on the hate train for whatever the villain-du-jour was. Of course it was Monsanto. Of course it was fracking **(fracking is not an internet term, nor is it, in this context, from *Battlestar Galactica*—fracking is the process of fracturing rock using pressurized liquid, to extract gas. Goddamn I sound like a textbook or some shit. *The internet* does not approve of your ignorance. iamverysmart.jpg)**. Of course it was the Republicans, the Democrats, the Jews, the Nazis back from their decades-long hibernation and back to take over the earth. Jesus, my medium of choice is a fucked up place a lot of the time, I know, but hell, it was interesting.

The Twitch streams **(Twitch is a service that lets people live-cast their screens, used primarily for spectator gaming)** for all the big gamers were insane. People watched *Starcraft* matches around the clock, which wasn't anything new, except that the people helming the matches were on for just as long. That shit is exhausting; I have no idea how they kept it up like that.

TF2 ***(Team Fortress 2*, an FPS [First Person Shooter] made by Valve)**, *Rocket League*, *CSGO* **(*Counter-Strike: Global Offensive*)**, basically anything with a loyal online fan base went wild. Games added new hats. New hats! Players love new hats. New game types sprung up, fan-made and player enforced. Most were called variations on GO TO BED. One of the areas of a map was designated the bed, and players had to get their whole team to be on it, in the form of bodies. So the opposing team would try and prevent them from dying on the bed. Someone at Valve had the wherewithal to actually insert an actual bed into the game, big and soft looking, with a comforter adorned with the face of their founder, known as Lord Gaben. It was fun at first but after the days wore on it got too depressing, so they switched back to good old CTF **(Capture the Flag)**–style games, or just Slayer.

YouTube was full of every kind of thing under the sun, as usual, with a heavy emphasis on talking about sleep and sharing possible solutions. Or just ways of trying to keep your chin up.

Twitter and Instagram were insane. They were already insane to begin with; the short-form videos on Twitter, Instas were usually kept short as well; the brief flashes of commentary was an inexhaustible flow of insight into our situation. I've seen some hilarious stuff on there. For a while, posting videos of people sleeping was a thing. We all knew it wasn't real, but it was oddly comforting. Then the ones of people being woken up started to trend, and those few-second clips had more of value to say about what people were going through than any of the news media were capturing in their round-the-clock updates.

Not that there was much to update . . . And still the hoard sought out explanations, or at least scapegoats. Tumblr and the chans **(community of message boards, famously known for 4chan)** got into an all-out digital war over some pretty crack-pot theories. Enough that it leaked into the other areas of the net, and people started to assemble real explanations, real plans.

When the internet vigilantes got it in their heads that somehow there was a vaccine, or a cure or some shit, god help us. I mean, the internet, our collective wisdom, our collective stupidity, had had real life ramifications before. I'd helped flood a children's oncology ward with pizza once. I participated in the world's largest Secret Santa every year. Fuckin' 4chan solved a goddamn murder once. For real. We did good, but the things that float to the top are the times we screw up. Ruining someone's life, you know, like the fuckin' Fedoral Bureau of Investigation **(fedoras = neck-beards = NINJAs [No Income No Job or Assets, a primarily Millennial demographic on the rise before the apocalypse])** on Reddit mis-IDing the Boston Bomber, that sort of shit.

So of course there was a cure, or a vaccine, or some goddamn *expecto patronum* that we could use to fix it all. After just a few days into it, people were desperate. Rumors spread fast when they're something everyone wants to hear.

We organized raids. Loosely organized, you understand. We had times and places, but it was anarchy. It was a bunch of kids. The oldest among us were the man-children too stupid to stay away from it, or too desperate to join in the madness that they would finally leave the solitude of their battle stations **(gaming**

setup—the hardware and software involved in a life of "professional" gaming).

As if they, the people in charge of public health I mean, didn't anticipate it. They knew the danger they were in. They had no cure. No treatment even. And it's not like they weren't also on the internet, on the very boards that were orchestrating the attacks. So they were ready for us.

I say *us*, but really, I wasn't a part of all of that. I mean sure, I was there, but I was trying to document it. For the hoard. Video of what happened was actually working at counterpurpose to their intent; show the internet what happened when "we" took on the CDC, and it did more to deter further action than anything else could have.

Keep in mind that this was early on in the crisis, when the riots were in full swing and everyone was on three or four nights without sleep, before the curfew. We were all severely impaired by this point, basically stumbling drunk, unless we had some uppers to kick our noodles into gear.

My footage began with the first people rushing up to the locked front doors and lighting their homemade bomb. They hustled away and hid behind a newspaper box—as if that would protect them from their clearly overzealous amount of explosive material in the bomb. Those stupid Guy Fawkes masks they wore (a symbol of internet vigilantism) hid their expressions from my camera, but their shaking hands and erratic movements told all we need to know. That kind of fear anger is a whole-body response. Arms spaghetti.

The newspaper box was way too close to where they lit the bomb. Fucking amateurs; what did they think would happen? They fell before they even heard the blast, but it allowed the others to pour out of safer hiding places and towards the now open doors. Those charging forwards didn't notice the carnage that had begun before they were even faced with the defenses of their target.

There were a few hundred laying siege to the CDC building. Large enough that they felt like they could do it, large enough that their insanity spurred one another on; even when the gunfire started they stayed the course. The internet brought guns too; guns with real bullets, not the rubber bullets the CDC force was using. There was tear gas, but, the internet being the internet, they'd come prepared even for that. For what moron vigilante *doesn't* have a gas mask in their riot kit?

Another bomb went off, taking out a section of wall to add another entrance into the building so they could flank the defenders, who unknowingly outnumbered them three to one, and had proper weapons and training. I would call it a massacre, but those people defending the CDC never left the confines of the walls. They never advanced, only prevented further infiltration from the crowd of idiots getting pocked with rubber bullets and trying to keep their masks airtight against the gas.

Right as that other hole was blown in the wall, a fresh busload of some much more organized forces came to join the melee, armed just as I'd expect a collection of gun-happy crazies to be. Automatic rifles sounded out, grenades were thrown into the building, and then the defense really kicked it into gear.

No more rubber bullets. No more tear gas.

I caught footage of someone inside unable to continue firing on what were clearly US citizens, and half of them just kids. That man inside held my camera's focus for longer than a lot of the shots of the action on the front steps—his lips moved constantly with some hurried speech, a litany against fear or a prayer for safety perhaps.

When I took my lens back to the front steps, there was a kid with his guts out all over the ground, screaming. I wondered if it had been him who'd thrown the bomb that'd undone him. A bullet caught him square in the head, and from the way the splatter of brains shot from his head, there's no doubt it came from inside the CDC. A mercy killing? An execution?

Then there were those ones with the riot shields working their way into the hole that had been blown in the wall. Here was perhaps the greatest show of force I witnessed; there was a loud clap and a bright flash, and those guys with the riot shields dropped down to the ground screaming.

This was a time to see all sorts of previously secret weaponry. I'm sure a lot of it had never been tested on human beings before; this was an exciting opportunity for weapons developers, no doubt.

Mostly it was just the good ol' fashioned bullets that did the trick. A few of the more flashy things the CDC used maybe saved some lives; after those guys with the riot shields got hit with that weird light like that, and no one knew what could have done it, a lot of the attackers fled.

Those that kept it up were dealt with more swiftly. Bodies started hitting the ground at regular intervals. Every five seconds maybe. Long enough that it was an obvious, deliberate pace, short enough to keep it urgent. It caused even more people to flee. No one that ran was fired upon, no one that held their hands up in surrender was harmed.

Except for one, who held his hands up and walked into the building.

"*Bomb!*" came the yell from inside.

Gunfire. A blast. The sound of a million pieces of debris flying out of the building. Screaming. Coughing. Shouting. Blood running in a thin trickle across the dusted ground, dribbling down the top step, onto the next, down the next and the next, a line of red falling away from the now silent CDC.

Anyone that was left on the steps was there because they couldn't leave. I got footage of someone's blown-open ribcage, their heart still beating, bubbles frothing on their lungs where the shrapnel had done its work on the soft spongy tissues.

Yes, it was graphic, and some of it might have been unnecessary, but I wanted to really drive it home, be really, *really* clear that it was a bad idea. Some of those screams were so horrible; you can't un-see those images, can't un-hear those terrible cries, in English, in words that sound like your own. It was real, and hammered home the message way harder than it needed to, to make sure.

It was fortunate I lived nearby one of the first buildings to be hit. Let me set up my cameras early, let me have a place to fall back to position as well, for after.

I think my footage did more to prevent further internet vigilantism than any stupid press release, any official statement. It may have also been the impetus for The Curfew that blanketed America.

Seeing those couple of Guy Fawkes masks, either blown apart or with a bullet hole in the forehead and splattered in blood, was a clear, direct message. Notice the grey matter spattered just behind them?

Do not try this. This doesn't work. Your body is a fragile mass of meat, and you will end messily.

Very swiftly, the internet drew a line connecting me and the CDC. Said I must have known, and wasn't it weird how I wasn't hit? True, I walked away unscathed, but damn, it's not like I was up close and in the shit for most of it. My camera had a great zoom, and I had two other stationaries set up to get master shots. Christ, I could have filmed it from the safety of my own home if those damn trees weren't in the way.

But after it had quieted down, I was able to get some pretty awesome shots of the carnage. And yes, some of them could only be acquired from the inside. I think the CDC saw how it could have helped them. I wasn't working for them, but I certainly wasn't one of the ones lobbing Molotovs through their front door. And they saw what I was up to. So yeah, they let me get some footage from inside, and sent me on my way. Another in a series of smart moves.

I had to flee pretty soon after my video reached a million views (in only, what was it, four hours?). I knew they would come for me. They always do, when it's something that bad. The amount of hell they can cause a person is not to be underestimated; when it was just words being lobbed around the response was insanely disproportionate to the offence. Now they had a real live witch to hunt in lieu of their scapegoat for the whole insomnia.

It's all right though, I don't even think I mind. At least I wasn't home when they torched my house; I was hunted, but I think I saved a bunch of their stupid lives, so it's okay. How many attacks fell through after my footage got into their brains, when they could hear those screams and imagine it was their own guts laying on the ground like that?

God, the internet is an asshole, but I'm glad I helped save them. Even as they were chasing me across the park when they finally found me, late into the Longest Day (god they were relentless) I was glad, glad I had played my part.

I didn't stop being glad until they lit the blowtorch.

FIVE PASSENGERS, $50,000.00 CASH, DESTINATION: GARRY, INDIANA, USA PLEASE, WE HAVE TO GET HOME.

—Banner hanging in Los Angeles International Airport

Us night-shifters over at New Bangkok International were already pretty close. Panuwat, the guy who had the com to my left, would bring the coffees from the staff room every evening so we could start our shifts with a hot drink. He and I had started there at about the same time, and were at the same rung in the ladder of seniority. Nat, the older lady to my right, had been there forever, and would always say the same things to us throughout the day.

"Let's get these planes in the air," was the one to kick us off.

"Whelp, time for a little in-flight meal," was to let us know she was going on her break.

"Back to the ol' gyroscopic stabilizers," or some variation on flight gear, when she rejoined us.

"See you gentlemen tomorrow," in parting. Every day, Punawat and I could count on these four lines, or variations on them, to be heard. After a while, we made a game of keeping track of which ones. I made us Bingo cards, and we filled them in within a matter of days. I made new ones with words rarely used, and some of her standard gestures. She sometimes did a Fonzie slap on the dashboard and pointed at a plane she'd just cleared as it took off (old American shows have gained quite a following with some of the older generations in Thailand, and Nat was making her way through *Happy Days* after work). Punawat and I would exchange a smile and tick off things on our respective Bingo cards. It was good-natured fun.

I liked them both. We had each other's backs. We learned each other's jobs, too, when there was time.

"Keep the headset half on, half off," said Nat, showing me her right ear, uncovered. "Then you can hear everything."

We were the first ones to be affected. Work was either 9:00 a.m. to 6:00 p.m. or 1:00 a.m. to 10:00 a.m., depending on that week's schedule. When it happened, Punawat, Nat, and I were on the 1:00 a.m. to 10:00 a.m. rotation. We'd get home around eleven in the morning, have our dinners, and got ready for bed with double curtains drawn, which would block out the light but was insufficient in keeping out the sound of children playing outside. We'd sleep our eight hours, get up, and have our evenings to do things before coming to work.

We knew right away something was wrong, even though the Eastern Hemisphere didn't get their first night of insomnia until what was Day 1 for the West. Air traffic chatter was all over it. Our employee online hub was rapidly filling with nocturnal pilots and attendants trying to find someone to take their flights after missing their sleep during the day. Problems with passengers were all over the place, and things were going wrong in every department. With over fifty million people coming through each year, our city of an airport couldn't just shut down. We were a hub for all of Southeast Asia. Everyone was told to do their jobs as normal.

For some reason, the night owls, the people who were used to working while most others were asleep, became like something out of myth. As if we were coping any better. We still needed our sleep; *when* we usually got it had nothing to do with how much we needed or how poorly we functioned without it.

But all of a sudden, it was "Punawat'll do it, he's used to the odd hours," or "Nat, you don't mind staying another hour do you? I can't even see straight." It seems off now, but then, we never even got a curfew like most of the rest of the world's governments decided to enact. How could we have been so pigheaded?

We would cast sideways glances at each other, worried at what we had become in the minds of the day-shifters, but we soldiered on and did our best to pick up the slack that they couldn't. We should have been deliberately bad, should have screwed up, or flat out refused. But we didn't. Our little team of three ended up becoming the gods of the air traffic control tower at Bangkok.

Our managers would fumble through their shifts and we'd point out their mistakes and try and keep everyone afloat.

It was only six days in when it became apparent that we had made a grave error. Not a specific error I mean, but the overall, big-picture one. The one where we rationalized the need for air traffic to keep operating.

Sure, getting people home to their families was great, but after a few days of those emergency flights, we should have called it. It was only a matter of time. And with tensions mounting quite close by, both on the border between India and Pakistan, and the huge kerfuffle shaping up in the Suez Canal, we should have known to bring things to a controlled stop. Instead of a consensual winding down, what we got instead was a great big slam into a brick wall. One that totaled us.

"Time for a little in-flight meal deal dool dowel," said Nat. Our speech patterns were getting increasingly inane. I've translated it for you into something similar, but you get the idea. Rhymes that led nowhere, random words; our mouths were suddenly unlocked and our tired stupidity was leaking out of them.

"Roger, Roger," said Punawat.

"What's our vector, Victor?" I added. Nat wasn't the only one that liked Hollywood's offerings.

"Green shrimp by bear balls," replied Nat.

I'm surprised we were still able to push buttons, let alone sit in our chairs and extrapolate flight paths and keep planes separate on their landings and approaches and all that jazz. *Arai wah*. Essential service, my ass. I started keeping a tally of things in the control tower; cups of coffee spilled, knees bashed on consoles, toes stubbed, minor meltdowns and memory lapses. Severe impairment transitioning into full-on signs of dementia.

Planes told to land at the same time before someone corrected them, multiple planes directed into the same runway, planes given all sorts of directions that didn't get anyone killed, just worried.

There had been those little fuckups, sure, all over the place. And that one slightly larger fuckup in the United States that everyone chalked up to terrorism; we never found out if that plane crash was intentional or accidental. I'm sorry to say that what needed to happen was a *big* fuckup, and, well, Bangkok was the unfortunate sacrificial lamb. Not on purpose—*kuay*, I didn't mean it like that, but, well, it had to happen somewhere. We were all out of our minds, and no one was really able to make that call. As long as we were putting planes in the air, and bringing them down A.O.K., we would keep right on doing just that.

The last day that there were civilian transport planes in the air, Nat, Punawat, and I were still at it, still keeping it together at Bangkok.

"Bat-cat-rat," said Punawat to Nat. "What the hell is going on with your shoes?" he asked, pointing wildly at her feet, fingers rapid-firing stabs at the two mismatched shoes.

"Punawat-what-what, you've never seen two different shoes before? Gods laughing!" she said, smiling at the heavens. Somewhere behind us, someone dropped a glass and swore. Nothing new.

I saw her radar. I *saw* it. But I mean, like, the light bouncing off the console and reflecting color into my eyes, sure, it was making it to the receptors of my visual input systems, but there was a problem somewhere between them and my brain. The optic nerve couldn't've been the error, because I knew what I was seeing. The disconnect was somewhere even further down the line, somewhere in the ability to extrapolate meaning from it. As it was, it was just two signals converging on one another. What they represented did not compute, as the cause-and-effect portion of my brain seemed to be malfunctioning.

What a Chinese military transport was doing landing at Bangkok, on a civilian strip, we may never know. It came in the wrong way, just as a Boeing 737 was taxiing for takeoff. Both were full. And I mean full; flights were getting scarcer, and the Boeing didn't have an empty seat on it. All those people eager to get to Frankfurt and transfer over to the last leg of their flight.

So I saw the display, watched it even. Like some part of me knew what was happening, but I was unable to articulate it. Nat and Punawat were exchanging further banter about her shoes, and neither noticed that I was staring. My mouth started having a go at sounding the alarm, but all it did was open and close; no sound came out.

"Haha, Komsan's a fish, fish Komsan, fish Komsan," said Nat. I managed to point. Just as they collided, I pointed. Somehow they got it much faster than I had. They stood, looking out the window to the tarmac below, where the fireball erupted.

Some of us stared. I finally managed to scream.

Back into the earth it goes
—Graffiti near the rupture on the Kirkuk–Ceyhan Oil Pipeline, Turkey

I was the strongest and doing the best, so I went to get help for my family. I had two children, a daughter and a son, my wife, her parents and one of her uncles, and my parents and one of my aunts with me on the farm. We were relatively okay there as things were getting worse and worse in the world, but when Jiaying started trying to climb up on the roof, I knew I had to see if there was anything that could help her. Seeing her up there was just about the most terrifying thing—her foot was scrabbling at the gutter and she'd very nearly found purchase before I scrambled after her and pulled her to the ground. She'd cried; it had hurt when she landed. Then she asked why I had pushed her down. She has no realization of her actions, which made a ball of anxiety start to churn in my gut, and a hot ball of anger form at my inability to affect my situation, my complete helplessness to keep her safe.

I packed a backpack and headed to the dam. If I could get across it, there was a pharmacy which would have things I could use to help my family.

The checkpoint to get across the dam would be a problem: they had been turning people away, and there had been fights as people were denied crossing. How they could have caused us such trouble over the simple act of crossing the dam during that terrible time made my blood boil. Was my country not better than that, than attacking the people instead of standing back so they could help themselves when no one else would? A heat rose up the back of my neck and drove me towards the guard post with a fight ready to erupt, every muscle clenched with the anger of being kept in that powerless terror.

Anger always finds a target.

As I neared the checkpoint with that heat spreading up my neck, down my arms into my fists, I clenched my best knife in my pocket. What good would a kitchen knife have done against their CS/LR rifles? I didn't even think about that, just that it was somehow important that I also had a weapon. My fist tightened around the grip as I approached the crossing.

But I soon found that it had only taken a few days for order to break down—the checkpoint was empty, save for a single soldier who had not even seen my approach. I crossed freely and without showing any identification; the solitary guard didn't even acknowledge me until I strode past him. I waved at him when he looked, and he blinked slowly, then gave a slow nod, which I took as the only sign I needed to pass. I let the grip on my knife in my pocket slacken with each step I took away from him, and I felt my anger begin to fade into something different as I left the lonely guard at his post. To be on your own on the dam while your country was dying, while your family needed you—what was that guard sacrificing to be there? What was he even doing there still, when it didn't matter that he was there? Maybe it was his last sacrifice.

I tried to leave my melancholy on the dam, but it followed me when I made land on the other side.

I was hoping to find something at the pharmacy in Zigui, right on the Yangtze River, by the dam, when I saw the barge go by. At first I thought it was just a normal cargo barge, but then I noticed there was no one on it. No people at all. And so near the dam?

I'm talking of course of The Three Gorges Dam, largest hydroelectric operation in the world.

Largest fucking Sword of Damocles in the world, more like.

I watched that barge pass by and knew something was up. My hindbrain was still functioning on some subconscious level that saw it, maybe saw some wiring or wondered what all those barrels were for, and knew something was about to happen. As the current floated it gently headlong towards the dam, thoughts of the pharmacy vanished from my addled brain and I could only watch the barge.

I think when I hit my head, either on the ground or from some flying debris, my short term memory didn't make it into my long term, so I don't remember a good twenty seconds right before the blast. I remember watching the barge, right before it got to the dam, thinking, *That doesn't seem right*. And right after I regained consciousness, it was chaos—I woke from being knocked out—it must have only been a minute, maybe two—and saw the watershed emptying. All the water stored to be let out in a trickle, suddenly freed to go where it wanted. That much water moving that quickly terrified me in some deep inner place that I'd never felt before. It was like I got cold, just looking at the water rushing, emptying, sending a torrent of death to everywhere downstream. I got cold to my core. I never realized how big water is before.

I looked across the river to where my home was. It was safe from the water. But now, it was on the other side of the world. With the dam out, I had no way to cross.

Within a few hours the vast lake would be a stream—I figured maybe I could cross it once it had drained away. As it did so, I sat on the steps of the pharmacy while it killed all who lived beyond the mouth. That mouth that had once been sewn shut now lay as an open maw, twisted steel and jagged concrete the teeth which could now only open wider, never closing, spewing forth the cause of, at that point, the single greatest loss of life in human history. The record, as you know, didn't stand for long, but on that day half a billion people were snuffed out as the stored watershed with the Yangtze behind it came crashing down.

First would be Yichang, almost a million, then Jingzhou, 1.5 million, Wuhan, 10 million, etcetera, etcetera, etcetera—all the way down until that water hit the ocean, it obliterated every town, every city, every single thing in its way was sloughed off the face of the earth and carried away in a gushing wave of water and debris.

Sometimes being in the belly of the beast has its advantages—after the hours of it draining, the water level lowering almost imperceptibly at first, then each minute seeing the far shore grow and grow, I felt a sort of calm come over me. I was on the wrong side of the river, but at least my family and I were upstream of the dam. I had a bag full of medicines. There was food in my house.

The erosion that the reservoir had already caused, before the dam was blown up, was only exacerbated by the earthquakes it also caused. It sat on top of not one but *two* fault lines, and the weight of it was actually enough to make the area geologically unstable. Not exactly what you want for such a delicate piece of infrastructure. So as the lake drained and drained, all that silt and debris became visible on the banks and all the way down the steep slopes to the valley below.

Old houses and buildings emerged as the silt settled, their geometry warped by the years under the water. A mucky forest, a mire of farms, all the things that we'd built along the river before we were displaced became visible again, a grotesque vision of what they had been.

I had to watch as the rushing outflow took every boat that had been upstream with it. There were many: ferries, barges, all sorts of vessels, but the one that sticks with me was just a wooden raft with a single person on it, standing at the bow. They had accepted their fate somewhere well upstream, and were ready to meet death through the burst dam with peace and clarity. Or at least, that's what I chose to believe I was seeing from a distance. They certainly looked peaceful, standing, facing away from me as they watched the far shore streak by them, taking in the sights while they readied for their end.

The water level fell and fell, and I started trying to imagine how I was ever to cross such a disgusting waste. I made a few tests near the edge, seeing what the consistency of the silt and muck was, but I uncovered some twisted steel, a discarded ship part perhaps, that made me fear for what else might be hidden in the muck. It was slippery. It was filthy. Looking down the banks, I would have to pick my way through the wreckage of a once-inhabited village, through the dead trees and houses . . . and then what? Somehow cross whatever water would still inevitably be flowing?

And then the earth began to shake.

I scrambled back up the shore towards the pharmacy. I sat on the steps, away from anything that might fall on me, and watched the silt spring to life. Tendrils began sprouting from it, globs dancing upwards, black and grey putrefying arms of the dead shaking towards the sky in a curse. Cursing us for that place.

And no, I wasn't hallucinating, not yet—the silt and muck was a sort of non-Newtonian fluid, and the resonant frequency of the shaking was animating it into that tendril alien dance. The whole place became a carpet of jittery tendrils raising up, fragmenting, raising higher still.

The dam itself was only built to withstand a magnitude 6 to 7, so it would have probably gone eventually the way things were going. But I can tell you it was sabotage. That barge was full of explosives, I saw it. The earthquake was after. The earthquake was enough to turn what had been a huge hole in the dam into an all-out catastrophic collapse of the remaining structure. It was also the earthquake that sent the silty plateaus of the surrounding valleys sliding into the water, to be rushed away and scrambled through the hell of the collapsing remnants of the dam.

I didn't look at the chaos. I went to the observation binoculars nearer the dam and turned them towards the far shore, where my farm was, where it had been.

I could just make out the ginkgo tree, the one my great-grandfather had planted. In that instant my vision shrank to a single point, and my mind decided that it would be my mission in life to get back to that tree. If the tree still stood, perhaps my family was somewhere safe. If my family was somewhere safe, I was needed. The medicines I had were needed.

As the water level fell and fell, a cluster of boats and part of a pier washed down and got caught on some structure that was emerging from the depths. I grabbed an umbrella from the pharmacy; it was long and I could use it to poke and prod in the silt to make sure the way forward had footing.

With more bank for them to catch on, the boats became more stable. I used the hook end of the umbrella to help scale up onto them, crooked and tilted bridges across the surging death that lay between me and my family.

I became a machine. I knew I had to be slow, and careful. Every meter I gained was simply part of my mission to get back to the gingko tree, and as long as my goal was realized it didn't matter how fast I was. A long as I was steady and relentless, I would get there.

I climbed the caught ship and traversed the deck. I was vaguely aware of some of the crew still in the helm, watching me.

On the far shore I found myself knee deep in the muck, and going was extra slow as I sunk the umbrella in before me, then had to pull my leg free of the sucking mire, then find my footing all over again, blind to what lay beneath.

On and on, a seemingly never ending journey: probe, pull, plunge, probe, pull, plunge.

I had, in the bounty from the pharmacy, and at my wife's request, secured a bottle of amphetamines. When I probe-pull-plunged and found myself unable to continue, I hazarded a glance upward to check my progress. I may as well have been on a moon of Jupiter; alone, stuck in the silt, surrounded by the ghosts of how we were before the water rose, I could not see the gingko tree. I became a robot again, and turned my inner memory to the picture I'd stored there, the picture of the tree. Somehow my family was there, I could see them, all around the trunk and standing on the deep roots.

But even robots need fuel. I set the backpack onto the muck and fished out a pill to take. The effect was almost immediate. But where I had blessed energy, I was also cursed with a clarity of sight that I wish I could have forgone—suddenly I could see the bodies around me, caught on old houses, stuck in the silt where they had met with the shore as the falling water had carried them to their final resting place.

I stabbed the umbrella down, found a place to get my next step, yanked my leg free, and plunged it back down for the next step. Over and over, forever and ever.

When I ascended the far shore and the silt began to be shallower and shallower, I was able to go faster. When I made it back onto land, I had to stop. I collapsed and lay, facing away from the hell I had traversed, to rest.

At the gingko tree I had to fully become a robot, and relied on the picture in my mind's eye to get me through it. I fixated on the idea that if I waited at the tree, my family would come to me. It became my home. My view was the destroyed dam, the carnage of where the water had been. My back pressed against my tree, my supplies at my side, I waited for my family.

It's like, everything's foggy. Not vision, though that too, but my brain. It's a thick sort of stupidity. Things take so long to think of. Words take ages to form properly. Trying to pluck the right word out of myself feels like wading into a swamp and brushing aside not just plant detritus, but terrible forms obscured in the murky depths.

It took me, just then, several minutes to remember the word "detritus." Several more to figure out what appropriate adjective should go before "depths."

And this, from someone with a shelf full of literature awards sitting next to her.

What a shame. But also, and better, what an opportunity to record. I shall never, I hope, have this chance again, to record what my brain is like under these circumstances.

It has been a full hour of trying to remember the word I'm looking for, but it escapes me. Such frustration, to have spent a lifetime amassing the perfect vocabulary to use as a tool kit for my trade, when here I am, reduced to ruin by the absence of sleep. God it makes me furious; the anger being stoked in my gut feels like a furnace, painful and growing with each word that gets tossed into it.

And here I am, losing even my own voice I fear, in favor of what last I read—for Coriolanus is fighting in my mind, where Shakespeare has taken up his post to try and see me through. It's easier to think with him at the helm.

Oh Queen Mab even you I would welcome grace this muted scribe.

But not muted yet.

Not yet.

But how I wish the world could be muted—how loud is everything. The birds which still have cause to sing, awakening from their night's slumbering, greeting the dawn that mocks us with another false start. The loudness of it all is as knives into, not just my ears, but my very brain. Such pain have I experienced these last few days, that I fear something must be going wrong with the tool I've honed to be my life's work.

And save it yet I cannot. I've tried crosswords and Sudoku puzzles, hoping against treacherous hope that I could fend off this wretched deterioration. And then knives in my temple. Behind my eye. Sometimes at the base of my neck, where my skull rests upon this column of old bones that houses the cables to convey electrical impulses to control my earthly form.

And in this sleep of death, what dreams may come when we have shuffled off this mortal coil?

I know that soon, for me, I shall come to the end of my tolerance for this hellish madness. If it takes too many more words from me I shall have to kill it, and with it, me, before it has a chance to take them all. I shall never surrender the tools I've stowed so deeply in my heart, but which this accursed thing is tearing away from my enfeebled grasp.

You cannot have them.

Acquit. Fecund. Zephyr. Defenestrate.

You cannot have them.

Rescind. Obligation. Morass. Jubilation.

You cannot have them.

Reciprocity. Calligraphy. Herpetology. Sommelier.

You cannot have them.

PART 3
"SOLUTIONS"

West wind, summer streams, them's the cure right there fam, boy howdy thanks Emily **Bro**n*të.*
—Permanent marker on a white board, Carlthorp School, Santa Monica, California, United States

My team and I were on it on Day 0, even though we didn't know we were doing anything but our regular job. My lab was already doing sleep studies in a large population trial (Phase II, two hundred people), as part of the approval process of a new sleep medication.

I guess everyone wants to know what was being done to find a cure, right? I think there were two kinds of paths taken. One was where the government swooped in and tried to do what it thought it should do, which usually ended in a travesty of human rights violations. The other path was like what happened with me and my lab, where we knew what we were doing and we were left alone to get to it. We did have people from the CDC show up, and various officials, but they were observing, staying out of the way. Thank Christ; at least I could make a go of working at finding a cure and keeping my ethics while doing so.

On Day 1, after the first night of insomnia, we were joking about out fortuitous situation at first; but as the day wore on and each time we checked online we saw just what kind of phenomenon we were dealing with, we got much, much more serious. At 5:00 p.m., when we would normally be packing up to toodle-oo for the day, we held a powwow in the break room.

Right off the bat we scrapped the double-blind nature of the experiment, and opted to divulge all information to the researchers and make it a single-blind. The subjects remained unaware of their treatments, but by revealing what had once been secret to those running the trial, we could better understand what was happening.

We split our group in two: one-quarter of the participants were kept as planned, continuing treatment with this new experimental drug that we were tasked with vetting. The other three-quarters, well, they had already signed all the necessary consent agreements to be experimented on for the purpose of sleep research. We divided them up into three groups and began running different streams of therapy on them.

None of the subjects knew about the insomnia affecting the whole world. Their whole existence was a controlled laboratory setting, which included no electronics, where all their information was controlled by the researchers. It was a perfect setup to find out what was taking away our sleep, and we had it all ready to go right off the bat, no ethical dilemmas or anything.

So we began with the four groups, which eventually split into sixteen when we realized that nothing was working to put them to sleep.

I won't repeat what the Sleep Report has put in the forefront of everyone's minds, but I will remind your readers that humans have three separate and distinct modes of consciousness: REM sleep, non-REM sleep, and being awake. Suddenly we were only able to experience one form of consciousness: being awake. Parts of our mind process were suddenly cleaved away, leaving us with what we think of as the human experience, the waking part of our lives. And even that third is further divided into two, with the two halves of our brains existing in completely different modalities.

With sixteen groups, twelve to a group, we had either "leftovers" which we made into a thirteenth group.

It's just how the numbers worked when we started with two hundred. Group 13—lucky, or unlucky I wonder? They were the exciting ones. We had them sign additional consent forms. I think they must have known something was up, but we still kept them in the dark as far as connections to the outside world went.

They didn't interact with us face-to-face, so they couldn't have seen how awful we were starting to look from the lack of sleep.

They were isolated from each other, so they couldn't have shared their ideas about why the change in their study had occurred. They were trapped in their sleep labs, so they had nowhere to go and nothing to do but what we allowed them.

We had two hundred people and we started trying out all sorts of drugs, alone and in combination.

Near the end we started killing people and bringing them back, making wagers with Death to see if there was some switch that could be reset. We managed an eight-minutes-dead resuscitation: on a warm person it was impressive in and of itself, but then we started really pushing the bounds. The lower the temperature of the person, the longer they could be clinically dead before being brought back to life. It had been done with animals before, but I think I managed to document the first instances of some amazing resuscitations on humans. With a core temperature of 52°F, I managed to revive a woman who'd been dead for 91 minutes. I pushed further with another, dropping them to just 35°F, and managed a revival after 182 minutes of death—over three hours.

It didn't matter how long they'd been dead, or how functional they were when revived: the ones we brought back were still unable to sleep.

Nothing worked. None of it. If anyone, anywhere, had actually been able to produce genuine sleep, it would have been shouted from the rooftops.

~~Anger is useless, it has no value - The Dali Lama~~
PRUNE JUICE IS A WARRIOR'S DRINK
—Graffiti, Grand Rapids Buddhist Temple and Zen Center, Michigan, United States

When none of us slept, we knew. The connection we shared by doing the work together made it impossible *not* to be able to feel the change in each other.

Guru Loka felt the change even before that first sleepless night. He had cultivated such awareness that he was able to feel the moment when we stopped being able to sleep, even though it was midafternoon, and none of us were trying to sleep. He didn't tell us right away, but he did discuss it with Guru Paul. Guru Paul also felt something, but neither had known what it meant.

The next morning, though, they knew. We had a group sit, the whole temple, to explore these new feelings, and then to talk. The meeting was not to discuss that we would be inundated with people—this was obvious—but rather how we would accommodate them.

We had the news on of course; we were not locked in the dark ages in an ancient temple away from all the comforts of civilization you understand. We avoided the television, but sometimes it provided useful things, like lectures on the work, and yes, news. We didn't want to be ignorant of the state of things, not when we knew we would develop a target on us.

Every temple where people did the work developed a target on them.

Some were overrun by desperate people, and they were unable to keep out the masses with their misconceptions and hunger for a solution to their pain and death.

But we were accustomed to the tour groups. We could guess how it would go.

We did the work, but we also made the temple look the most wonderful it would ever look, as part of the preparation for welcoming the New Ones.

I spent an afternoon with beeswax polish and made the main hall doors' woodwork shine like glassy obsidian. The tree had been old, had seen the growth of our civilization all around it, and had soaked up the early air of our industry before we had cut it down to be a part of our temple. With each carved leaf I went over I remembered with the tree, saw how the mill worker had stripped off its living bark, planed the wood to get this very thickness of door. I also saw the carver at work, how he had moved his hand just so to get this vein to appear, how he had curved the chisel in behind this leaf to lift it away from the background. And I marveled at the bees who created more honey and wax than they could use, letting us harvest it, while we tended them and provided them with the flowers of blueberries, herbs, and apple trees. I worked with the miller and the carver and the bees to make their work shine. And when I stood back and saw it polished anew, it was them I thanked, for I had only maintained their creation, brought it back to what they knew it could be.

The next day I helped beat out the rugs. I did not see sheep as they were sheared. I did not see the threads as they were spun. I did not see the dye maker blend the beautiful colors. I did not see the creativity in the design that had been woven. I didn't even see the hands that had tied off the final knot. All I could see were the thousands of shoes that had walked upon it, the sand, dirt, grit, ash, and dust that had accumulated on it. When I beat it out, I was in that unproductive place of grumbling obligation.

Everyone has their off days.

Give us a few nights without sleep and us *pre-enlightened* can become a little irritable, just like the rest of the world.

Guru Loka was there, a hand on my shoulder, and all it took was for him to say, "The hands that made this knew it would be walked upon." And just like that, I remembered the wool workers, the dye blender, the weaver.

Awareness practice, and the practice of loving-kindness, was so deep within me that it took only a few words to remember it, if I forgot it at all.

The New Ones that came to us had the potential for awareness and loving-kindness, but it was buried under so much other baggage that it would take much longer than they were willing to take to bring it to the surface. Instead, the thing that surfaced *was* mostly the garbage that would have to come out before they could shine. It was very unpleasant for them.

When the New Ones came, a trickle at first, like the tour groups, we were tested again and again. Their distress was so overwhelming that it brought some of us crumbling down in the face of such pain. Perhaps not if we had been in our normal state, I mean, with proper sleep to back us up.

The lack of sleep was such a devastation to us because it hindered our ability to concentrate on the work. Where once I could drop into the state of calm, the silence where I could hear nothing, no words, no sounds, no thoughts, absolutely nothing, became harder to find. I had trained my mind well, and, while it took longer, it managed to follow the path I had worn in my mind with many, many journeys before, to that state. Practicing patience was the name of the game for most of us. When you see your life's work become harder, harder than we were used to it getting, it can incite panic, but we used the work to deal with that, too.

I'm sorry if this seems all so abstract. I am used to talking with people that know what I'm talking about. But as the New Ones came, we had to adapt and express these grand concepts, these ideas which take a lifetime to explore, in bite-sized pieces, breaking them into small ideas. And your people, your city dwelling anger-as-a-mask-for-pain people, were harder to teach than anyone I've encountered before or since.

We did though. We taught. At first it was like the tour groups; they would arrive in little fits and starts. Sometimes as an office retreat, still utilizing a booking made months before, sometimes a family, and always the trickle of one-by-ones, people that had been wondering about what we did, and really they'd been meaning to come and ask us about it, but they were just so busy. But now, they had so much time! They could finally do all the things they wanted!

Challenging them on their justifications was difficult; we wanted to help them, get them asking themselves questions, so it needed to be done, but we had to be so gentle so as to not drive them away.

Our Loving-Kindness practice was tested to the very limits as we explored every facet of those trying situations.

The news of the terrorist attack in Phoenix sent more our way. Shaky handheld footage of Americans killing Americans. Those seeking escape from the violence the world was churning out came to our temple, and we received them with open arms.

Then they started showing footage of monks doing the work, trying to explore possible options for relief. Sitting against beautiful backdrops of mountains with sunsets, in the snow as it fell all around them and melted against their shaved heads, on the sidewalk of a busy city. It all looked so peaceful. They must have a secret. *We* must have a secret. Then the masses *really* came.

Anyone who was perceived to be able to somehow manipulate their mind, or other minds, was a target. Not for elimination of course, but it might as well have been. The hunger for knowledge was so great that the crush of desperation destroyed whatever the public set its sights on. No one could hope to handle the numbers.

We had a huge property to work with. The temple's gigantic grounds could hold several thousand people, and once the footage of those monks appeared on the news, we knew it would be utilized.

I helped move the bee hives to the other side of the temple grounds so that they would be away from the field. I was only stung a few times, and each time I apologized to the bee for causing its death.

We made a sort of stage, just to raise up the person who would lead the sit. The sit. The work. The practice. I still resist calling it meditation, because of the connotations the world has put on that word. We took that tact with the New Ones as well. The notice on the temple doors read:

We are not sleeping either.
We welcome you with open arms.
Come join us in awareness practice
and cultivating loving-kindness,
for the benefit of all living beings.

We held many levels of sits. Guided sits were led, taking half an hour, to help develop the techniques that people could use to learn the work. The energy changed dramatically when our numbers swelled. Yes, it was stress and fear and anger and pain, all those things, but also the excitement of learning, and the relief some people were feeling for the first time was palpable. There were a lot of questions and a lot of tears.

We couldn't hold enough lectures. The New Ones were so eager for knowledge that there were never enough talks to satiate their curiosity. How wonderful to find you have a cup that can never be filled! Wonderful for some anyway, frustrating for others. Others that were used to *Step 1, Step 2, Step 3, Finished!* No such system, bub.

We had many rooms to work in, and could offer many levels of sits. There were some more advanced meditators who joined us, and some even helped us manage the influx of New Ones. Those times when we, the ones that had been practicing before the event, could sit together were really something special. We developed a bond that went very deep.

The largest sit we ever held was on the back field, but also spilled around the temple and into the hall inside, and even in the little parking lot down the embankment of the garden which used to hold tour busses and then held a tent city. Someone went up to the roof and took panorama photographs of it, of the sea of people crashing against our life raft, unable or unwilling to see that it was also sinking. We estimated nine thousand people were in attendance.

Guru Loka led that sit, and it was quiet. The sounds were quiet, I mean. The energy was almost louder than I could tolerate. He led them from a basic level on to complete silence, utilizing a microphone which connected to speakers that extended his guiding out into the crowd.

The following paragraph is an example of what he said, but realize that it was said over the course of perhaps twenty minutes. Each sentence was slower than regular speech, and there were great pauses between each one to allow the participants to take in and address the instructions as they were meant to be explored.

"Become aware of the smells around you. Explore what they might be. And then, there's taste. Maybe it's the coffee you had earlier, or just the innate flavor of your mouth. If your eyes are open, you take in what you see without focusing on what you see. If your eyes are closed, notice the darkness behind your eyelids.

Take a moment to notice the way the clothes feel on your skin. When you breathe, the fabric moves with you and brushes against you. Feel the breeze play across your face. Is it warm? Is it cool? Is it neutral? The sounds around you wash over you, coming and going without disrupting you. If one of these senses detects something which you feel yourself drawn towards, answer it with an, 'Oh, isn't that interesting,' and continue on your way, acknowledging it, but not dwelling on it. Lastly, feel the earth under you. Your weight pressing down onto the ground, which holds you, and has always been there to hold you. Your entire life it has been there, ready to catch you, and now you feel its support, unconditional, constant. Now, focus on your breath."

The sit had been silent for another twenty minutes after Guru Loka finished leading it, and he chimed the bell to signal to the participants that it was coming to an end.

Just after the first chime, a man in the middle of the field stood up, flipped a switch in his hand, and blew himself up.

Nails and ball bearings exploded away from him and went ripping into the people that sat nearest to him. I dove for cover around a giant planter near the back steps, on the edge of the field. While I was steadying myself to stand, becoming aware of the ringing in my ears, another explosion sounded out, from the other side of the temple. Two bombers working in tandem to end their lives, and end the lives of whoever happened to be nearest them.

I waited to see if there would be another blast. My ringing ears slowly let other sounds filter in; terrified screaming, people moaning in agony, shouting. I stood from behind the planter and held on to keep myself from falling back down as I physically recoiled at the sight of the blast.

At the very edge of the radius, people were sitting on the grass, clutching their wounds, which didn't look severe. I didn't fully realize then just how dire any wound was in that time. I went towards the blast center to see if I could do anything to stabilize someone long enough for better help to arrive. I came to a man whose left arm was severed, his bicep hanging in shreds.

I'd never before successfully envisioned the human body as meat, just meat. But seeing his arm like that, just, bits of meat swaying with every move he made; then I knew it.

"Just keep still," I said.

"Where's my arm, do you see it?" he asked.

I stepped over someone with nails protruding from the side of their head to retrieve a belt from another body. I went back to the man looking for his arm, and slung the belt up as high as I could around his arm, pinching his armpit and the top of his shoulder.

Guru Loka approached.

"Good," he said, louder than his usual volume, "good, yes, see how many we can save. I will tend the dying," he said, striding further forwards to the heart of the blast.

I went to another person and pulled a nail out of their side, stripped them of their shirt, and got them to put pressure on the tiny hole.

Such tiny holes, deceptively small wounds. Even if the nail hadn't been terribly long, it was enough. Breaking the skin turned out to be problematic enough; we were about to find out just how deadly it was to have any sort of molestation of the flesh.

Guru Loka was speaking loudly, not shouting, but trying to have his voice reach out to everyone near enough the center of the field blast that they were beyond physical help. He took them through a fairly accelerated version of dying rites, to try and bring them some peace in their last moments, amidst the screaming and moaning.

The other monks helped me in my task of stabilizing whomever we could. Once I got someone out of the immediately-dying zone, I helped them to the temple. The upper rooms were soon filled with injured people.

"How long until the paramedics arrive?" I asked one of the scribes as soon as he hung up the phone at the front desk. His face was ashen.

"No one's there," he said.

"What?" I asked. "What do you mean no one's there? Where are the ambulances?"

He gulped, then shook his head slightly.

I went back out onto the field.

"If anyone has any first aid training, please, we need your help," I said. Obviously there were some that did, as they were already helping tend to people. But some had been shocked into a stupor, and my call to action seemed to bring a fresh surge of people out into the bloody mess to help.

"Got any medical supplies?" asked an elderly man as he climbed the back steps. I nodded and took him to the temple first aid kit, which was, as most casual kits were, woefully inadequate to treat such wounds as had just been dealt. He took it and then asked if we had sheets. I showed him the closet and he got to work ripping them into bandages.

Guru Loka was still in the center of where the blast had been, still calling out rites and visualizations for those who were dying. We worked around him, clearing those who might make it to a room in the temple, staying with someone if we thought they were in their final moments.

I was with one such person, an older man with stubble on his tense face. His neck had been wounded by shrapnel such that he had bled out gradually. He realized he was near the end, and took my hand and squeezed it. I was about to offer some words of comfort, but he preempted me with a chilling portent as the last of his strength left him.

He squeezed my hand tighter.

"The body needs sleep to heal; all these you have saved today will die slow and painful deaths."

I smiled, trying to exude the loving-kindness I had spent my life cultivating, despite the nature of his prediction.

"Kill them, mercy, mer—" he said, then was unable to continue. I kept my eyes on his as the life left him. I saw the very moment of his death, the exact time when he ceased to exist. And I saw a truth that had been hidden from me before: that when we die, we die. I did not see any sign of continuation, or any sort of transformation. Not that I had thought before that such a thing would be visible, but somehow seeing the moment of death, of looking into his eyes when his life ended, I knew in my core that there was something false about what I believed.

A crisis of faith on the battlefield, hardly a new experience.

I had to save it for later; there was too much else to do. I continued on, managing to salvage a last few survivors, until the blast area was littered only with bodies and limbs, and was still.

Guru Loka remained standing in the center, his arms stretched upwards in his final blessing. I saw that he was wounded—a small patch of his saffron robes, just under his right collarbone towards his shoulder, was dimpled inwards; the head of a nail was just visible amidst the folding towards the center.

"Guru," I said, attempting to draw his attention to his wound.

He drew his arms down and smiled at me, radiating such a calm that I could not help but accept some of it into myself. He simply reached up and plucked the offending nail from his chest, holding it up to get a better look at it. It was a small finishing nail, silver and thin. It didn't even have any blood on it.

"It's all right," he said. "There's much to do." I nodded, and together we went to the temple to help with the living.

It wasn't until that evening when we had most of them stabilized that we began tending to the dead.

The crowd had dispersed; many of those with medical training stayed to help us, but the others fled. We didn't have a large work force, and so we opted for a pragmatic solution to the one hundred and seventy three people who had been killed outright by the blasts; we made a large pyre at the center of the bomb site in the back field. The one around the temple had gone off too close to the building to light a fire there, so we took the bodies to the back field for a single pyre.

Each body underwent the same ritual.

I searched the pockets first, and took out anything I found in them. And because I was unable to stop my well-practiced awareness, I saw into what their lives had been as I stripped them of all evidence that they had lived. Movie theatre ticket stubs from a night out with friends merely a few days before. A hair elastic with a cartoon character on it, ready to secure the hair of their child. Breath mints to cover a coffee addiction. Shopping lists of all sizes for all households. Their wallets, each in a style that had appealed to that particular person, saying something about the aesthetics of their eye, the color pallet of their lives. Then I took off any jewelry they were wearing. Watches from loved ones for anniversaries. Necklaces of favorite animals. Earrings of birthstones. Glasses, some scorched, some broken, some as intact as the day they had been purchased.

The women with purses had all these things put inside their bags. Men without any sort of bags got a Ziploc from the kitchen to contain their effects.

With each one, I took the pad of sticky-notes from my pocket and wrote on each one.

I simply took down their name, birthdate, and other vital statistics from their driver's licenses. I put the note in the Ziploc bag, facing out for easy reading, and put the bag in a large bin that had once held extra sheets. The purses got the sticky note stuck to the inside of the main compartment.

Then, with a helper, I moved the body to the pyre we were constructing.

Once every person had been dealt with like this, we had several bins, and one suitcase, full of the purses and Ziploc bags.

We lit the base of the funeral pyre at several places just as it was getting dark.

Human fat kept the flames fed for hours and hours. No one could escape the smell, a smell that we would all become far too used to in the coming hell.

The ones with more serious wounds were the first to show infection. The more of their flesh was compromised, the quicker all the microscopic predators that wait for human weakness took hold inside them.

The man with the severed arm died that morning, despite one of the first aid attendants doing an admirable job of cleaning and dressing his stump. If something got into the blood, there was nothing to be done.

Nails that went in even a mere centimeter were enough to push ravenous attackers into the body, enough to undo even the healthiest person.

Aside from those with major wounds, the others began to fall ill as well.

Scrapes didn't heal. A redness grew out from them until it was a throbbing, hot patch of infection. Simple nail punctures became like bullet wounds, rendering first the nearest limbs sore, then immobile, and then the mind shut down as fever destroyed their brain.

We eventually brought those with fevers outside on the back steps, to hose them off, trying desperately to cool them down. I had to duck inside, hiding the sudden alarm that washed over me as I remembered the dying man's portent.

Without sleep, they will not heal, I thought.

And there was Guru Loka's hand on me once again.

"We are here to ease their departure," he said. He knew what I knew. I put my hand on his shoulder to thank him, and he was unable to cover a wince of pain. I insisted on seeing his wound, but he refused.

"I will not be here long. I request only a small amount of time at the end for myself, to make ready." I shook my head, wanting to say some nicety and deny his assessment, but we were far too honest with each other for such a lie to hold any sort of comfort. I smiled.

"Of course my friend. I will stand at your door, or hold your hand, or whatever you desire," I said.

"Ah, desire," he answered, "even with so many years of practice, I still feel that tug of *want*."

And then I began **bargaining**, but not with him, for some comfort—with myself, desperately trying to ignore that feeling I had felt while I'd looked into a man's eyes the moment he died. Guru Loka was preparing for a journey he would not make. I had only a short time left with him, and a selfish snarl of *want* roiled up inside me. What was the point of it all, what had any of it meant if we were just snuffed out like a candle? He put his hand on my shoulder again.

"It's all right," he said, "you have done very well." He went away then, to help treat infection and oversee the functioning of our death temple.

Somewhat surprisingly, but welcomed none the less, some people still came to the temple. We held sits and lectures and guided meditations, but it was for dozens, not thousands. We were upfront about what had happened, a letter on the door proclaiming the previous and possible still-present danger of gathering at the temple. People came anyway.

Those with small wounds fell prey to the relentless infection and sepsis and necrotizing bacteria that had been waiting for our complacency, the failure of our immune systems.

And then as time went on, after the bomb victims had all perished, and they realized that *we* were dying too, we were down to only a handful.

Back home, they were being sent off with sky burials, taken away by the birds and ground animals of the steppes, as was our custom. The New York temple made a graveyard at the edge of the grounds as people died one by one. But in the end, when we were down to just a few, and we were so weak that we couldn't dig, all we could manage were small pyres.

And when it was just me, I couldn't even manage that.

I don't know what all the fuss is about;
I finally have time to read.
—On an otherwise blank page on the story wall of Champs-Élysées

My art contributed to making Paris into what is being called the largest art installation in human history. I orchestrated the Champs-Élysées Sleep-In. There were Sleep-Ins on every major street, and virtually all the city came out to partake. I had a team of ten people I could order around to help with the mission for Champs-Élysées, and each of them had a team of ten, and each of those ten had ten helpers. Us thousand roped in thousands more to partake.

The beds on the street were done up in the most opulent fashion. Voluptuous pillows, luxurious quilts, candles on the beds with posts to hold them. We were dragons, our treasure hoards pillows and blankets.

People wanted to make the performance their own, and asked to put up pictures and stories. I convened with the other artists coordinating the Sleep-In, all in charge of other streets. Victor-Hugo was to be for children: toys and pictures and children's art, shrines popping up to children as they succumbed. Wagram transformed into a bulletin board; storefronts were plastered with news and art and messages of encouragement for the living. I decided Champs-Élysées was for stories.

Le Patio des Champs became its own entity, transformed into the mustering station for all postings and memorials regarding terrorist attacks. The plane crash and explosion in Phoenix had brought that edge back to Paris, that edge that felt so familiar and so close, an edge we did not want to have to touch again. But when more and more small-scale attacks took place around the world as order broke down, we who had felt the sting of that edge cutting, and cutting deep, posted things in solidarity.

When the conflict between India and Pakistan over water rights started to heat up, when the words "nuclear threat" made its way into our lexicon once more, dredged up from days of Cold War past, I took myself out of the loop and focused entirely on the people of Paris. What did they need? How would this art save them? I narrowed my attention to the beating heart of the project and how I might affect it best.

I directed a bed to be placed under l'Arc de Triomph and we made it the centerpiece of the work. L'Arc itself became plastered with stories. It spilled out from there down Champs-Élysées, every available space playing host to papers with tales from any citizen that wanted to participate. I maintained my attention on the bed under l'Arc. Empty. We kept it empty. All the beds around it were filled, every bed along my street was constantly occupied, part of the work.

I managed to obtain a pallet of LED lanterns that were not too garish. Solar powered, they could be stationed along the street every few beds, and both stayed lit at night and posed no threat the safety of the city or the performers. They were a soft yellow glow that nicely complimented the sodium-vapor orange of the street lamps. And when the street lamps went out, that's when the piece really came into its own. When it became more than what I had envisioned.

I managed to get some gigantic pillar candles, real ones instead of LEDs, and thought, if I was very careful, if I kept my eye on them, I might put them at l'Arc with the empty bed. I moved them one at a time from the truck that parked as close as it could to the art. The candles were logs; I carried them one by one across my chest from the truck to the bed under l'Arc, where I rested near the bed between each. When I had picked up the fourth and final pillar candle and was shuffling, near exhaustion, towards the bed, I saw a procession coming from the other direction, from Victor-Hugo.

How long had it been since I'd seen a child? Days certainly, maybe weeks? It's all so hard to peg down the timeline of when things happened.

She was in her early teens. She wore a white gown. Her hair was tied in a ponytail. As I carried the candle towards the bed, she carried her own burden: another child, limp, dead, in her arms. When I saw this I stopped, not wanting to interfere with the evolution of the art, finally seeing a participant with a contribution to the piece that would not be matched by any other.

She walked slowly to the bed. The procession behind her kept its distance, and they stopped when they reached the outer circle under l'Arc, to give her space. We watched as she put the child, a girl, into the bed. She threw back the covers and then adjusted the girl under them before getting into the bed herself, pulling the blankets back over them both, and curling up next to her.

All were silent and still, all watched the comforter rise and fall on one side of the bed with the single breath of life. How many breaths did I watch? How many breaths were we all silent? Those were the breaths that constituted the greatest work of art humanity has ever produced. That comforter rising and falling, those papers covered in stories attached to l'Arc flickering in the breeze, those silent tears. Pure expression, made complete by the two girls in the bed at the center of the whole piece. One alive, one dead, all our present and futures, an act of kindness, an act of resignation, an act of love, an act of suffering.

I was spellbound. Eventually (and again, how long was it? Hours I think), one of my staff came and took the pillar candle from me, which I had put down at some point in the holy mass that was happening all around me. My staff took the candle and completed the center of l'Arc by lighting all four of them. She paused at the bed and stepped towards the girl—I gasped; I felt that at this point it would be criminal to interfere with the work as it was unfolding. She went no further, and instead retreated away from under l'Arc, to a safe distance, where the crowd stood in a respectful circle, watching.

In the daylight, the spell was broken, and one of my staff did go to talk to the girl. I watched him lean in and speak to her, then pull back a corner of the blankets, then replace them. He strode swiftly away from the bed and came directly to me. His face was ashen.

"The older girl is dead too," he said. I nodded.

"Thank you," I said.

"What . . . what do we do?" he asked.

"Why would we do anything?" I countered.

"But, they're dead."

"No one is to move them," I directed. I pulled aside another passing staff member and reiterated the situation to her.

It's not like we put up signs saying to leave them there; it was just the same continuation of the art, the evolution of the largest performance piece ever undertaken. They lay there at the center of Paris for the entirety of the crisis, a shrine building up and out from l'Arc, spreading down the streets. Others started dying in the beds on the streets. The ones closest to the monument were filled first, then grew outwards and outwards.

You die if you stop / you die if you stop / you'll never die if you never stop
—Chant that could be heard on the bucket line during the Cape Town Fire

How much did you love your job? When it came down to it, when all the pieces started falling away, how long did people cling to their work? People that had loved doing what they did for forty years seemed to hold on to them for longer. It gave them direction, meaning, focus. But I was part of a generation that couldn't fathom that sort of job security. Being in a single job for more than a few years was becoming rarer and rarer, so having a Jack-of-All-Trades background wasn't so unusual to me.

I had just moved to Seattle, and had just got my license to drive city busses. Before, I had been a forklift operator, a flagger, and even a barista. I wasn't attached to any one thing. And when all the pretenses fell away and the motivation left, there was really nothing for me to do.

But I had other things going for me; I liked to build things. I always had something on the go; helping a friend rebuild a car, fixing up an old chair, assembling a kegerator for home brewing. It wasn't the job that kicked in, it was the instinct. The instinct to fix, and to help. In all my jobs, helping was key. It sounds corny, but we're well beyond any judgement for that now. Corny things got people through it. Corny things saved lives.

So I quit driving my bus, because driving was pretty much a no go after a few days, let alone driving a bunch of other people. But I had to find something else to do. At first it was just helping in the neighborhood, walking people to their doors. Haha, I still wore my bus driver's uniform, as if it made me seem official in whatever I did. Things made sense at the time.

So there I was, wandering up and down my street in the 'burbs of Seattle, helping people carry things, helping them up when they stumbled, offering them a smile when I could, which was often, because I was doing something I enjoyed. I was helping.

When the Staring started, I helped them like anyone else.

My landlord, who lived upstairs and rented me his basement suite, was the first. He was an older gentleman whose name was Stephanie Civock, but who everyone called Mitch (I never received a good explanation as to why that was, or what kind of parents would name their *son* Stephanie). He had come home one day, but not gone inside. Poor Mitch, I'll never forget the first time I saw him like that. Just standing there, midway down his front walk, a cement path that led from the curb to the front door of his house.

It had started to rain, but he was standing there out in the open, getting drizzled on. His faded teal pants were growing darker by the second as the rain started coming down at an angle, and by the time I reached him, his loose khaki shirt was soaked.

"Hey Mitch," I said, putting my hand on his arm, which felt thin and limp. "Mitch?" I asked again. He didn't move, didn't look at me, but did gently blink as a droplet of water trickled down his forehead and threatened to get in his eye.

I led him to the door. Our neighbor from across the street watched from the window as we went. Other people had dealt with Starers, but not me, not yet. Mitch was my first. We stood at his front door, which was locked. The rain began to pick up.

"Mitch, do you have the keys?" I asked. He never responded, never moved on his own. "Okay Mitch, well, I know where your spare key is, but I don't want to get it with people watching, so I'm going to check your pocket, okay?" I did as I said and soon enough we were inside. I led him to the living room and went to get a towel. When I returned, he was exactly as I'd left him.

"Damnit, Mitch," I said softly. I'd heard that once this happened, people didn't come back from it. But I had to try. I dried him off. I went to find dry clothes, and again when I returned, he hadn't moved. I maneuvered him to change him out of the wet clothes, leaving the only slightly rained-upon boxers. I wasn't ready for that yet. Getting him into the pants was okay; when I lifted his leg to get it through a pant, he held it up just for a moment before putting it back down to regain his balance, like a horse teasing his farrier as he was being shod. I pulled the fresh shirt over his head and folded his arms so I could push them through the short sleeves. It was awkward, but we got it done.

"What, you got nothing to say to me? About me being here, picking out clothes for you?" I said, doing up the shirt buttons at the neck. For the sake of this story, just imagine that whatever I do or say, I manage to illicit no response from Mitch.

Not when I sit him down at the kitchen table. Not when I drop one of his special plates on the floor beside him. Not when I sweep it up. Not when I cry on the floor.

He became part of my routine. There was no morning, not as we used to have it. No start to our day, because there was no end. But I did like to still have a sort of order to my time; beginnings and endings went a long way to maintaining, if not sanity, then at least a routine. And through routine, functionality.

At first the beginning was a walk, but after I saw so many people doing yoga as the sun came up, I joined in. The whole street was lined with people doing yoga on their front lawns. Probably a funny sight, but at the time it was just nice to be a part of a group activity that made any sort of sense, and that felt good.

After yoga was "breakfast," which wasn't really a breaking of a fast at all, but I couldn't think of anything better to call it. Meal finished, I would sit Mitch in his living room, and begin my troll up the street. After Mitch, there were others that stared, stopped in their tracks whatever they were doing at the time.

I found them watering their lawn in the rain. Standing at the window inside. Sitting behind the wheel of their car, which was just as likely to be running as not.

Eventually I started knocking on people's doors to check on them. If they didn't answer, I would go inside. It was almost never locked. If it was, I found another way in.

Mostly people weren't home, gone god knows where. Sometimes they'd bit a bullet in their bathroom or taken pills in the bedroom. Lots of people went out with sleeping pills, taking so many that they had to have known it was the end. One last F.U. to the insomnia plague.

But if the house was empty and they weren't just out or dead, then they were staring.

When it was only a dozen, I kept track of them by putting a tea towel on their front door, jamming it in the mail slot.

The middle of my routine was filled with gathering supplies. Food, water, anything useful, I brought it to Mitch's. I left a small patch of lawn for me to do yoga on, but the yard turned into a mustering station for everything under the sun. Eventually I let it spill over into the little park next door to us. Rubbermaid bins full of odds and ends. I put most of the food in the garage, so it wasn't just out in the open, but I had more than enough, and some of it I left out, in a big trunk labelled *Help Yourself!*

I always watched the sunset. From a roof, usually.

Then the night was for resting. I was no less tired, no less exhausted, from our activities. And, while I couldn't sleep, I could sit down, maybe rub my feet, rest my head. Listen to the radio, until the horrific world events overtook even my easy-listening stations and I had to switch to using an old CD player. I think I stopped tuning into the world right around when that mess in Pakistan got so gruesome. I'm sure you'll have others that can tell you about that stuff, but I didn't want to know about it. All I could do was keep my routine; a constant commentary on how the rest of the world was imploding would likely not help retain my sanity.

After resting and music, when the sun rose, yoga.

There were fewer and fewer of us doing yoga. And more and more tea towels hanging out of mail slots in doors. It became too many. I couldn't take care of them all in their own homes, there was just not enough time. It made more sense to group them together. So I took them to Mitch's.

"Hey Mitch, we're going to have company," I explained. "I'll tell them not to make a mess," I said sardonically.

His small living room could comfortably hold a dozen, arranged in a circle at the edge of the room, allowing me to get access to them from the inside of it as I moved from one to the next with a water bottle and a bowl of porridge.

I moved others into the houses nearby. The next door neighbors'. The house across the street. Dozens, standing motionless in living rooms, and then bedrooms, hallways.

I left a note in every house I found a Starer.

"*I found them staring, took them down the street to XYZ Stoney Lane.*"

Only one person ever came for them.

I was doing yoga when a car pulled up. Christ, someone driving; that was a danger we didn't need on our street. I walked over to tell them off, but a man hurried from the driver's seat and into the house across the street. By the time I arrived, I could see his passengers: a woman, staring, and a little girl that, if the circumstances had been different, if I had been a toll booth attendant and they were passing by, I might have mistaken for being asleep. But the color was wrong in her face.

There was muffled screaming from the trunk. Thrashing. Someone in the throes of a living nightmare. A Dreamer.

"Don't touch my family," said the man, pointing a large gun at me as I backed away from the car window. He had an older gentleman's arm draped over his shoulders as he led him out of the house. He advanced slowly, gun shaking. I put my hands up as I continued to back away.

"It's okay. I take care of the Starers here," I said.

"I found your note," he said. "Thank you. But I'm taking him now. He's my dad, he should be with us."

"Okay," was all I said. He got his father into the back seat, next to the lifeless little girl, and shut the door after him.

He put the gun in his belt and got back behind the wheel. He pulled out into the road and sped away.

I went in to check on the others inside, and they seemed fine. Unfazed in every sense of the word.

For a few minutes, I indulged in reminding myself that they were awake and alive. To accomplish this, I raised their arms up in front of them at ninety-degree angles and watched them slowly drop back to their sides. I tried to make a sort of synchronized pattern, making a circle of slowly falling arms that was like a slow motion wave all around me as I twirled in the center of the circle.

It made sense at the time.

There were fewer and fewer of us doing yoga in the sunrise. One was a nurse several doors down. I had an eye on her before, flirted every now and then, but nothing had come of it. Unless you were on drugs, which I wasn't, you didn't feel much like flirting, or sex, or anything really. But especially sex.

She was looking at me more these days, when I did my walk up the street, when I went to check on the many houses full of Starers.

There were too many. It was starting to eat way into my resting time, feeding them, taking them each to the toilet. Dozens of them. It made sense at the time. But the exhaustion was wearing on me, and I began to despair. Sometimes I'd catch her looking from her front porch, which she was converting into a greenhouse, and it would brighten my day.

I'd incorporated a stop to her porch into my routine.

Our conversations went like this:

"Hey Ash," she'd say.

"Hey Willow. Team Tree still going strong?"

"You bet. Want any—" (and here she'd insert her herb-du-jour).

"I'm good, thanks. You want any people to stand and stare in your living room?"

"No, I'm good, thanks."

"See you beautiful."

"See you handsome."

Seven lines between us for every day that we both lasted. She saw me growing more and more exhausted as I tried to keep up with the huge number of Starers that we had on our street. It had grown into a seven house operation; seven houses full of people that had to have everything done for them. It brought an order to my world, a routine that was helping people. I was keeping them alive, at the cost of my own health and sanity.

But it made sense at the time.

Willow came by after yoga one morning.

"Ash, you've got to stop," she said. "You've done enough. You need to cut back to just however many you can handle."

"Thanks, Willow, but I'm helping them."

"Ash, you look terrible."

"Terribly handsome?"

She smiled, and as most nonmedicated smiles were in those days, it was sad.

"Sure, Ash, sure. You take care now. See you on your walk," she said.

I did my walk, passing by house after house with various markers on them, markers whose meanings I had adapted after I moved the Starers into the group houses. The neighborhood was empty now. Either the people had left (tea towel), offed themselves (candlestick with a burned-down candle), or were standing in one of my safe houses, near Mitch's (tea cup). The reason I used those objects was because every house had tea towels and teacups; no one took their teacups when they were fleeing the end of the world. And the candlestick with a burned-down candle was something I did for the dead; I couldn't bury them, but I could light a candle for them at least.

Then it was just Willow and I. I stopped by her porch, as usual.

"Hey Ash," she said.

"Hey Willow. Team Tree still going strong?"

"You bet. Want any rosemary?"

"I'm good, thanks. You want any people to stand absolutely still and stare in your living room?"

"No thanks, I'm good."

"See you beautiful."

"See you handsome."

And I went back to the houses of Starers to take care of them. It ate well into my resting time, but I managed to sit for about two hours. Two hours in my basement suite, in this beat-up old armchair that I'd worked a nice butt-groove into, twiddling my hands around a Rubik's Cube for fun. I wasn't trying to solve it. Had no idea how to. But it felt wonderful, flipping the layers of cubes around and around, clicking the colors in and out of alignment, sliding them into place to form a perfect shape in my hands, and then throwing it into disarray once more. Over and over again, flip, turn, click, slide; methodical, mindless.

At the sunrise, I did my yoga, surrounded by the supplies on the front lawn.

I set out for my walk. Tea cup, candlestick, tea cup, towel, candlestick, towel, towel. On the way back, Willow wasn't on her porch. Instead, there was a little bundle on the railing, a floral print handkerchief tied with a blue satin ribbon. Beautiful. There was a note.

"Fresh mint for tea. See you later, Ash. I did it to save you, I'm sorry. I hope I left you enough."

I was puzzled, but not worried. Strange notes were all the rage. When your brain doesn't work properly, it prioritizes things in odd orders. Mint might have been important to Willow, but I had no idea what to make of her note. I took the bundle of fragrant greens and made my way back to my house, to start the routine of caring for the Starers.

I went into the first house and gave my usual greeting.

"Ash Ash, here to help," I said automatically. Maybe Willow was right, I was taking on too much.

The living room circle was in disarray. They had decided to lay down. I was excited; it was the first time any of them had moved on their own. But then the stench hit me; the smell of dozens of bowels and bladders having been emptied where they lay. Their faces were slack. I'm sure I knew they were dead, but I couldn't quite get my whole brain on board with it right away.

I lifted one of their arms and let it go. It fell heavily to the floor. I did this to all of them, all of the bodies lying in a rough circle in the living room.

They seemed whole and perfect. No obvious gunshot wounds, no bashed-in skulls, no bruises around their throats. Just a single pin prick of a needle entry point in their necks.

Then the panic hit. I rushed out of the house to the one next door, another Starer house.

It was the same there. All dead.

And the next.

And the next.

All of my houses, except for Mitch's house. More than a hundred dead.

I stood in the middle of the circle of Starers at Mitch's house. Twenty left. Thirteen in the living room, four in the den, two in the hallway, and one, Mitch, in his bedroom.

I pulled the bundle of mint from my pocket and read Willow's note again.

I hope I left you enough.

I pressed the mint up to my nose.

"Who wants mint tea?" I asked. I went around and raised up each hand, one by one. They fell back to their side slowly.

"Everyone! Wonderful," I said. "Willow picked this for us. We shall share a hot drink."

I made mint tea. I fed it to them, then fed them lunch, a feast of macaroni and cheese. I took them all to the washroom. I changed their clothes. I combed their hair. I put on some music and moved them around, not quite dancing, but sort of leading them in a circuit from the living room, down the hall, into the kitchen, in a tight circle in the mud room, down another hall, around a bedroom, and back to the living room.

Twenty times I did all this.

And by the end, it was time to rest, and I could.

Those twenty were far better cared for. And I didn't die of exhaustion.

I didn't save anyone, but Willow managed to save me.

Beware frauds! Trust your instinct, or if you're too out of it, come and ask me, Knowledgeable Nolan, and we'll find the truth together!

—Sandwich board outside of Nolan's Books,
Moscow, Russia

When I got hired on at Club Petrichor, I was just one of the guys that helped with the lineup. Those times when I could be inside were the best; Berlin has some not-too-great weather, sure, but mostly the club was inviting, warm, and the carpets were literally works of art. You'd think it would get old after a couple of days, but just when my head was down and something was eating me up, I'd see some new pattern, some new way to fit the pieces of it together to make a dog's head, a tire iron, a fish, and I would feel better.

They told me you were translating the non-English works—I hope my English is good enough to not need it. If there's mistakes, leave them in, maybe it'll be funny. Germany had a huge percentage of English speakers, and Berlin was a growing tourist hub that was starting to rival London in international draw. It was good I learned to speak it so young; I had to interact with the wealthy traveling class that had been slipped the Club Petrichor card and wanted an adventure.

The poor people from the puritanical colonies . . . Do you know bars in Canada close around 2:00 a.m.? And most had to leave before then so they could catch the last train home? These people had no idea what they were getting into! Petrichor was just getting *going* at two in the morning. My typical shift was the 1:00 a.m. to 9:00 a.m., so I got the brunt of all the crazy shit that went down in the night.

The English tourists were, while perhaps unprepared for what lay ahead of them, quick to join in when things got rowdy. So I'd have a bunch of regular clubbers and the dub-metal crowd would trickle in after one concert or another, and sometimes they'd sing and sometimes they'd fight, and the tourists would join in, and always I was there to help out.

At the end of it I'd sit on this camel saddle in the hall. What a camel saddle was doing at Club Petrichor in Berlin, I'll never know, but it was there, in this little alcove, and I would sit on it and lean against the wall and catch my breath. If it had been bad, I would lean forwards instead and hang my head, and stare at the carpet there.

I got pretty familiar with that patch of carpet.

If it hadn't been on the news, we might not have noticed. It was perhaps just slightly busier at the club that first night. And then after, when we knew, it got really busy.

Boss closed off one whole section of the club. We thought he was mad, when our lineups had never been longer, to take away capacity. But he told us he had some sort of plan, that Petrichor would need to adapt and he was creating something even better.

There were these dividers that rolled along a track in the ceiling that he used to cut the club basically in half. New workers came and went through a door that connected to a little coat room that served both halves of the club, and thus served as an entrance to whatever secrets lay beyond.

One day these guys came in carrying huge sheets of acrylic or bulletproof glass or something like that, sheets and sheets of it. The boss waved them in and ushered them down the hall and into the secret part of the club, the part he was obviously upgrading for something or other. Those guys didn't even *look* at the carpet. That night there was a fight and I looked at it long enough for all of us.

It was a few days of nonstop work, whatever he was up to. Power tools could be heard, and then strangely, *nothing* could be heard. Still those dividers stayed up. Our capacity was reduced, and we were busier than ever. We sort of fudged our attendance to let more people in than we should have; a disaster if there had been a fire, but the bigger disaster would have been not serving the function we were there to do.

The escape offered by Petrichor was simple, and people continued to flock to us, and all the other clubs for that matter, to escape the night. We didn't have a curfew like most other countries; Germany carried itself with decorum throughout, though there was much worry of the Turks and other foreign-born nationals causing trouble. As long as we kept things civil we could maintain our freedoms. What do you do with all that time suddenly on your hands? When dancing to a raging beat is the only thing that makes sense; people will dance.

Once the staff started not showing up, we hired some new people for lineups, and I moved inside for good. I had good earplugs, a good spot near the entrance hall, and a good view of the whole club. Well, the part of the club that was still open to the public.

When the boss opened up the rest of it, he didn't tell us. No staff meeting or anything, no explanation, he just removed the dividers that had been hiding his renovations for days. And he did it in the middle of the night, when we were so busy we were full to bursting.

The dance floor was one writhing, flailing mass of flesh, jumping up and down to the beat, lasers and spotlights trailing over their heads and cutting through the slight fog of the artificial atmosphere. Once the song ended, it would usually have transitioned to another one seamlessly, so the club wouldn't be interrupted in the slightest by the cut. But this time the revelers were jarred out of the trance of screaming sweating dancing as the music *stopped*.

No fanfare, no announcement, no nothing. Construction guys came out of that little coat room and then moved the dividers to reopen the club. But it was still sealed off; in their place were panels and panels of clear dividers, bulletproof glass held in place by formidable framing. Not just one, but *three* layers of glass.

The new part of the club was hardly lit. There were soft spotlights that fell in a regular grid, onto beds. There were several dozen of them; single beds, extra long, each with a medical monitor next to the headboard. At the front of them all, near the glass, one of the beds was occupied. It was parallel to us so we had a side view of the occupant.

It was a little girl, and she was asleep.

The crowd jostled for position to see the new part of the club, but when the whisper traveled throughout that the girl was asleep, things got rowdy. People pushed and shoved to get to the front to see the little girl in that bed.

Her golden hair lay still on a white pillowcase, and the royal blue sheet on top of her rose and fell with her even breathing, which we could see clearly. The medical monitor was hooked up to her arm, and it told a tale of her blood pressure and pulse, that steady blip of her heartbeat bobbing up and down in a line which we could barely believe.

"It's a trick!" said someone in the crowd, as was natural.

My boss came out from the coat room and stood on a raised part of the bar.

"It's not! Try it yourself!" he shouted at the one who had voiced his doubts. The man in the crowd smirked.

"I'll try it just to see what your trick is. If I don't walk to that bed on my own volition, you know something's up!" he shouted at us. We generally agreed, curious, hopeful, and glad to have a guinea pig to test out the what what.

I knew the man in the crowd. He was a regular, but I don't think the boss paid him or anything. So when he went into that coat room and the crowd held their collective breaths waiting for him to emerge on the other side of the glass, I was right there with them. Duties forgotten, most everything forgotten in the wake of *oh god please let it be real.*

The man from the crowd emerged on the other side of the glass and was led to a bed next to the little girl. He got under the sheet, lay down, and rolled his eyes at us, like he didn't think it would work. It took perhaps a minute, but, while my boss hooked up the medical monitor, the man in the bed blinked heavily once, then again, then looked wide eyed at us on the other side of the glass. He wriggled himself into the sheets and bunched the pillow into the shape he wanted. He smiled, and he fell asleep.

The boss waited a moment, and turned to us and raised a finger to his lips, playfully, telling us to be quiet. But by then there were the fakers, the artists, the people just pretending. How do you prove to a crowd of skeptics that someone is actually, genuinely, asleep?

He slapped the man across the face and he woke up. We saw his blood pressure spike, his heart rate jump. He bared his fists at my boss, who laughed. They exchanged some words, but we couldn't hope to make them out—it was quite soundproof. My boss nodded, the man smiled. He gave us the thumbs up, then laid back down, and fell back asleep. It could have still been an act, so we waited.

The monitor showed his heart rate slowing back down, his blood pressure falling slightly. His breathing came deep and regular. My boss leaned in close to him and snapped his fingers right by the man's ear. He didn't flinch.

My boss came back out and addressed us.

"Obviously he could be faking it. I have not been able to come up with any method of demonstrating that someone is actually asleep, to the satisfaction of onlookers like yourselves. So I offer twenty spots. Twenty people. With that many, surely, if I am a fraud, one amongst you will get up out of the bed and tell everyone.

"Do I have any volunteers?" he asked.

About half of the hands in the club shot into the air. Those that didn't were snuggly tucked in crossed arms, or clenched into fists.

Twenty were picked out, and I could see clearly that they were not from one particular clique, and almost completely separate. There were two that got in together that were regulars, Jill and Jim, a nice couple that came to dance the night away when they felt the spirit move them. But other than them, none of the others knew each other. They were all simply club goers. Some I recognized, some I didn't.

They went through the coat room, went to one of the many beds, and laid down. Jill and Jim laid across from each other, impish smiles on their faces, as if they were about to be part of some punchline in a prank. My boss stood by the door with his arms crossed, watching as they got comfortable. Jill's eyes drooped, but then shot open in surprise, staring at Jim. They talked animatedly. Jim held his hand out across the gap between them, and Jill took it. When they fell asleep, their hands slipped from each other's grasp.

My boss smiled and made his way through the beds to Jim and Jill; he gently took their arms and tucked them back onto the bed so they weren't hanging down. He put his hands on their foreheads and smiled down at them.

The other occupants of the beds were similarly settling down, each with surprise or glee written clearly on their faces. Several didn't seem to react at all, and simply settled in matter-of-factly, getting down to the business of falling asleep. We were watching people falling asleep! Surely out of the twenty strangers, one of them would have told us if it wasn't real. What had they to gain from such a ruse?

My boss surveyed the sleepers, nodded with satisfaction, then made his way back to the doors and out of the room.

Then it went insane. The club goers pressed forwards to the coat room door, everyone wanting a spot behind the glass. A whole bunch of armored guards poured out of the little coat room, making everyone back up and make some space. They set up stanchions, to make a lineup. My boss came out.

"For them it was free. But now, I must pay for my club. All are welcome. Race, class, age, none matter here. The great equalizer is money, and every bed is the same price."

He named it. There was disgust, but some in the club took advantage of the price shock to surge forward again, hands in the air, shouting "Here, here!" or "Me, I'll pay it!"

We filled the beds, and it was only a few hours before the news media showed up.

The lineup outside got insane. We erected pavilion tents all along the sidewalk to keep the rain off as people waited. The street outside turned into one big traffic marmalade until it was cordoned off altogether. I helped keep the peace inside, and the lineup guys had their work cut out for them outside. We worked out a rotation so that the beds were in constant use, but not by any one person for more than twelve hours.

I only got short glimpses from then on as I managed the club floor and the front of the lineup. People in medical outfits, wearing masks and full body scrubs, carried people off of the beds and onto stretchers. They were taken out of the room, into one of the back rooms beyond, out of sight, to be woken up and sent back out into the world.

We didn't see any of that first batch afterwards, but no one cared; everyone was so eager to get a spot in the beds that they didn't ask questions. Well they did, but no one answered. I was left to field their concerns and infinite questions, for which I had no answers. My boss gave us nothing.

Where are the sleepers now? Can they tell us how the sleep was? Did they dream? Do they sleep normally now, are they cured?

Apparently the mystery of it helped spread the word. It lasted long enough for my boss to get rich, and I mean *rich*. There were maybe fifty beds. And twelve hours of sleep each . . . Jesus.

There were sleepers that shared their stories, and they varied wildly. I don't think I'd ever seen them before; I was good at remembering faces, but by then my brain was getting pretty addled, so I couldn't be sure.

I ripped up that section of carpeting and took it home with me. I look at it every day, to remind myself. You'd think I wouldn't need, with our history, god. God!

When I learned the reality of what I was helping orchestrate . . . the guilt was immense. Still is. I should have asked more questions. I should have tried harder to investigate. But I was only the gatekeeper, trying to maintain the peace in a time when everyone was losing their heads. There were guards everywhere. And I don't think they knew what was going on either. I don't think any one person had all the pieces to put it together. He made sure of that.

It was rather ingenious. We didn't think it was gas because he was going in with them. And the medics even, taking them away! I was the one that followed his paper trail to the doctor that fixed him up with that hellish implant in his windpipe. The doctor was long gone, so I'll never know if he could have had it properly removed, or if he was sentenced to a life with that thing in his throat.

One of the things we knew from Fatal Familial Insomnia was that putting someone into a coma to treat that kind of sleeplessness actually accelerates the symptoms; the brain still cannot achieve the lower-wave sleep states that produce dreams and allow the brain and body to repair itself, and for some reason the coma state makes everything so much worse. Turns out it was the same with our apocalyptic mass insomnia.

At least my boss had people in place to take care of them afterwards. I hope you'll remember that. Even after he took off, someone was there to change their IVs and turn them so they wouldn't get bedsores. He'd set it up so they would be cared for in that warehouse he took them to once they were done "sleeping" on display.

In the end, as you know, it didn't matter. When it got to what we thought was surely the end, people stopped showing up for everything. Those people died, sure, but they died in a coma. I think they had it better than most of the rest of us that died. Jim and Jill sure did. The last thing they saw was each other.

Since the Indus Waters Treaty does not address the sharing of waters between India and Pakistan with the provision of effects of climate change, the two countries need to hold discussions on the treaty in order to make amendments to its present structure. —The Indus Equation, 2011
—A phrase highlighted on the only piece of paper left in the Wagah Border Stadium, Pakistan

I don't know if anyone's even left that can give you an accurate picture of what happened at the neck of the Red Sea, in the Bab-el-Mandeb Strait. Maybe you've got someone from Yemen or Djibouti that can tell you exactly what the fuck happened there instead of my layman's piss-poor guesses from the deck of a cruise ship. I was sloshed, trying to have a vacation and forget my mess of a life. But just in case I'm one of the only ones left that knows, I thought I'd write you and make sure you have at least this fragment. I figure, what the hell, at least it will level me up in my History-Keeping stats.

I was on a cruise, one of the ones making for the Suez Canal right when everything went to shit. Talk about timing—I'm not sure if it was better or worse to have been on the ocean, but I guess here I am, so . . . I got to experience Singapore before the end of the world, had a nice few days of open ocean, then saw Mumbai just at the start of it, when they were just getting the notion to riot. That was fascinating, and not terrifying, solely because I had a cruise ship to retreat to, safety amidst a foreign culture made slightly more predictable with the panic that binds all humanity into that single base emotion: fear. We departed and crossed the Arabian Sea, and were making for the Gulf of Aden, between the Arabian Peninsula, where the Saudis were building increasingly appalling monuments to man's arrogance, and the sharp horn of the most northeastern part of Africa, Somalia. The Gulf of Aden leads into the Red Sea, which in turn gets you through the Suez Canal and into the Mediterranean.

A man, a plan, a canal: Panama! I always thought Suez needed a snappy palindrome too. It came first but they really dropped the ball on it. Or maybe it would inevitably involve an old god's name in a region where we can't really talk about that? *Zeus, are we not drawn onward to new era? Suez!* Why all the preamble and geography? Did you ever really think about the route your goods from China took to get to your home? When was the last time you thought about the Suez Canal or the Panama Canal and thought, *Good gravy, if we didn't have those the whole world's trade system would be drastically different?* Well hey, in a world-wide crisis, those two canals became absolutely critical to secure.

So when our ship got to the Gulf of Aden on Day 5 of the whole shebang, I got to see a run-through of the start of World War III.

How much food do you have in your house? How many days' worth of food are in your city, if nothing more was brought in? How long could each country last as an island, a trade island cut off from the world? Throughout all of human history, it's been proven time and again that every kind of person across every culture in any time period will raid their neighbor before they starve. *Every single time* when it comes down to it, we pillage and kill to save ourselves and our kin.

Ships streaming through the Red Sea towards the Suez, bound for Europe, became gigantic targets.

Piracy was always an issue, but it was when governments decided to get in on the act, political ramifications be dammed, that things really all went to hell.

Before the apocalypse, four million barrels of oil per day passed through that straight. *Per day*. About 10 percent of the all the oil in the world, squeezed through that little thirty-kilometer (twenty miles for those few from Liberia, Myanmar, and the United States) gap and into the Red Sea, onwards to the Suez. So there was always that incentive. But combine it with the threat of trade stopping altogether, and we essentially had a noose around the neck of the world, and every country wanted to grab the last gulps of air.

And, since everyone reading this will either have been born after the insomnia, or were born before it but not too much before it, I know that none of you were around for the British defending Suez from the Ottoman Empire in WWI, the British defending it from the Axis attempts to capture it in WWII, or the Suez Crisis and the subsequent Arab-Israeli Wars of 1967 and 1973. So because you weren't around for any of that, or at least old enough to care, what I'm trying to tell you is that one of the most important trade features in the world has been fought over for the entire time it's been in existence.

The insomnia apocalypse was no different.

Day 5, when my cruise ship tried to get through the Bab-el-Mandeb Strait, we slowed and dropped anchor to watch the start of one of the largest naval battles the world has ever seen.

Every country with an interest in trade through the Suez showed up. We were only there long enough to realize that the shit was about to get real ugly, and that there was no way we were getting through, so we turned back.

Back to Mumbai, starting on Day 6. Another five days of crossing the Arabian Sea. I listened to the radio and managed to piece together that China had bombed a bunch of the infrastructure needed to coordinate the shipping through the Suez; Saudi Arabia, Egypt, and Yemen all saw missiles pepper their cities in an attempt to keep the shipping artery open. Not that it did much good; the ships that encountered the blockade and subsequent battle turned tail and got the fuck out of there, and by the time it was safe to go through, no one was competent enough to be captaining anything.

While we were crossing the Arabian Sea, we heard (and felt—oh god, the shock wave was incredible) the blasts that could only have been the nuclear exchange between India and Pakistan. That was day . . . 7 I think? A week of it was all it took for the water wars to begin. From that point on I wondered about air currents and the jet stream and how radioactive particles travel . . . I can only surmise that I was upwind of the exchange.

I stayed in my room. I cannot tell you of the chaos that brews on a cruise ship when the apocalypse strikes; I'm sure it was interesting, but I wanted no part of it. That microcosm of mutiny and intrigue on the high seas meant danger and death. Hearing the gunfire and the sporadic PA announcements urging calm was enough to know that the safety of my room was the best way through that hell. I had a box of protein bars, a fruit bowl, and booze, and on Day 4 I had managed to empty out the vending machine on my floor, so I had a little stockpile to ensure I didn't have to venture out. I thought if I could be good, if I could just stay put and stay out of trouble, maybe I could get through it.

By Day 11, when we finally made it back to land, no one was left to operate the ship with enough clarity to avoid crashing us into Kegav Beach, having missed the crucial turns into actual ports.

Not that getting to the actual port would have done us much good—with the shit going down in the straight and the Suez no longer an option, any ships that had been trying to get through had to go to ground. Everywhere was full.

A lot of the cargo ships were just washed up on the beaches; we passed close by to one that had smashed into the tip of part of Mumbai that sheltered the port, so close I could read the serial numbers on the crates, and it was swarming with people. It must have been there for at least a day; all of the spilled containers were open and emptied. One of them was still full, but . . . it was full of bodies: women, and a few girls. How many had been crammed in there, being smuggled, before they died of neglect, suffocation, dehydration . . . People were crawling over every inch of the ship, stripping it of anything useful. There was one container that had yet to be opened and there was a fight to control it as our ship sailed past (going much too fast now that I know what was going on at the helm).

Our boat hurdled towards the beach just as the first gunshots *pop-pop-popped* out over the ocean.

The smart (read: living, capable, still functioning) captains were dropping anchor far enough from shore to keep out of the grasp of the ravenous population of a city that was itself choked, starving, and desperate for anything on board any ship in sight.

There was no one competent left at the helm of my cruise ship. The crash was jarring but I made it through. Be good, stay put. Get through it.

I had pills with me enough to last more than my planned trip, so I was able to make a pretty good go of it. And when I found someone's stash in their room; good god, I bet half of the staff were already addicts of one sort or other. Not that I could blame them; cruises had started out as elegant luxury and had devolved into something far more resembling a floating shopping mall. How did staff get through confined hell on the high seas? Pills galore were waiting for me in a myriad of hiding spots.

I set about, quickly, as soon as we crashed, making my hallway inaccessible. I devised a way to use two doors that opened outwards to make a wall by fastening them together. There were gaps at the top and bottom, but I used part of my closet to cover those and make it look like a single wall. I did the same on the other end of the corridor, so I managed to have the whole hall, with several rooms, all to myself.

I had the land-side view, a barnacle on a beached whale looking out at the crabs scuttling over the surf's detritus, so I could watch the city of Mumbai tear itself apart. I'd missed the bulk of the riots, but even on Day 11 and onwards there was sporadic war in the streets. There had been a fire before my cruise ship had crashed, and twenty-two million people had to get out of its way, though most didn't. The various gangs fought over the ships washed ashore. I watched as leaders rose in the charred warzone and were gunned down, watched as people retreated, then surged back again when they had some superiority, watched micro wars being fought for valuable cargo containers. My ship was taken over, but no one ever got into my hallway. I lasted out the whole time in those rooms, being good, staying put, watching the outside world descend into chaos until there was very little to see. I sat by my porthole and stared out into the dying world.

Such death wow
many die
wow very tears
eternal slumber
—Graffiti scattered across Shibuya Crossing, Tokyo, Japan

>be 23
>be in gated community
>suburb pleb
>rich parents, still basement troll
>sucking teat of freeloading ‘murican freedom
>hear thumping, then explosion
>helicopter crashes on front lawn
>house catches fire
>try and save new battlestation
>dog saves new toy
>we watch our house burn down
>our favorite toys clutched against us
>forgot all the cables inside
>mfw

Behold, I tell you a mystery: We shall not all sleep, but we shall be changed . . .
. . . The dead will rise incorruptible and we shall be changed.
—Pamphlet handout of "The Lord Wants Us Awake," Sierra Leone

I'm sure every brand of church saw its ranks swell. Around the world, lapsed Catholics/Muslims/Wiccans, every church, every kind of follower, at some point tried to reconcile their beliefs, or seek solace in an abandoned comfort. Churches couldn't hope to hold the congregations that crashed upon their doorstep each day, each new morning when we *still* hadn't slept.

I was one of these.

My relationship to the church had been one of devotion and complete dedication, until my sister and I began a clandestine hunt for knowledge that led us down the inevitable path to the truth. I think.

We split the work: she learned about the church's history, the stuff they don't want you to know about, and our faith in the institution was shaken. I learned about all the other gods we'd invented over the years, and our faith in *faith* was shaken.

We worshipped Yahweh (finding out the name of our god was something that wouldn't have even occurred to me before—how ingenious to take away their names and proclaim them "god") purely because of when and where we had been born. Another time or another place, and we'd be singing praises to Wotan, Vishnu, Thor, or one of the thousands of gods worshiped throughout history and geography. Together we helped bring each other out of that haze of blind belief.

At great cost. They only shunned me. What they did to her was far worse, and, for the sake of this story, all you need to know is that I no longer have a sister.

But our secret info-sharing sessions live on in my memories of her, and sometimes, still, when I'm debating something with myself, it's her I have to defend my ideas to. An older version of her, the version they didn't destroy. She has tattoos and is a badass. She plays the cello and rides a motorcycle.

The times when I find myself most tempted to believe again is when my heart aches for her, and I wish there was a heaven. What a lovely fiction it is, that I could see her again.

But I can—she's here with me now, as I get around to telling you about all the cults and religions that sprung up around insomnia and sleep and the end of the world. I just wanted you to know that I've got church issues. Fair warning. I'll begin in a church, where I was, with who knows how many other nonbelievers.

It was overcast outside, but still light enough to make the stained glass rosary window glow brightly in the dimness of the church. Candle flames were steady and peaceful as we sat on pews or stood leaning against the walls.

Like I said, it was packed full. There was a sermon being given, on the righteousness of helping your fellow man. Not everyone was listening. There was a Starer at the back, whose family had brought her.

When it came time for communion, they led her up the aisle and the father helped offer her the body, which she chewed blankly, and the blood, which she drank automatically.

I didn't go up to receive the sacrament. I wasn't about to forgive them, even if it was the apocalypse. I was there because I lived alone (my girlfriend had up and left me to go and play "end of the world fuck-fest") and the world around me was in turmoil. The quiet of the church, just being there with other people, was comforting. I took solace both in the physical space, for it was a beautiful church, as well as the group of my fellow Galwegians (oh yeah, did I mention I'm in *Ireland*? Just pile on the church issues and when you think you've imagined enough, heap another dumpster-full on top of that). We sat listening, or just *sat*, and the silent hug of community acceptance was a feeling I had missed dearly.

I just didn't want to feel alone. I reckon that's more than the half of why various churches pulled a lot back in. Just sitting with other people, hearing familiar scripture, a kind glance, a tired nod.

The doors at the back of the church opened and banged against the walls as a dozen people surged inside. Roughly half of them had AKs.

I'd only ever seen an AK in real life once before, when I witnessed a sketchy trade-off between two vans that were parked ass-end together, four jittery men standing about and hastily transferring black duffel bags. There had been a noise down the street, and one of them pulled an AK from his coat. I ducked back around the corner I had been peering around, and waited for them to drive away.

I imagine it was the same for most in the church; there were weapons all around us, hidden or hastily tucked away from innocent eyes. We'd all seen them, and we knew they were in vans, in umbrella stands next to doors, taken up whenever the peephole was in use.

We weren't unaccustomed to violence either. IRA wasn't as dead as the international media would lead you to believe. It was not beyond the realm of possibility to see groups with guns. So these few men and women, half with AKs, the other half with hand pistols, were met with exasperation rather than fear. Mostly. Adrenaline flooded into my system as I prepared to fight or flee. Spillover of a riot? IRA? Something yet unforeseen? It was the latter, thank god, the latter, and it was quite benign.

A leader emerged from the group of interlopers and rushed up the aisle to take the pulpit. The father objected and tried to bar the way, but the leader, a thin man with long limbs, a shaved head, and many, many tattoos on display due to his shirtlessness, sidestepped him easily and took control of the congregation.

"Look now," he said in an accent that told me he was from out of town. A Northerner perhaps. "I understand why you're here. Community. Comfort. Solace. All that fockin' stuff," he said. A few in the pews that were still able to feel incensed expressed it with shock and grumbling.

"This is a place of the lord!" shouted a woman in the front row. "You leave here, Satan worshipper," she continued.

The man with the shaved head at the pulpit narrowed his eyes gleefully at her like she had walked right into a trap he'd prepared for just this particular prey.

"I don't worship Satan. What does he have to do with sleep or dreams? No, I, and many others with me, have gone back to the old gods. If you join us, we will bring them back, and receive their blessings.

"Our ancestors knew which gods needed placating to receive a good night's sleep.

"Hypnos, god of sleep, demands praise. We must transfer our attentions from this useless Abrahamic god onto the only gods that we need to appease now. Morpheus and Oneiroi, gods of dreams. They will be the ones to send us back into the sacred R.E.M. and, together with Hypnos, allow us the relief of a deep enough sleep to dream.

"We also worship one of the gods of Ireland's past: Caer Ibormeith." The shirtless-bald-tattooed man turned his attention from the woman to the whole of the congregation. "But these are the specifics of a much larger picture. I ask you to come with us, add to the volume of our voices when we call on these old gods. They will be our salvation, but we need your voices to rouse them from their long sleeps! We must wake them and let them know they are not leaving us again."

The congregation was awash in mixed reactions. Most were shaking their heads. As if a few sentences of heresy could undo a lifetime of religion. Imagine my surprise when I was the first one to stand up.

"What are your tenets?" I shouted.

The tattooed man grinned a wide grin and pulled a sheet of paper from his back pocket. He smoothed and folded it out on the pulpit as he answered me, long fingers smoothing, folding, smoothing, folding.

"We try different drugs to open our minds to the gods. There is a hierarchy with a military ranking system. The structure allows leaders to emerge and followers to do what they do best. We work together, but there is a strict schedule of prayer. We are trying out different methods. Instead of doing the same things over and over again with no results," he said, gesturing around the church, "we are changing it up, brother." He locked eyes on me, and they were intense, predatory, and I found it impossible to look away.

He flung something at me, and I flinched out of reflex. But a paper airplane floated over the pews towards me. I snatched it out of the air and found it was a flier, which I unfolded.

RULES OF THE WORLDWIDE OLD GOD AWAKENING INITIATIVE (WOGAI)

There was a narrow strip of wax paper with colorful dots on it tucked into the spine of the paper airplane.

"Any who wish to leave this place of ineffectual habits," and here he laughed, seeing a nun out of the corner of his eye who was glowering at him, creating a pun, "will find a place in a new group, one which is growing by thousands of voices every day, all around the world. Come, take an initiation dose and help us awaken the gods of sleep!"

"And if I want to leave?" I asked.

"Ask my men!" he answered. I stood and looked at the dozen or so men who were at the back of the church.

"Is this legit?" I asked. Several of them shrugged.

"It's better than nothing," said one of them.

"We're visiting churches for the rest of the day, seeing if anyone wants to join up. It can't hurt," said another.

"You can leave any time?" I continued. They nodded.

"Lost one at the previous church; he found some long lost family there and decided he wanted to be with them instead. No skin off our backs," answered another. The answer seemed genuine. I nodded.

I looked back at the leader at the front of the church. I raised the strip of wax paper to my lips and peeled off one of the colored dots. I let it dissolve on my tongue, a strange powdery feeling settling into every nook and cranny of my mouth.

"Who should I be praying to?" I asked.

"Try Hypnos," said the man. "Pray for sleep. But don't beg. Demand it! Take charge! It is your right!" he shouted. "We demand sleep!"

Two others in the congregation stood and looked to me, convinced enough to at least try something different. I just wanted an adventure at that point; I knew it was futile, but goddamn if it didn't seem like fun. The leader at the front seemed wild and intense, and I knew he would take me on just such an adventure. I climbed over the incensed parishioners to the aisle, where I met the other deserters. I offered them the flier and the strip of dots.

What followed was a wild ride of drugs and sex and violence. In my initiation trip, I stood next to Archie, the leader of that battalion, and in fact the leader of the whole of the Ireland faction, and echoed his pitch in front of a dozen other churches.

I'm sure it was funny, talking about worshipping these old, forgotten gods, but to me it wasn't any more ridiculous than the gods the church-goers were in the process of worshipping (Catholicism had ten thousand Saints, remember, essentially a myriad of gods to pray with, for everything as broad as *world peace* to specific as *straightness of wood grain*). But to me it seemed deadly serious. In the end of the world, I needed focus, and I wanted a group to belong to again; I would show them my strengths, and play the part of recent convert to help draw in new people to WOGAI.

It was a parody of those crazy American deep-south gospel shouters you see on Sunday morning television. The father would say something, and someone at his side would riff off it, adding to it or emphasizing by repeating words, hands up in the air *par-AAAY-zin' Jee-zus*. But, unlike us, it was probably that neither of such a duo was on mind-altering drugs, other than the ones their bodies were producing, I mean.

"Join us and awaken the old gods," said Archie.

"The old gods will save us," I added, hands up in the air, head bowed, offering praise to gods whose names I had only just learned.

"If we are loud enough, we will call Aengus MacOg to visit Caer Ibormeith and sing the song that will make Ireland sleep for three days and three nights!"

"Oh swan gods sing your song," I said, wondering at the colors dripping off of the stained glass rosary window, leaving it grey-scale.

Archie's tattoos swirled and dripped, his skin a mesmerizing display of animated pictographs and disruptive camouflage; for the life of me now I can't remember what they actually looked like. I only see them through the haze of all the time I spent tripping while watching them swirl and shift.

After a while, Archie let me do the main sermonizing, and one of the others in the group took over the role of echoing me. Archie watched from the sidelines, his approval and stoic admiration doing wonders for my confidence.

Those first few days were a hectic haze. When they gave me a break from the drugs (both disappointing and a relief—god, how I taxed my body in such a dangerous time), I had opportunity to learn more about the organization while we traveled. And in that brief window of cogency I learned of all the chaos that was descending upon every corner of the world—the attack and subsequent loss of that American city to one of their many militias, the explosion in Paris, the escalation of what may well be World War III in the Suez Canal and on the India/Pakistan border, and, closer to home, the destruction of the Palace of Westminster and effectively the British government.

It was perfect timing, as far as my personal psychedelic experience went; I had my wits about me enough to flee and survive when the chaos came our way, when IRA came and destroyed our HQ in Dublin. They came in with the big guns, "purging the lord's temple of the Satan-worshipping heretics," they screamed.

Archie was quiet for a long while after that; a lot of people died. But then Archie and I joined up with another group that had fractured off of the WOGAI, the Hear Us Hypnos movement, who were appealing to Thánatos, Hypnos's brother, the god of death. They hoped that if we got all of Hypnos's family on board, that he could be swayed to answer our prayers and give us back our sleep. Eventually it evolved into worshipping his three sons as well; Oneiroi, Morpheus, and Phobetor. Surely one of them would relay our message to their errant father.

We started up a faction, got it self-sufficient and self-perpetuating, and then moved on, new people clinging onto us and old ones dropping off at every new town.

My time with them was mostly spent outside, in fields where we set up rings of fire and candles in beautiful patterns laid out by a professional crop-circler. Archie helped mastermind the patterns, pictograms that made sense only when seen from high above. He drew up plans, and we wrote symbols in the grass in fire to call down the gods of dreams, nightmares, sleep, and even death.

One evening in the field as I helped lay out another pictogram, a plane flew overhead with a huge banner that read NASTASIJA, RUSSIAN GODDESS OF SLEEP, BRINGS HER FOLLOWERS DEEP SLEEP! PRAY TO NASTASIJA!

One of the guys in my battalion knew some Cyrillic, enough to write out the name of the goddess anyway, and we incorporated that into our design. The fields of Ireland still had their sheep wandering about, but also our messages to the gods, fires contained in borders of stones, with shielded candles and lanterns every now and then to keep fire always on hand. The flames flickered in the breeze as a line of people tended the fires, keeping them lit, keeping them within the stone borders.

We had a great meeting of the factions. When it was getting on in the Longest Day, when we were starting to go legit insane, we all came together to talk about our direction in the midst of worldwide collapse. And I do mean we were going legitimately insane; we lost many to becoming those Waking Dreamers and even more than that to that oblivion which was stopping and Staring. For the record, too, I feel like I should mention it wasn't just the Russians that had that rare dog-archtype, those ones turned totally feral and aggressive; we had one of our own go that way, and he ripped out someone's throat before he was put down. And in the midst of this we still came together for this other form of insanity.

Even as we dwindled, we kept right on going. To accompany our huge meeting, we had a rave in a field. Drugs flowed freely;

everywhere you looked there was fighting or sex or both. When people don't think there's a hope of recovery, they will do just about anything. We were all consensual though—not to be confused with those awful groups that went around raping and murdering, or Hunt-A-Human, or any of the other truly heinous organizations that emerged during the destruction. We were just there to have fun and to feel alive.

I was in the middle of something very salacious with about six other people (I'll spare you the details—or maybe *deprive* you of the details? God, it was good), when Archie pried himself from the fray and took the sound system off of the music to scream at us. Insults of every kind, about how we were just as stupid as the sheep that were in the churches. About how we weren't helping anyone hiding behind this farce of new religion.

"The old gods are dead! We killed them too! We cannot wake them because there is nothing there. If you continue on this path you are deluding yourself. Sheep! Fools! It's meaningless!"

They carried Archie away from the rave and let him weather out the drug cocktail in the quiet of an empty B&B that we had taken over for the meeting.

In the afternoon, when the drugs had mostly worn off, the leaders of the various factions met at the B&B. I woke up and took the water offered to me, but eyed the accompanying pills suspiciously until someone passed me the bottle they'd come from; common painkillers. Archie apologized and rescinded his words, but they couldn't help but feel that it was how he really felt, that he was done with the insanity of our old-world god cult.

"Even if it is true," said one of his right hands, "we still have each other. We don't need to be pretending to worship gods, we can just be a group. You're my only family left, and I'll be damned if I'm going to let us disperse because we don't have a thing to do."

Archie slapped his hands together.

"Right! So what now? What shall the Magnificent Old God Worshippers become instead?"

"The Magnificent Cunts!" shouted someone enthusiastically in my face.

"There's destruction enough as it is!" countered Archie with a harsh glare of finality. "We need a better path than that."

"I still think it's a good idea. What if it helps somehow?" I asked. "Worshipping the old ones, I mean," I said, softer, feeling an uncomfortable silence settling on those gathered.

"If it makes you feel better, do it," said Archie. "Let's keep the fires going. In the darkness of the nighttime, let's pretend. But let's also do something useful!"

"We're too out of it to do anything useful."

"Then stay here and worship your lies!" shouted Archie. He'd had it, they could see. But we'd grown to form a bond with that crazy group, and we wouldn't just leave it behind, not when it became apparent that we might never sleep again, and the end was nigh. So there was a compromise.

I followed Archie. The WOGAI and associated clone groups continued on in the fields, but Archie and I fled back into the cities, on motorbikes that we kept fueled by syphoning out of the abundant cars abandoned on the sides of roads.

We alternated activities. In the light of day, Archie screamed at now-dwindling church congregations, an AK in his hands to ensure he got to speak his piece. He called them liars, hypocrites, sheep, every name he could think of. He tried to get them to wake up and get out of the ineffectual system they were a part of to do something useful. He would always have a project, and he would always challenge them to do it. Sometimes it was gathering food supplies together at the church, or, probably about 50 percent of the time, it was to organize a clean-up brigade to take the garbage away from the town. Mostly they ignored him, but I saw at least a few times when he managed to spur them into action, to *do* something. So there was that, at least.

And when it got dark, it was my time to shine. I took over giving the orders, and Archie would follow me, just as I had followed him in the day. He helped me design and trace out the pictograms to awaken the old gods. In backyards, school soccer fields, in parks, wherever we were when it got dark, we would make the symbols and shout to the heavens, our faces licked with the glow of flickering flames and the smoke of petrol and whatever we'd found to burn.

We gained quite a following with this method. Anyone who'd had it with the church, or just wanted an adventure, as I had, followed us. They joined us either as Archie screamed at a church or even in the street, or as I chanted some Latin nonsense up at the old gods, the fires of the made-up symbols lighting up whatever field we'd settled on for the night.

I would love, please, for those that were still able to do satellite imaging at the time to see if they caught any of these things happening in Ireland. It would be lovely to see what they looked like from the sky. But if not, I know Karachi was in the spectacular process of burning to the ground right around then: if *my* fires weren't visible from space, that one sure as hell was. A time-lapse of the earth while we tore ourselves apart would be an interesting sort of forensic documentation of our last days. At least my fires were good, not destructive. I was trying to help.

It was during one of the final days, when Archie was preaching truth and awakening, seeing if he could make more people abandon the lies of the church, when he got shot. It had to happen eventually. There were enough armed parishioners that it was only a matter of time until one of them tried to put an end to his heresy.

I don't think I could have got through it without him. He was my salvation, my god that began as real and then existed only as part of me to get me through to the end. I wonder if it had been *me* at the helm and not him, who would be writing this? Was I him before, or was I me?

I still have the bullet in my chest.

I took the last of my pills to be able to write this. Otherwise it would be a sheet of paper covered in drool.

It's like—not breathing. Every moment I am awake my mind fixates on the thought of go to sleep. *If I held my breath, after a minute the urge to breathe would be less than this awful feeling of deprivation. I try and think of other things, have tried to read a book, but always this thought butts in of* go to sleep.

WELL I BLOODY WELL CAN'T!!! Get over it!

Can you just. leave. me. alone.

All the things I once was, who I am, or at least who I was before I became this monstrous thing, this barely-thinking, sloth thing, all those things are falling away from me now. Memories are slipping out of my grasp with each passing hour, each time my mind screams *at me to* go to sleep.

All my loves, the people, the hobbies, the passions which drove me to live a rich life, I can barely graze them as they fly from my grasp. Sometimes it's violent and obvious—one minute in the middle of the night I realized I couldn't remember my middle son's name. I could see his face plain as day, see how his eyes would crease in laughter at a joke, more often at my expense than not, but no matter. I love him, am so very proud of him, and yet, his name is gone from me.

I have seen a plaque on my wall which bears my name, but I have no recollection of receiving it. And why was I ascribed a strange nickname on it? A middle name inserted in quotation marks, to suggest that it was a joke, and yet there too, a hole. Maddening, to feel and be aware of this slow madness as it descends upon me.

At least I am warm.

And always this strange companion—a man outside my window and sometimes at my door standing, staring, and sometimes whispering at me that I need to go to sleep. *He tells me I'm going to die if I don't sleep soon.*

I know already!

And then the whistling! There's the sound of waves crashing on a shore, but I'm a thousand miles from the coast, and sometimes the sound of heavy rain, though it's a clear night. This great grey static noise fills up my ears, and then whistling. The man at the door.

There have been bells a few times, pleasant, deep chimes, and I've gone out to see where they were coming from. But everywhere I went, they were always that much further away. I can never catch them, so I think they must be like the waves and the rain—a product of my hallucinating brain.

I did ask the man at the door once, through the mail slot, if he could hear the bells. He only laughed and said that I needed to go to sleep.

And then there're some things in the room that I'm not sure are real. For instance this nice chair I'm sitting in, surely it, in essence, is real, because I am sitting in it. But there are jewels studded all along the arms and legs of it, and I'm not sure that it was like that before. They catch the candlelight sometimes and the glittering of them is quite harsh and bright, enough to make me look away.

I have a candle that wobbles back and forth like a belly dancer. She has a bead of wax for her belly button, and a tapered form which is strangely sultry. For a candle, I mean. Only when she is unlit though; I lit her once to see what would happen, and it stopped its dance. So I haven't lit her since. I've put her on the side table, next to this chair with its pretend jewels, and sometimes I watch her dance. Sometimes the bells strike a rhythm so it looks like they are either keeping time, or she is dancing to match their pace.

And at my feet, the ottoman raises one of its legs up like a dog and appears to urinate on the carpet. I'm pretty sure that's also not real. It shuddered once, when I put my feet up on it. And I apologized to it.

So my brain is inventing things, inserting new reality into my surroundings.

Before it got this bad, I set myself up rather well; all around me, the room walls are lined with canned food. When I am hungry, I have only to get up from this seat, being careful not to look at the chair if it's doing its blind-me-with-jewels routine, and take six steps away, so I am at the wall. I have seven can openers, or it might be eight I can't remember now, but they are all easy to see.

One of them spins all on its own, even when I'm not touching it, it spins. It woke me up once. But I wasn't sleeping, so that can't be right. It . . . it maybe broke my concentration, which felt like waking from sleep. It's not an automatic can opener. I don't know what's different about that particular one that made my brain decide that it would be the one to hallucinate moving on its own. It's just a plain can opener with olive green handles. And it spins on its own.

The man at the door has asked for some of the food.

He knows I have a gun.

He has also asked for a bullet. But I can't do that. There are a myriad of ways to do away with oneself in this catastrophe, I shall not be charitable and help him take the easy way out when he is still able to do it himself. Lazy ass.

The tin of pears I just ate was black, and tasted of motor oil. But I was sure that, when I put all the food against the walls, I was still able to read, and I could tell that it was all food I was putting there.

And yet now this taste of gross motor oil, of ash, of dirt, is in my mouth. I just looked at the empty tin, and there was only some clear pear juice left in it, just a few drops, but it wasn't black, as it looked before.

The man at the door is yelling now, screaming at me. He can hear the bells too.

The rain falls heavy outside, but this time I can't hear it—only see. And I went outside to put my hand in it, to see if it was real, and it stung my hand.

My skin is bubbling.

I cannot tell if it's real. The pain is quite real, but after these weeks of fighting go to sleep*, it is not so hard to ignore pain. Nor to invent pain where there is none.*

I'm fairly sure it's real now—my skin is sloughing off, and the blood is flowing from a few places.

So something in the air is killing me.

The man at the door tells me to go to sleep.

I ask him if he still wants me to shoot him. He says no. I might do it anyway; if I can muster the strength to open the door and see what he looks like—if he looks as terrible as I suspect I do, with these sores and skin peeling, and now my fingernails feel loose—then I shall help him.

I opened the door, but outside was only a mirror. The man there did *look like me, and had terrible wounds, and a tooth missing, gums bleeding.*

I will shoot him now.

PART 4
DEATH

Turn off your lights or I will shoot you in the fucking head!
—Fliers pasted up in Syracuse, New York, United States

Hopefully I can give you a bit of an info dump without it coming out like a pile of shit.

But really, it's about damn time you learned a thing or two about the power grid, isn't it? I mean, we probably saved more lives by keeping it on than . . . Ah well, whatever man. Just, I'll keep the civil engineering lesson short, okay?

There's three major power grids in North America, Texas not included. Texas has their own, because Texas. I was at the helm of the Northeast Power Coordinating Council, part of the Eastern Interconnection, which sucked power out of Canadian damns and pumped water into the Hudson Bay. We were responsible for getting hydroelectricity to seven states, New York being the most populous, and five provinces, Ontario and Québec included.

All told, I was in charge of keeping the lights on for over sixty million people.

Right off the bat we had it lucky. Anyone that relied on coal for their power grid got the big ol' F.U. of the dark ages within a few days. Coal took a lot of intervention. Coal had to be constantly dumped into those plants, a steady stream of people working, all the way from pulling it out of the ground to getting it into the damn burners. You just can't keep a system like that going when the world starts to end. Most of the United States relied on coal.

Can we use emoticons? Will you edit them out? Frowny face frowny face frowny face.

Despite a lot of industries putting on airs to switching over to renewable fuel sources, it was nowhere near where it should have been. I mean it's a laugh really; the last year that BP existed, it spent more money *advertising* that it was going green, than it did *actually going green*.

So most of the people in charge of keeping the lights on were doomed from the start. They tried, I know they tried. There were lots of people who didn't just fuck off, people who didn't need the government to mandate that they stay the fuck at work. They knew that keeping the power on was the most important thing. Some might argue with me, but they're wrong. What good are any of the other services they'd put before power, without power?

Electricity was the name of the game, and like I said, right off the bat, we were lucky.

Someday, the world is going to come for Canada's water. I don't blame them. We have more than our fair share of it, I think. But when it came down to it, we were able to keep the power running for an impressive percentage of our country, and seven states, because we used hydro power.

The places around the globe that used solar and wind fared even better than us, I imagine. They need even less intervention to keep things going. There are a lot of tidal power units, even more than before, and they couldn't care less about people doing whatever.

The only hitch in the system, every system, not just those of us putting a harness on whatever river we wanted, was that we weren't talking about normal power use. Before, we'd have our peaks and valleys, highs and lows of power consumption throughout the day. . . . But these were created from the constant cycle of waking and sleeping. Once people were awake *all the time*, once the night pressed in around them, and especially once the curfew started getting serious, the demand for electricity went through the roof.

It was not even a week into it, just five days of not sleeping, five days of people slowly dropping out of their jobs, abandoning their posts, when I calculated how long we'd be able to keep the power on for two-thirds of the country's population. Sorry to the rest of them—we had to focus on helping the most people we could, so that was my grid. I know the west managed something similar, but god help us we failed the vast expanse of central Canada. All our farmers, all our small town people—well, I'm truly sorry. Some of them kept the lights on, for sure, but mostly they just didn't have enough people with the expertise to keep the grid working. What small town can boast an excess of power grid technicians, when even before they'd had to import them in on a for-lend basis? If they were lucky, they had enough to get the system set up to last them as long as . . . well. We didn't know.

But like I said, I ran the grid which fed off of the dams that led into the mighty Hudson Bay. We worked against nature—capturing runoff water during the melt and storing it in the summer and letting it flow back out into the bay to power the turbines in the winter, effectively reversing the freeze-melt cycle of the largest freshwater system on earth. We were wreaking havoc on the North Atlantic and the whole of the Arctic Current, and thus, the whole earth's ocean currents.

Sorry 'bout that.

No one said it was perfect.

But hey, we could keep it running even on minimal staff. I made a plan to keep it going as long as possible, but we'd need the public on board. I chaired the meeting to lay out my timeline and my projections, and I think it was the meeting that saved the grid.

And because we controlled the water, we controlled the power. There was fear that the military would roll in and throw a wrench in our works, but we hoped to keep the juice going to Uncle Sam as well as us Canucks.

We could have cut them off, could have made it real easy on ourselves . . . Whatever we did, we tried to do the best for as many people as we could, border be damned.

God, I bet there's a ton of that to hear about, from those times. Sacrificing the needs of the few so the needs of the many could be met? Well I think we made the right choice. You can decide for yourself I guess . . .

There were a few empty seats in our shiny board room, white walls with recessed lighting along the ceiling. The window wall looked out from the second story over the lobby of the hydro building, increasingly sparse staff scuttling to and fro as best they could. This was the building where all the bureaucracy happened, quite removed from the operations of the dams and river turbines that fed it the juice.

"Where's Bill?" I asked.

"Had to help with his kids," said one of the guys from PR. I nodded. You can't make people work. Some people came in to serve the grid even when they had other things that maybe they needed to be taking care of, like family. A lot of sacrifices were made. But they had to be the one to make that call. Mandates don't mean shit in the wake of the personal tragedies people were beginning to go through.

"We need a slogan, something that pops and that people can remember and repeat. *Loose lips sink ships*, you know," I told them. My brain was starting to get that fog all over it. Like looking through one of those old telescopes a ship's captain might use to scan the horizon—grit around the edges, the glass perhaps a little warped along one side, and held with the shaky hands of someone whose teeth are loosening and whose men are thinking mutinous thoughts.

"What we want to get across is that the longer we can conserve power, the longer we'll have it," said one of my engineers. My first mate. My navigator. Her fingers shook as she ran them through her hair, which was caught in a collar button; she fumbled with it to untangle her hair, and ended up tossing away a piece of knotted locks, ends squiggly from where she'd pulled them from the offending knot.

"*Loose lips sink ships*," I repeated, as though it would clarify everything.

"How do we tell people to live in the dark?" answered one of the public liaisons. "Watching television is the only thing keeping them from rioting," she added, disregarding the massive riots that had already happened despite the power holding steady.

"Look," said the PR guy, "we cut the power. We keep it off for a day. We let them see what it will be like when it goes out. Then we tell them, *Hey, we figured out a way to keep it on, but you have to follow our instructions to the letter, or it won't work.*"

"What instructions?" said another engineer. "There's no way we can keep up with this demand. Lights on in every city, *all night*! Televisions going, heaters going, goddamn video games going, twenty-four hours a goddamn day!" Mutiny stalking around, barely below the surface, a fin breaching here and there.

"I've got a plan," I said, my hands shushing at him in what I hoped was a gentle way. "I've worked out a sensible schedule that I think most people would think is fair. Each household basically gets one light on for twelve hours a day, one television on for eight, and the regular usage for appliances and hot water."

"They'll never do it voluntarily," said the engineer with a frown.

"That's why we cut the power," said the PR guy. "We need the message to hit home. We need them to see what it will be like if they don't do what we say." PR guy, an unlikely hired gun. But he knew, maybe more than most—he'd been in the control room with me, been there when we saw how fast it'd be going dark. He had kids at home.

"It's cruel."

"It's effective," he countered.

"The lights go out. And when the power comes back on, we still need a message. We need a concrete plan and we need to follow through with it. And we might need to set an example of someone that doesn't follow the plan."

"We could encourage people to report those in noncompliance," said another engineer.

"And turn neighbor against neighbor? Everyone scrutinizing each other's power use? *The Johnson's light is on again dear, won't you go and say something?*"

"And why shouldn't they say something!" shouted the increasingly irate engineer. "People are going to start dying when the power goes out! It's going to get bloody cold. We're going to go out in the dark, huddled around a candle as the only thing to see us through the death in the night!"

"There's even another question: can we tell people to use candles? There have been an awful lot of fires already; people just aren't paying attention like they should be, and a knocked over flame could be a disaster."

"Less homes to power. If everyone didn't live in their own home, if we could get them to double up, triple up, maybe have one house on the block with power or something—"

"Jesus, man, that would never fly." PR guy was going too far. The fins were breaching the surface further and further, the water beginning to roil with discontent.

"Look," I said loudly to regain the decorum of the meeting, "we go with my timeline. It lets people have the most power for the most time, in their own homes. As long as our automation works as we've told it to. First, we cut the power," I said with a nod of deference to the PR guy, "and when it comes back, the TV has every channel on a message from the government, both governments, telling them how it's going to be. We need a slogan, and then we need people to follow the plan."

"You think we should just tell them," said the PR guy. "It would incite panic," he added shaking his head.

"People are already panicking," said my engineer. "If they know the plan—people love plans. They'll follow it," she finished, looking at me eagerly to continue.

"I agree," I said. "So let's get crackin'. We need the CBC in here to film our message, and we need a script. We need a slogan. We cut the power in twelve hours," I said. They dispersed as if I had banged a gavel on the table. Maybe I slammed my hand down, I don't remember now. If I had, it didn't hurt, didn't even feel like anything. I remember seeing some comic of a dinosaur, a long-necked one, and it's only two panels: it steps on a sharp rock, and then in the next panel it's walked quite a ways away from the rock, and it says *OW!* That's what it was like then. Things took longer to feel. My neck getting longer and longer, the signals having to travel farther and farther from my hands to my brain.

Not that that's what dinosaurs were like. Will you have any other amateur paleontologists in your volume though I wonder? I wonder how many of us are left. I also wonder if fatal insomnia had ever been considered as a cause of mass extinction before this. Sorry for the digression . . . I know what you wanted me here for, so I'll stick to that.

My plan to keep the power on. Everyone went to do their job and more—getting the press release video together was harder than I imagined it would be. The CBC sent a skeleton crew over to make a tape, and we were still struggling to come up with a punchy slogan to get our message across.

We also realized at the last minute that we'd have to make it work for both the Canadian and the American viewer; we added a local art decorator to the team and she hurried to get the necessary props together: hockey things, eagles, American flags, maple leaves—visual shibboleths for both nations. We'd wanted to make two videos, but man, there just wasn't enough time. We tried to dress the set in as much dual-nation background stuff as possible, hoping each nation would see their own things there and make it theirs.

But before we shot we had to finish the script. The boom mic operator watched over our shoulders as a writer worked with me on a white board, various words and phrases circled, scribbled out, surrounded by words that rhymed with them.

Seeing people work under pressure is amazing, but when your work relies on your mind, it is a frustrating thing; creative genius under the strain of that fog of looking through a long lens, seeing only a small circle of horizon, I have no idea how anyone creative was still able to put ideas to paper. Perhaps it wasn't done as effectively as he'd been able to before, but he got it done. Well, he was getting there.

If we'd had more time, or maybe an ad agency helping us, we could have come up with something better. But as it was, we only had to come up with something *good*. Something clear and honest.

"Look," said the boom mic operator, clearly getting frustrated at seeing our dysfunctional creative process at work before him. He snatched a white board marker out of my hand and used his broad fist to wipe off a section of the board to work on.

"Lights Off, Power On," I read. "Not bad." The writer's eyes went wide as he saw the slogan, then narrowed as he glared at the unlikely man who'd contributed it. Robert, if you're still out there, don't worry man, you did the important work. Those videos, your writing, saved a shitload of lives, man.

"Thanks," said my engineer to the CBC crew man, visibly relieved, perhaps not noticing the daggers being stared at him by the writer.

"No problem, buddy," said the boom mic operator. "Hey Felix, we're good to go here," he called to the rest of his crew.

I know the audience for this collection is international, and not everyone will have seen the message we broadcast. If you happen to meet a Canadian though, ask them, and I'd be surprised if they didn't know our little advert line for line, mistakes in diction and all. If they don't, then they're part of the population that their country let down, left in the dark, and had it way harder than anyone who can recite our message. Anyone with a New Yawk accent should know it.

We recorded it, and watched as one of the crew of the CBC edited it on the fly. We had a satisfactory bit of propaganda when she was through, and we sent them off with it to get approval from higher up.

The next day, we cut the power.

Sixty million people. Ontario, Québec, New Brunswick, Nova Scotia, Prince Edward Island, on the Canadian side of the 49th, and Maine, Vermont, New Hampshire, Massachusetts, New York, Connecticut, and Rhode Island to the south. Northeast Power Coordinating Council don't fuck around.

Hospitals had backup generators that kept them going, or at least, kept them going *enough*.

But everyone else was in the dark. Twenty-four hours of dark, cold, boring, terrifying, powerless existence. And I don't think I'm conflating the reality of it. Before the fall, if you'd lost power for any length of time, you probably remember it, right? Mostly it meant that your devices couldn't charge and you'd be running your laptop off its battery for a while, reduced to eating cold food for a meal.

Well I wanted to make us realize what we were doing, the hell we were inflicting upon people. I didn't think we had a right to be making the choices we were without going through the consequences too, so we tried to emulate the experience of the public by limiting ourselves to what we thought they had on hand. No special treatment for the power grid gods, no sir. I sat in the dark like everyone else. Had to leave the control room (what kind of power control center would cut the power to itself? I had to find a room to have to myself and manually flick off the lights).

I had a flashlight; certainly most of the houses that went dark had flashlights. I had a blanket. I had an energy bar. I turned off my flashlight to sit in the quiet dark. I used my other senses for a while; I felt the raspy fibers of the blanket against my fingertips, unwrapped the energy bar and listened to the way the wrapper crinkled as I moved it, and held the pressed bar up to my nose. It smelled like wet cardboard, and peanut butter. It tasted only like the peanut butter though, thank goodness.

My ears were ringing. In the quiet I could hear them clearly—an E flat, not an unpleasant tone. I experimented with humming along to it for a few minutes, the ringing my drone while I toyed with a melody around it, like bagpipes.

I stood and played with my sense of balance. Standing on one foot for a while, or rather, trying to, made it abundantly clear that my motor skills were taking a hit. I sat back on the ground and looked at my watch.

I did a double take at its face. Had it only been an *hour*? Jesus, what had we done?

I wish I could say I stayed in that quiet, dark room for the whole time, but I couldn't. I got a taste of what my plan had visited upon people, my people, my charges who I was supposed to be protecting; any longer and I would have gone fully insane from the guilt.

Instead, I went and micromanaged the engineers as they recalibrated the system during the down time.

Cut the power for twenty-four hours, during what was already a crisis, and we punctuated our point quite well. There were a few minor riots, but both governments had our back. Good thing we did it that early, when there was still a semblance of a police and military system remaining, with the warm bodies to back it up.

When their lights came back on, when they rushed back to their televisions and radios, we were on every channel, every wavelength, AM and FM. Everywhere the NPCC reached, there was our video or the audio from it.

We chose a woman's voice for the message, friendly and warm, but with commanding notes of stern tut-tuttery in it, to strike a balance between friend and boss. On top of it, we gave her a British accent, a surefire way to add credibility to someone and make them seem more intelligent. Using stereotypes could be helpful. Maybe it wasn't as good for the American viewer, but their culture still put the Brits up on a pedestal, would still listen to anything in that accent. Documentary narrators, car enthusiasts, villains . . .

"Lights off, power on. Lights off, power on." She said it rather flatly those first two times. But then there was a sincerity in the next repetition, a longing, an urgency there that demanded attention. "*Lights off, power on.*" She paused for a moment, then continued on in a friendly tone. "If we keep our power usage to a minimum, we'll have access to electricity for longer. Do your part. Turn out your lights. If you're able, you may help by going into empty houses and turning off all the switches in the fuse box. Turn off every switch you can find. Wear more clothes to keep warm. Conserving power now will save lives later. Lights off, power on. Lights off, power on. Lights off, power on."

It ran on repeat for a solid hour. Step one of our propaganda plan.

And then it was back to business as usual. Everything that discussed the message elaborated on it. There was carefully crafted opposition, so it didn't seem so biased, but every channel and frequency tried to hammer home that it would be best if everyone could do their part and turn off as many electrical devices as possible. A lot of the discussion conflated the idea, equating turning off your lights and bundling up with being a hero. Saving lives, just by turning off the heater? Who wouldn't be into that?

We ran the message every twelve hours, and each time after the first, we followed it with a little fluff piece that the CBC skeleton crew helped us put together.

The first was inspiring: "Mr. Johnson of Washington Street turned off the lights of more than *two dozen* empty houses today. It's because of him that now two dozen houses with families in them will have electricity for light if they need it."

Cut to three adorable young children, two young boys and a girl, huddled around a single nightstand lamp with a shade printed with a pattern of hockey sticks, snowmen, and red maple leaves. Their smiles shone and they waved at the camera and said in unison, "Thank you, Mr. Johnson!" It was so sweet it almost made me barf.

But people ate it up.

"YOU can be like Mr. Johnson: turn out lights and save lives!" Cut to a row of suburban houses with all their lights on. This segment we managed to film twice—in one version, American flags flew, and in the other, there were no flags, but a hockey net and two sticks outside of one garage. One by one the lights wink out until there's only a single room lit in each of them. Cut back to the three adorable children. They laugh and wave at the camera.

It made my heart glow a little, even though I knew what a contrived piece of bullshit it was. Goddamn, we were good.

We saw an immediate dip in demand. Across the board, people were using less power for everything, all the time. As soon as we saw it start to rise again, as soon as we saw the complacency begin to creep in as we knew it would, we began phase two of the plan.

We cut the power again. Another twenty-four hours in the dark. Another beating to teach them a lesson in their animal brains; brutal punishment would have to suffice instead of gentle niceties. We just didn't have the time.

That time, I didn't sit in the dark. I couldn't. My posture was becoming reminiscent of a caricatured laboratory assistant, my legs were feeling heavy and weak, and the ringing in my ears was getting worse. I tried to keep busy with maintenance, helping where I could, getting my hands dirty.

When the power came back on, every TV channel was on our new ad.

The three children huddle alone in the dark; there is an infrared filter on the camera to capture the images in the dark, showing them only in tones of grey against the blackness, bright, washed-out grey in the center of their pleading faces. Their oh-so-Canadian night-light is out. They shiver and rub their hands together. One of them is crying.

"Mr. Johnson, why did our light go out?" asks the youngest, looking balefully up at the camera. A high angle, looking down on the little boy, makes him seem weak and vulnerable.

"We're so scared!" says his only-slightly older brother.

"Please turn off your lights and heat and only use what you need," says the older sister sternly, chastising us in the audience. "We only need this one little light, but it's not working. Can you help us?" she asks, this time with the exact right amount of childhood innocence and vulnerability.

"Please," says the youngest, tears spilling down his tiny face in the grey glow of the infrared filter.

There was a goddamned riot in Montreal after that aired. Their **sorrow** was brought to a head and there was no other release valve for such an awful epiphany as the children made real their worst fears.

But then, after the violence died down, people were on power conservation like flies on shit. Neighborhood patrols were organized to check all houses for occupancy, so that the fuses could be switched off if no one was home.

Thousands of hot water tanks were turned off. Thousands of power suckers, all the electronic devices that use power even when they're not on, were suddenly removed from the grid. We saw usage fall dramatically again. Whole blocks of New York City organized patrols to ensure compliance.

Our ads returned to offering the carrot instead of the stick, showing the three little children laughing around a book, playing a game of Go Fish, coloring in a coloring book, smiling and waving at the camera.

We did feature pieces on people that had turned off houses' fuseboxes. Most were shy and humble, but we also showed footage of interviews of people expressing their appreciation for their efforts.

"Marjorie and Jack are heroes," says a burly bearded man in a plaid flannel shirt, suspenders holding up tan work pants. "They came by to see if we were home, and asked us to turn off one of the extra lights we had on." He gives a gruff grunt, as if to say that he'd never been confronted before in his life. "Well, she was right. We *didn't* need as much light as we were taking, and they reminded us of that fact. It takes courage to confront people, but Marjorie and Jack did. And because of them, the power will stay on that much longer." He looks at the camera, deep brown eyes stern and commanding. He points at the viewer. "It's not too late to turn off a light."

Every twelve hours we tried to add to the narrative we were crafting for the country. Making ordinary people out to be heroes for turning off fuse boxes and living with very little light and heat. And always that oft repeated, "Lights off, power on," slogan before and after everything we shoveled onto the program.

Eventually the population began to dwindle and the power usage began to fall even further. People were still doing their duties at the end though, going into houses with bodies in them and flipping fuses to conserve power.

"Wear a face mask to avoid the smell," we had the British-accented lady add with concern. "And put something on the door to let everyone know you've already done your duty in that home." Cue shot after shot of front doors marked with everything from a duct-tape *X* to a spray painted lightning bolt.

When we realized that we were in a better position than we'd hoped for (because how could we have anticipated such a horrifying mortality rate into our calculations), we used our propaganda machine for another purpose.

Cut to the three little children reading around their night lamp.

Into frame floats Mr. Johnson, a ghostly apparition, blue and grey wisps floating languidly off of his semitransparent skin. It was a crude effect, and sometimes Ghost Mr. Johnson didn't quite interact with the scenery as he should, but we got the idea across.

"Hello children," he says in a friendly tone, voice in a reverb chamber to give it even more ghost-cred.

"Mr. Johnson!" they say with glee, rushing up to hug him. Their hands pass right through him.

"Oh no Mr. Johnson, did you die?" asks the little girl. Mr. Johnson answers with a somber nod.

"But don't be too sad," he says, "because you know what? Now I know you can have another light. Or a video game or something. Is there a treat that you've been missing that takes more electricity?" he asks, a twinkle in his eye as he glances at a shelf of DVDs behind them.

Cut to the children, backs to the camera, arms around each other, as they sit silhouetted in front of the glow of a television, DVD player beside it busily scanning the disc so they can watch a cartoon. Winnie the Pooh.

Cue Ghost Mr. Johnson putting his unearthly hand on the youngest boy's shoulder lovingly as he watches with them.

Cut to a splash screen of text which reads "*Treat Yourself, Canada!*" or "*Treat Yourself, America!*"

Of course we had another video prepared, one of Ghost Mr. Johnson with the children, turning *off* their cartoons and returning to using only the single light, back to conserving power—I'm sad to say that it never aired. It would have meant we were using more power than the grid could handle, and that we had to ask the public to end their excess usage. But so many of us died that the extra demand for power during the splurge didn't cause us to go past the threshold that would have necessitated urging conservation again.

We kept running footage of the three children watching their cartoons. Near the end, we had clips of them on the hour. A lot of repeats, but some new stuff interspersed. Even the clips from the cutting room floor were used; ones of them laughing, picking something out of their teeth, adjusting a shoe.

I say it was new footage, but of course it had been recorded weeks before. *All* of it had been recorded weeks before, over the course of only two days of shooting. We tried to get as many little vignettes captured as we could think to craft. I think we got it mostly right. There were some we didn't use, but we still managed to scavenge shots from them to add to other things.

Those three children didn't know each other before filming, and I doubt they knew each other afterwards, taken back by their families who began the long haul of surviving the apocalypse.

They were awarded the Order of Canada, posthumously, for their contribution to saving the lives of Canadians by tugging our heartstrings to get us to turn out our lights.

The NPCC grid didn't lose power once, save for those two times when we intentionally cut it to punctuate our propaganda.

I know my plan worked as I designed it to, nay, *better* than that, because of my inability to soothsay the scale of death we would face. I wish I could have told you how it failed, how our power went out because of so many people sucking juice from the grid. I imagine the world would be overrun with horses right about now, if wishes were horses.

"Cheer up cunt!"
—*Last headline of* The New Zealand Herald

After I had my car accident, I had to relearn faces. Not just who people were, but what expressions meant. What facial cues were and what they were trying to say. So many subtle social cues had to be relearned, from scratch, without the facial-recognition part of my brain functioning.

After my accident and subsequent brain injury, microexpressions became my waypoints. Microexpressions are the split-second tells on people's faces that give away their true intentions. They give me a better sense of what was really going on with them. People can't hide behind fake expressions with me, because they can't stop themselves from subconsciously exhibiting their true emotions. That split second lasts for ages for me, rolling around in my head as I piece together the true sense of the person I am looking at.

When people get tired, microexpressions take longer. And they get much more pronounced.

Everyone knows what tired looks like, but I got a pretty intimate look at it. People trying to cover up their emotions, their exhaustion; none of their tricks worked on me. I saw their madness before they spoke. I saw their intent to rob me before they had even made the conscious decision to do so. Once I even saw someone's death before their eyes rolled back into their heads. So I guess if I make it into your collection, it will be as a record of what the human face truly looked like, what we look like when the world is ending, everyone around us is dying, and we are dying. For it's not enough to say that we looked tired.

It was like we were dead men walking. The slackness in our faces was broken through by microexpressions of extreme anguish and terror, and above all despair. Such despair that it broke my heart. Everywhere I looked, people were deeply frightened and inconsolably sad. Covering it up with their fake faces, those masks we wear to show others, and ourselves, how we want to be perceived. They couldn't hide it from me. Even though *they* believed it, I couldn't, not when the truth was so plainly written on their faces.

The masks though, they were flawed enough as it was. Deep sunken pockets under their eyes, black from old blood pooled there from the strain of missing REM sleep, sometimes with swollen and red patches stretching out from the black. Eyes constantly veiled by drooping, puffy eyelids. Bloodshot eyes. Slow blinking. Extreme tension held in the face, just beneath the horrid skin, teeth clenched behind taut cheeks, mouths held in grim lines to keep from screaming. And those were the faces that hadn't given up. The ones that had were all that but instead of tense they were slack; the face of living death.

I had to stop looking at people's faces, it was too much to take.

Near the end, I was with a friend of mine, Gareth. Casual acquaintances and neighbors became friends in those times when we were in the trenches together, fending off the army of all things trying to kill us. Just having someone in the trenches with you gave you a leg up, I think. I was glad Gareth was there with me, but I had to stop looking at his face just like all the rest. It was too awful. His face itself was handsome enough I suppose—crisp green eyes, bold cheekbones, and a square jaw ending in a slightly cleft chin—but those were just pieces to me. I didn't see faces as a whole any more, only what the individual parts were doing; they still tried to make a face, but not all of the bits and pieces could be assembled appropriately on time, in the correct setting, and truly his was the face of madness as World War ZZZ's casualty count went up and up.

And when I could still look at Gareth, it was a fascinating look at the disconnect between his subconscious facial control and the mask he wore. Jaw tensing up between words. Cheeks puffing out with the exhalation of frustrated anguish. Crisp green eyes that flashed in and out of despair and pain during every conversation we had, then softened deliberately to tame them. The blackness under them, the old blood, could make it seem I was looking at a skull.

He couldn't understand that this was how I saw him. He did ask me to try and explain one day, when we were outside and the sun was shining and he was smiling. We were watching a cheeky meerkat trying to get into a trunk, which we had used to transport some canned food we had found.

The meerkat poked its nose at the seam of one of the corners of the trunk, found his efforts to get in fruitless, and moved to the next corner. And it continued around, checking corners—I suppose he wasn't keeping track of how many he'd checked, or maybe the smells from inside were so intoxicating as to warrant a double-check of each possible way in. The critter eventually leaped up on top of it and rolled around on the lid, perhaps in frustration, but, while its long body flip-flopped back and forth as it rolled, the light fur on its tummy puffing out, it did look rather cute.

Gareth laughed, but that made it even more obvious how much pain he was in. Maybe not to someone who didn't know him, someone who didn't know what Gareth's laugh should have sounded like. His big barrel chest should have produced this huge laugh that boomed in my ears. That hollow laugh on that sunny day was instead the laugh of pain and madness.

"Why don't you ever look at me?" he said after I failed to join in.

"I can see your pain," was all I could say.

That evening though, as we sat inside, he asked me again.

"Goddamnit man, I am dying, I accept it. Please, just look. Brave it, for me, my friend, I cannot bear it," he said.

I knew I owed him that much. We hadn't been close in our years of being neighbors, but we were still friends. Friends enough for me to force myself to look at his face and see his true self. The face of pain and anguish. He had a smile stretched across his lips, as though it could hide the truth from me.

But I'm glad I looked. It meant I was there for him when he died, and when his face relaxed and was finally free of all that pain, I saw it. I saw a few others later on, and it was more of the same. Our bodies were shutting down and our faces could not hide it.

"Prions can survive cremation! Don't burn the bodies! What if it's prions!?"
—*Final headline of* The New York Times

No one was prepared for this amount of bodies. Sure, things got sloppy; some of the records aren't exactly perfect. But what do you expect us to do, when there's a body in the street and there's no ID on it? It wasn't optimal, but it's no fault of ours that so many went unidentified. We simply didn't have the manpower or the resources. We were just glad to get them off of the streets. Shàntóu had five million people and shrinking; we had to dispose of the dead as fast as possible, to keep the living safe.

All over the world, the death toll was rising, and how we treated the dead would continue to affect the scope of the disaster. There was an outbreak of gastroenteritis in Jakarta from all the bodies near their water supply; the horror of rabies swept across India from the animals growing ever aggressive and competitive for the corpses in the streets. But by far the greatest danger posed by the dead is psychological; in fact it is a myth that bodies spread disease. If they had a pathogenic disease in life, in death they could spread it. But when they were otherwise healthy, and had died of insomnia? Something everyone already had? The threat the dead posed was to our psyches.

Coupled with the growing number of domestic attacks, opportunistic skirmishes between governments clashing over supplies, or enacting operations they'd had planned out for years, the instability of life translated into the horrific degradation of how we handled the dead among us.

Everyone had their own way of dealing with it. Some have attributed the high rate of suicide in certain cities to the mass pyres, or the "death carts" that they brought around, actually calling for people to bring out their dead. It was the Dark Ages all over again. Such foolishness! So cruel!

We, my team and I, the whole city of Shàntóu, took a different tack, trying to be quiet about it. The dead were ushered away silently, respectfully, in exchange for a form that we hastily drew up so there was at least *some* record of our duty.

Mass graves were convenient. So savage we had become that it didn't matter to us that we were literally dumping our loved ones into pits like garbage. We were just lucky to be getting them out of the city, away from people, away from the aquifer. We were grateful to have access to a stockpile of lime, which we put to good use. The smells of decomposition—putrescine, cadaverine, and the lime we sprinkled over piles of bodies were a cocktail of smells that punctuated the worst times in our history. It was savage, but it kept the horror out of sight.

Can you imagine if some disease, other than the insomnia, managed to take hold, adapting in our severely weakened state? Certainly there were local outbreaks, but a global pandemic would have been the end of us; accidentally, incidentally, intentionally—it didn't matter. One maniac with a vial of Ebola, one dreamer letting out the infected research animals, one misguided mass experiment, one military coup using biological agents. Our drawbridge was down and any old something could have wandered into the sacked city that was the human immune system. I think we very narrowly escaped extinction, not because we survived the insomnia, but because no disease stepped up to the plate to take us out while we were at our most vulnerable. It would have been an easy massacre.

As it was, there were dead aplenty. At first it wasn't so many. More than normal, sure, but it was manageable with the systems we had in place.

I'm sure if you asked the general public to list what they thought the "essential services" are, you'd get a pretty consistent answer. The big three of course: hospitals, firefighters, police. And then those which are perhaps even more essential but less obvious when they're working as they should: running water, electricity, sanitation. Everyone notices when the garbage men go on strike, but no one thinks of the coroners. But when garbage men don't exist and there are bodies in the street? Whose job is that?

This is one time when we were essential, no doubt about it. And we are not squeamish around death, and in our actions we created a sort of ripple effect wherever we went. We gained many among our ranks during that time, people that found they had what it takes to be able to take a body out of someone's home and have them thank you for it.

It was built right into our anthem: *As the Chinese nation has arrived at its most perilous time / Every person is forced to expel their very last roar.* We banded together and would fight to keep our country together. Keeping the coroners' services together was my *last roar*. I think it was loud enough to save the city.

We get our fair share of weirdos too, though. I mean, you have to expect that we'd attract some nutjobs. Certainly during those times it brought out the best in people, but also the worst—those ugly, dark parts of us that we keep covered up to be able to function in society. But when that facade is no longer needed? When things are crumbling all around you? When people started dying, *really* started dying, all bets were off.

I'm sad to say that Jeff Zhang Li was one of us from the start. He had been a coroner for even longer than I. Perhaps it was his tenure that blinded us to what he was doing. We didn't see how off his rocker he'd gotten; he was actually quite a dedicated member of the team. He had a suave way with people and would help ease the trauma of taking the dead away from their loved ones with some simple words, a gentle hand on the shoulder, sometimes a sad smile. He even had premium incense to light at people's shrines during his visits.

In the grand scope of everything that was happening, people were trying to keep things functioning on such a basic level, that, once someone was dead, it's not like they mattered. I mean they do, of course, you have to keep up the pretense that the dead matter, but here, after, when I'm not standing in front of the recently deceased's family, I can tell you: the dead do not matter. Not really. Oh god, can I be worse at this? Explaining this, I mean. The dead matter to their loved ones, but as an idea. It's not like when we ineloquently bump them against a corner it's a problem. We try and shoot for a certain amount of dignity, but that standard falls away once you hit a certain tipping point. We had to get them out of there, out of houses, away from people. The living. The living matter.

Though, it's not entirely true, is it, that the dead didn't matter? When people became too exhausted to deal with their dead? When they became a psychological horror, the horror of being proximal to someone you loved after they die and remain uncared for? Sometimes people were lucky to get them out of the house and into the street. The dead mattered; they mattered *differently* in those times. They became a monstrosity, a foe, a growing horror.

Bodies would have been everywhere. As it was, The Ones Who Went Away were everywhere, standing in the streets, staring. The Ones Who See were everywhere too, dreaming their false realities, running or screaming. But the dead, no, we could at least handle that.

One of the warning signs had been when our teams were out in the city, making the daily sweep for the dead. I had a sector of the grid that neighbored the one Jeff Zhang Li was working. We each had a helper, to assist us with the hopefully dignified-looking maneuvering of the dead into our carts. *Covered* carts, with official insignia on them, each with a small flagpole and our flag flying.

No rickety open-topped wagon would be ferrying away the dead of China.

My assistant, Tzu, and I were bringing our cart to the main load, a large truck which amassed all we brought it until it was full and another took its place, when we spotted Lam, Jeff Zhang Li's assistant. He was pulling his cart on his own, and struggling. We asked him where Li was, and he frowned and said something about Li attending to something else for a moment. His gaze darted down one of the streets in the sector he was sweeping, and I nodded and took off to find him.

I saw Jeff Zhang Li come out of a ground floor café. Its windows were boarded up. I asked him what he was doing, and he told me he was saving them for later. *Saving who?* I went past him and opened the door to the café. Inside were five Ones Who Went Away, standing still in the dark, staring.

I frowned, but could hardly argue. They would be standing out in the elements otherwise. And we did have the Gatherers, a sort of volunteer organization that was picking them up and putting them in places to care for them.

"Do you want to call the Gatherers, or should I?" he asked. *He* asked. So normal. So caring.

I gestured for him to call. He smiled and accompanied me back to the main cart to help unload the finds of our sweep.

His smile told me there must be more. He'd never mentioned finding Ones Who Went Away. I asked his assistant.

"He's been putting them safely away for pickup, more and more," he told me. "Yesterday he called in more than a dozen."

I called the Gatherers. A harried sounding woman answered, out of breath and flustered.

No, they had received no calls that day for our sector. The day before? No. And if they had, they wouldn't even be able to pick them up until tomorrow, or the day after.

No, I didn't know anyone that wanted to join the Gatherers.

After I hung up, I lamented that gathering up the dead was going to last longer than gathering up the living.

Tzu and I took a gun and followed him that night. You don't really take a gun unless you're sure, but then, you want to be *sure*. I knew I was getting addlebrained. I knew I could just as easily have been inventing insanity in another, where my own was growing. I had to be careful. My assistant would hopefully be a second voice; surely both of us would be able to see what was going on without inventing the same madness. So we went together, silent dread overtaking the slightest of hopes that it would not be as terrible as we feared, that his madness was something we could tolerate, that he was a monster we could let be.

The factory Jeff Zhang Li claimed as his own had been halfway completed before construction halted on it. There were ample building materials around the site, and a mostly finished storehouse that was several stories tall and waiting for finishing touches. There was even spare fuel with a backup generator. We followed Jeff Zhang Li at a discrete distance; he led us to the storehouse and pulled open the metal doors, on smooth sliders that we couldn't even hear over the buzz of flies. When he went inside, we crept to the doors and looked at the scope of his madness.

Tzu and I watched from the doors as Li went to another part of the storehouse, sliding open another set of steel doors that opened up the whole other end of the half-finished factory. We followed him inside as quietly as we could, skirting the edge of the building, staying away from the perimeter of horror that stretched out in a puddle under the trees. When we peered across the threshold at the next room, any movement that would have betrayed us, and even the horrified moan that let slip from my gaping mouth was covered by the noise of his creation.

It's not as though *all* of them were still alive; he had chosen them because they were so far gone that they were easy to handle, easy to string up. Mostly it was Ones Who Went Away. There were a few Ones Who See, moaning and, from one man, terrible screaming that sounded out intermittently as he thrashed, trying to bat something away from his face.

There were six "trees," constructed out of the abandoned building materials. The trunks were steel girders that had beams of wood attached to them, branching out and out, some suspended by cables hanging from the roof. Covered in people. He said in his journals that they were an offering to the god of nightmares, that he was being tested to see if he could rival what the god of nightmares could do in our sleep.

Six of his *trees*.

We watched, horrified, as Li knelt in front of the tree and bowed several times, head touching down to the dirty concrete, a small patch swept free of the carpet of dead flies and maggot husks, as he made silent prayers to his god of nightmares.

It was obvious what he had done; my colleague and I exchanged a single glance by way of sentencing, to make sure we were both seeing the same thing. I readied the gun I had brought, and Tzu nodded. I walked up behind him to get close enough. I'd never fired a gun before. I'm ashamed to say that I didn't confront him; I shot him in the back of the head before he could turn around.

I would have thought I would have felt something immediately, from killing someone like that. Someone I knew. Someone I had shared meals with. But the hell of that time was that it gathered up all that horror and saved it for later, slowly releasing it, revisiting choices and actions that I wish I could have done differently. But at the time . . .

And then what to do about hundreds of people strung up to those metal girder trees? There was nowhere for them to go, no one to take them and care for them. We could have left them, but that would have felt wrong. It all felt wrong though. How do you deal with something like that?

I stepped forwards and crunched a hundred dead, dried flies. The screaming started as that One Who Sees began fighting some dreamed demon as it attacked his face.

"You may leave if you wish," I told Tzu. He shook his head.

"How good a shot are you?" he asked me. I showed him my gun, chamber open to show four rounds, all I had.

"I didn't hoard ammo; I just found this on someone we picked up last week," I explained.

We tried to consider what to do without looking up at the trees. So many people. Their voices are still in my mind; a lot of it was indistinct screaming or moaning, but there were some words. Ones Who See didn't really make any sense, but that didn't stop my brain from trying to hear them. I wish I could have tuned them out, but that part of me was gone.

Without another word, Tzu walked over to the generator and hefted one of the gas tanks towards the base of the nearest tree. He could barely manage it though, and I went to help him without really considering what we were doing.

We put gas tanks, big metal canisters, up against all of the trees.

Tzu slipped in blood once, and his vomit on the floor wasn't even a notable addition to the myriad of disgust on the ground of that place. Everything the human body can expel was on the ground there, layered with dead flies and the crawling things that eat them.

Li had successfully called the god of nightmares, for we were inside him.

We hid behind a wall at a distance we hoped was safe, and I took aim. I missed the first two shots, which sounded hollow and sad amidst the screaming and moaning and buzzing.

The third shot hit the tank in the middle of the factory and the sparks were enough to set it ablaze in a small explosion.

Tzu and I hurried away, hoping the first tank would be enough to set the others off.

They *popped* with each ignition, coming more frequently as we fled, until we were safely away and the final chorus of explosions came all at once in a crackling boom. There was a clear line of sight to the factory below, but I didn't look. I only saw it reflected in Tzu's face as he watched the walls fall away, watch the trees burning, their fruit writhing in their final moments as the flames consumed them. Even that shadow of what we had done was enough to almost push me over the edge. The flickering glow glinting off his cheeks, the way his pupils shrunk to pinpoints.

Tzu ended his life that night.

He was the first in my cart on the morning's pickup round.

Live Vegetables For Sale. Next Right.
—Banner hanging on overpass, the I-5, Oregon, United States

The last day I showed up for work, one of the lieutenants shot up the start-of-shift briefing. He got six headshots in before I even got one, but it was all I needed. I went straight home and locked myself in my apartment, then pushed the couch up against the door.

Other cops kept going to work. I wasn't one of those cops.

As things ground to a halt, I stayed safe in my second-floor apartment. It was a mixed bag of garbage-y emotions doing savage battle with instincts I'd trained up to be in law enforcement; when I heard screaming the first time it just about damn near made me check out. Why would I go and help if someone who was just like me, who I'd come up with, could turn their gun on their friends? Could end the lives of good men and women who were only there to help?

If I had been sitting one row closer to him. If I'd've seen him reach for his gun instead of seen him pull the trigger. If I wasn't in this stupor, if I could have comprehended it sooner, if my reflexes weren't dulled to shit. Garbage-y ifs, garbage-y emotions, garbage I was suffocating under as I heard screams from outside.

They stopped.

Others came on and off, different people, running from different things, real or imagined.

I tried to shut it all out. When it came time to do my job, I failed. I am not one of the success stories. I am not a hero. I did not do the right thing.

But here I am all the same.

Now, do you know what a slack line is? It's like a tightrope, but with tons of slack, and it's usually set up just about a foot or two off the ground. People set them up in parks, between trees, and test their balance and reflexes by walking a slack line. If they fall it's no big deal, because the ground is right there. A lot of people say that living through the insomnia was like walking on a tightrope, where one wrong step, one slight breeze, one aching muscle tremoring at the wrong time could send them hurtling to their death. Way I see it, for me it was more like a slack line. The ground was right there. It would be so easy to just step off. One side or the other, just a single step and I'm off the rope. Being on it was me shutting myself away from it all. Stepping off one way or the other, well, I could go do my job, or I could put my service weapon to use one last time.

I was content to just wait it out in my apartment, and when screaming happened, or gunshots, I just put my good headphones over my ears and played some loud music. That slack line got pretty comfortable.

Until it wasn't. I could feel myself slipping away. What if it stopped? What if suddenly everything was back to normal, and everyone was talking about what they did during the crisis? It's not that I didn't want to help, it's just . . . well fuck, I don't have to justify myself to you. I know there's shit like Post Traumatic Stress Disorder and all sorts of other fuckery I was contending with. Just, when it's happening, it doesn't feel logical. It feels like failure.

So I stopped being a cop. I lived on that slack line and tried to ignore how the rope was fraying. But then my neighbor came to me for help, and he managed to convince me to be something else, some*one* else. Someone more helpful than a shut-in.

I don't know how much you need to know about Anna to care about this story. Maybe it's not her you need to care about. I'm the one telling you shit, I'm the one who made it through, so maybe all that's important is that she mattered to me. She was real nice. She brought me soup when I was sick a few times. She and Burt were my neighbors, and they were as kind as you find 'em. Maybe in their 60s? Hard to tell. They acted young but I knew they were older. They had me over for Thanksgiving last year. If the whole world was people like Burt and Anna, there'd be no need for police.

It had been quiet for a while. No screaming at least. In the distance sometimes I could hear gunshots, but I didn't have to drown them out with music. I was perched on my slack line, teetering, trying to hold it together in the solitude of my apartment, when Burt knocked on my door.

I think I had one foot off the slack line then; one foot on the ground to test it.

"Jim, I need your help," said Burt, after I had slid the couch away from the door enough to see him. When he saw my face he started back. Or maybe it was the smell.

"Burt, I, uh," I didn't know what to say. I think Burt was on a slack line too; he had one foot on and one foot off, and when he surged forward into my apartment, he stepped off it and hit the ground running.

"Jim, there's still running water. Come on over here now," he said, taking my wrist and leading me towards the bathroom. He'd been in there before, to fix my sink. He turned the tap on and got the shower running.

"You get in there this instant," he commanded. "It'll be cold, but I know you can do it."

I stripped and got in. It was cold as fuck.

"Scrub," he said from the other side of the shower curtain.

I could go on about how he made me shave, how he fixed me some proper food, how he held my hand when I told him what had happened at the station. How we cried when he told me that Anna was missing. Bottom line is, I joined him in stepping fully off the slack line. When he handed me a backpack and a bottle of pills, that's when *I* hit the ground running. First forty-eight hours is critical. I would find her, and I would bring her home. That was the ground beneath my feet, and that was the path that I found to get through it.

I'll skip to the interesting bits. Tracing her movement wasn't too difficult. I managed to pinpoint her disappearance to somewhere between her sister's on Moberly Street to the diner where she worked on Pike. I started walking from the diner to her sister's and back, taking different routes each time, to see if I could see anything. But then, I was thinking like me; I was adding a few extra blocks to the trip because I was staying out of the edge of the industrial zone that the walk skirted. If I thought like Anna, I would shave time off and walk amidst the warehouses, past the metal factory and old machine shop. So I did.

I took a pill. A stim. Burt had given them to me to help, and I gotta say I don't know that they helped more than they hindered; I was pretty keyed up when I heard the gunshots. I pressed myself flat against the warehouse for cover, instinct kicking in against the chemicals coursing through me. *Find Anna, find Anna,* was all I thought.

The gunshots got closer, and I slid against the wall until I found a set of doors.

Most of us had never smelled death up until the sleep apocalypse. It was hidden from us, the world sanitized of any hint of that indignity. And now none of us are able to pretend we don't know. I had smelled it once, at a crime scene, an old murder that had gone a few days before being called a crime scene at all. I should have known what the smell was, but the stims, and maybe the psychological junk too, was keeping me from realizing what it was as I slipped inside the huge, impersonal metal doors of that industrial building.

I grabbed the flashlight from my bag. I swept it around. I was in a receiving bay, bare concrete walls on bare concrete floor.

There were large industrial shelves, the kind meant to hold crates of boxes of heavy things, and at the base of one of them, I found the source of the mysterious smell.

A body.

Bloated and swollen, quite a few days old, no doubt. There was dried blood all around it.

It. It's much easier to talk about dead bodies by calling them it. But this *it* was a her. At some point she had been a her. Just exactly *when* a body goes from being a *her* to being an *it* I don't know, but this body had gone over that line quite some time before I found it. I walked closer, tentative steps, towards a strange thing I've never seen before, even though my stomach was churning in earnest.

I gagged at being so close to the smell. And again when I saw the maggots.

Death and decomposition would become constant companions to us all in the final days, but in that early time this was my first exposure to it in the wild, as a civy, without backup or accountability or procedure. I think everyone remembers their first. For some it was fast and shocking, like having someone jump from a building and land right next to where you were walking, or seeing a body cart go by as they tried to keep the dead out of the city. But for me, there in that receiving bay, it was slow, and I could approach on my own terms. I did. The cop inside me was still there, and I started taking in information. *Find Anna,* kept thinking the keyed-up part of my mind, but then another part was trying to slow it down with, *This could mean something.*

And there was foul play afoot: bloody footprints around it told me someone had been there when the blood was still fresh. I shone my flashlight beam around and scanned the scene. The crime scene. The footprints were big; work boots, perhaps, more than likely from a man. I went into Investigation Mode. I tried to slow down but I was getting jittery from the stim.

Bloody handprints smeared on the wall next to the shelves. A high-heeled shoe several feet off from the body. This had been a violent, struggling death. And someone else had walked away from it.

I shone my beam around the concrete industrial bay. I was in a large enclave of a receiving bay; the shelves that bordered the bay stopped by a door into an office. There was an exit sign above it, though it wasn't lit—another way out, should I need it. At the edge of the shelves by the door was another body. I went to it.

This body was newer. Her skin was pale but not rotting. Her cheeks were bruised. One of her eyes was hanging out of the socket by the optic nerve. Her hands were bound behind her back and tied to the shelving, so she was in a slumped-over sitting position. Her insides sat puddled on the ground in front of her.

I reeled away and threw up.

I hurried to leave. Anna couldn't be here. She was somewhere else. I had to find her. I heard a shuffling scrape, and then a woman's laugh. I pressed myself up against a wall, heart hammering, stomach writhing, mouth stinging with bile.

Just as I reached the metal doors though, another sound from outside made me stop. Not a gunshot, but the woman's laugh again. Then a gruff man's voice, right from the doorway. I couldn't hear them well enough to get the words, but I didn't need to. My gut knew what was happening, and knew that I had two options before me. I could retreat back into the bay and exit through the office, or I could investigate what was likely a murder in progress.

There was no way the newcomers didn't smell the smell. And if there were two bodies already, from different times, there would be more, and more and more until whoever was responsible was stopped. This was someone's killing room.

I turned my flashlight off and slunk along the wall until I found the office doorway. I slipped inside it to keep myself hidden, watching the way I had come in, where I could hear them coming in. I pocketed my flashlight and knelt on the ground, peeking through the door which I left slightly open; there were no windows to see through, and the darkness behind me would keep me hidden. Or so I hoped; I'd never been that close to danger before, never watched as a monster went on its hunt, so close to where I watched.

A voice came inside and I could make out the words.

"Double patty, extra cheese, no pickles, comin' up!" said the woman. The man was silent. He led her into the bay and shut the door behind him.

"Chocolate milkshake, comin' up!" said the woman cheerfully.

I reached down my leg and pulled out my gun. I'd never fired it outside of a firing range before, except that once, in the briefing room. I suspected this would be the time for it.

The man and the woman came fully into the loading bay where the other bodies were. He held an LED lantern up in front of him as he went, and he had her by the arm, leading her. She walked along slowly, taking small steps, but she looked relaxed. He let her go and put down the lantern. He stood still, she was in constant motion.

She sort of shuffled side to side, and then started doing things with her hands, miming some vivid dream action. I recognized her then—Anna. *Found Anna, found Anna.* How long had she been with this . . . this thing, this monster? I didn't know what kind of monster he was yet, but I could feel him, his shadowy tentacles writhing in the dark.

Oh god, how much of those drugs had I taken? But the evidence was there—even if maybe I was freaking out a little, it doesn't change that there were bodies there. I know, because I went back to be sure.

"No ketchup, got it, Ralph?" said Anna cheerily. She continued on acting out what I gathered was pouring coffee, taking a side step to another spot behind the diner counter she knew so well in her mind's eye.

"Ralph, no ketchup, you got it?" she said in a singsong tone, louder.

The man stood still, so still, and just watched. He reached to his side and drew a long hunting knife.

Anna moved in her dream, unseeing, unhearing. My gun had already been raised; as soon as I'd seen the knife I was ready. Yet he didn't advance; he watched her move, just staring. Do I shoot? Do I wait until he lunges? Even though everything I had seen was telling me, *This was the guy, this was a monster*, I was still held back by my training. He was just standing there with a knife. I didn't *know* he put those other bodies there.

Yes I did.

He took a step towards her.

I shot him in the head.

Anna didn't flinch, didn't react in the slightest, as her would-be killer dropped dead to the ground next to her. My pulse raced. Adrenaline coursed into my blood even after I'd done the deed; who knows how it was reacting with the drug I took earlier. I went to her.

"Hey Ralph, throw on those onion rings, too, or they'll go to waste. Adam likes onion rings, right?" she said. Her eyes scanned along in front of her and she reached out, manipulating an imaginary coffee maker into brewing another pot.

"Anna?" I asked, to no response. "Anna?" I tried again, but she didn't seem to be aware that I existed, or where she was, or what had just happened to her.

"Adam, how are the pugs doing?" she asked with a dopey smile. She waited, nodding as she listened to the dreamed response, then laughed. "He'll get over it." Her eyes were open. She moved perhaps a little slower than normal, but she was competent in her spatial maneuvering.

I put my foot between hers to see how she would react, and she stepped over it gracefully.

“Interesting,” I said.

I plucked the lantern from the floor and took Anna by the arm and led her out of that place of death without another glance at the man I’d shot. I had zero guilt about it. Even now, none. Some people gotta be put down, and I was the only one available there to do it that time.

I walked out into the industrial street with her, stopping to listen. It was quiet, but then the rain started. The streetlights were harsh then, all the light burning my retinas until I had to squint and shield myself from it.

At least we had the place to ourselves. And then she changed modes—instead of making coffee and sending up orders in her diner, she began dancing. Huge steps, waltzing in wide circles, footwork practiced and graceful as she went through her dream routine.

“Burt, my love, let’s dance forever,” she said. There was such love, such warmth in her voice, that the sorrow of losing her hit me in the gut. She was still up and about, talking, walking, but she was gone. I steadied myself against the building, finally having to sit down. I watched her dance for a few minutes while I waited for my hands to stop shaking, my pulse to stop pounding in my neck, my eyes to stop gushing tears.

It didn’t even matter to her that I had just saved her life. She wasn’t there anymore, what did it even matter?

I walked her home. We made it to her front door and I let her dance while I buzzed Burt. There was no power, I don’t know what I was thinking; but then he was there anyway, tears welling up in his eyes. The fuck *it didn't even matter*, of *course* it mattered. It mattered to him. It mattered to *me*.

"Oh, thank god," he said.

"You must keep her inside; someone tried to hurt her," I said. His eyes narrowed and he went to Anna, who was still dancing in the empty street. When she didn't acknowledge him, all I could do was mutter a soft, "I'm sorry."

"Burt, my love, let's dance forever," she said.

Burt maneuvered himself into her arms and fell into step with her.

"Yes, let's," he answered.

At last, the insomniacs' time to shine! Eat it, conventional sleep cycle people!
—Full page advert in the last issue of the
Metro Daily Newspaper

When I was littler, I used to think that kids didn't need to sleep. Only when we grew up and our brains got big, they were too busy to get all the thinking done that we were used to. I thought it was a problem I'd face when I grew up, having to sleep.

I did sleep, just not enough. Before we found the pills that would help, I had nights alone to myself for days on end. When everyone joined me I thought they would be happy. I had way more time to play than they did!

At first everyone was upset. My mom and dad tried to hide it but I guess it got so bad that eventually I saw it. Never upset with each other. Only with other people. A woman at the supermarket tried to take something from my mom, and my mom hit her. Later, as she was checking my seatbelt in the car, she put her hands on my cheeks and looked me in the eye.

"Honey, what mommy did was wrong," she told me. "We don't hit people. But that lady was trying to do something even more wrong, and that was to steal something that we needed. I'm sorry you had to see that. I'm just trying to make sure we get through this, baby," she said. "We're going to be okay."

I heard that a lot, from a lot of people. *We're going to be okay.* Most of them didn't believe it. Some of them died. But I believed it. I knew I could go a long time without sleep, because I already had.

Early Onset Chronic Insomnia. They used to think it was pretty impressive that I could say that. Now of course it doesn't matter what I say, people look at me with this weird awed expression. Like everything out of my mouth is a big word from a toddler. Being an orphan isn't so rare, I don't know why I get the special treatment.

At first everyone was upset. They were finally getting a taste of what it felt like to be so tired that it felt like fingernails on your face, that everyone's voices sounded like shouting, and that the light sometimes stabbed right into their brain like a knife, bright and sharp and painful. Once they understood, maybe it was better for me, but it was so much worse for them. If only they could have slept.

During the upset times, there was shouting and fire and once someone laying in the street, outside my bedroom window, with blood around them. That night, my dad came in from work and his hands had blood on them and my mom helped him wash them in the sink. He came to see me afterwards and touched my cheek very softly and said, "Daddy's not going to let anything happen to you, honey. Don't open the door for anyone."

The next day they told me that things were dangerous, and that there would be some bad people that might ask me to go with them, but that I shouldn't go. Even if they said that mommy and daddy said it was okay, I shouldn't go. We picked a password, just in case they really *did* need to have someone come get me. We repeated it three times, and said that it was secret-secret, and we couldn't tell anyone else about it ever. So I can't tell you, even though they're dead now—I told them I would never tell.

We never had to use the password. People did try to get me though, twice.

Once was an old man with scary eyes. He was like a shadow man, with grey and black over his face, except his eyes, which had yellow where they should have been white, and cloudy grey over the parts were he was looking out of. My parents went into a gas station after we packed up and drove away from home. The old man with the scary eyes opened my car door and said I should unbuckle my seatbelt, because my mommy and daddy and I were going to be riding in his truck the rest of the way.

I asked him for the password. Even though I knew he was lying.

He told me to unbuckle my seatbelt.

I screamed. He ran. He got into his truck and drove away.

A big man with tattoos came out of the gas station with my dad, and they asked me what happened. I told them, and the man with tattoos was upset. He wasn't yelling, but I could see that he was angry. But also something on his face I didn't understand, like he had to do something he didn't want to do. He got on a motorcycle. He went away really fast, following the truck.

The other time it was a lady. She was really nice. She had a white dress with red polka dots on it, and a really shiny red purse that looked like lips. She walked with short steps that made it easy for me to keep up with her. I didn't know what was going on at first, because she was so nice. I started to help her find her lost glove. She showed me the one she still had, and showed me the bushes where she thought she lost it. It wasn't far from the car, so I helped look. She was really nice. But then there was a man, and his hands were strong. And she helped him and they tried to put me in a different car. I screamed and screamed and bit the lady's hand.

There was a loud bang and the man let go and the lady was screaming as my mom picked me up. My dad said some things softly to my mom and she took me to our car. I couldn't see the lady, but she was screaming up until there was another bang.

I was pretty protected, from all of it. I mean, now I know what actually happened, that my dad shot some people, so that they wouldn't try and steal other children. That the tattooed man on the motorcycle went and chased after the old man and probably killed him so he wouldn't do that too. But then it was just confusing and scary. Seeing my dad's eyes: they'd changed, and he was like a different person then. He smelled smoky, but it was only the gun in his belt.

We drove to my auntie Donna's in the country, and stayed in a room upstairs. It smelled like carrots and there were a lot of new books for me to read.

They asked me what I did on those nights when I couldn't sleep—before I mean, when I was awake and they were in bed and asleep. I actually kind of liked it, that I was an expert, I mean. They all listened to me as I told them my secrets. I told them that sometimes I would draw, or read my books, or play with my toys. Sometimes I watched them sleep, watching as their flower-patterned comforter went up and down slowly as they breathed while they slept.

When I was scared I would watch them.

I used to think that kids didn't sleep, and that when we grew up, that our brains got too big to be awake all the time so we had to sleep. I used to think that when we were kids, we had magic, and as we grew up we forgot it, and forgot how to stay awake.

And then I found out none of the other kids in my class were awake as much as me, and they found out that I didn't sleep like they did. They asked a lot of questions and it was mostly about what I did with so much extra time.

Then *this* happened, and they all got to invent their own answers.

After the upset time, everyone got scared. And smelly. I don't know why, but everyone smelled bad. They had showers and baths, it wasn't like they smelled bad because they were sweaty and gross. Some people did—smell because they didn't have a bath, that is—but everyone else smelled bad a different way. It was something else, and not everyone seemed to be able to smell it. But to me, most people smelled bad. Aunt Donna smelled the worst. I think she knew it too, because she had more showers to try and not smell so bad. And she used this perfume that smelled like acid and bee stings, but I think it was supposed to smell like flowers. It didn't to me, though.

She turned into one of the staring ones. Mom and dad tried to take care of her, and I helped. But after the scaredness turned into the stupid times, it was harder to. They made all sorts of mistakes. I got mad at them a few times, because they were doing dumb things like burning our food and it was running out. And also they tripped a lot. Like going up the stairs had to be done on their hands and knees, like a doggy.

I didn't realize that they weren't eating enough and that they were getting weaker and weaker. I could tell that something was wrong though; their faces were wrong. Like after my dad had shot his gun. They looked like different people. It was scary.

I don't remember if they were still there when it happened. By then we were with some neighbors and I had all these stuffed animals all around me to make a bed. People kept touching my face, which was annoying, but it seemed to make them feel better so I stopped fighting it.

Then I was in another living room, in another house.

Oh, I messed up before, when I said we never had to use the password. But then when my parents weren't there, I screamed. I screamed and screamed for them, and one of the neighbors, a nice man who was with us at the end, had to shout at me, and he shouted the password over and over, until he was crying as he was shouting it. I didn't understand at first, but my parents had decided that someone should take care of me if they weren't around, for whatever reason.

I didn't talk for a long time after that.

Maybe there's more kids somewhere, like me, who had sleeping problems in the Before. If so, could you please get them to write to me? It would be nice if we could meet and talk. So far there's no one even close to my age here and it's lonely.

There was a big weird thing a while ago, where I met an old lady, and they got us to shake hands and people took a gazillion pictures of us. No one tells me anything, but I've learned that she was the oldest person to survive. They didn't tell me, but I've figured it out by now, that I'm the youngest. But that means there's others. I don't mind being the little kid at the table, just so long as I'm at the kid's table again, please. I'm so lonely.

KEEP OUT! TRESPASSERS WILL BE SHOT
—Painted on the drawn drawbridge at
Malbork Castle, Poland

I am dying.

I'm the only one here. Here. I wasn't even supposed to be here. Once things started to go all Pete Tong, I booked a flight home. Home is Bristol, the UK. Please don't let my family read this. Just tell them I tried. Daddy tried.

My flight had a stopover in Frankfurt; it was the only one I could find. It was just after we landed that the shit went down over at Bangkok. After that, the skies were clear. Clear of commercial travel. Well of course there were flights, private flights, and I spent three days at Frankfurt trying to secure one.

North Americans don't understand what Europeans think of as a long way. Nor can we fathom what it means to them. Frankfurt to Bristol was several hundred kilometers, really just a few hours' drive, but to me it may as well have been the moon. Even before the Catastrophe, it would have been impossibly far. Where I had countries, North Americans had states or provinces. Ask a Canadian what it means to be that far from something, and they'll probably laugh and say they're driving that far to their Aunt's for dinner next weekend.

The small private flights were supremely dangerous. Not just that they were crashing with regularity—even getting off the ground at all was a feat. All us thousands of international travelers (and that's just at Frankfurt—around the world it's way more, millions. How many people are trying to travel right now, I wonder?) all trying to get home, were all in the same boat. Ugh, were that I had a boat!

It's a wonder any pilots even offered their services at all. They stopped trying at Frankfurt, certainly they stopped after we killed that one. He was flying to London, and he announced it over the goddamned PA of the whole airport. Said what gate he was at and everything. The idiot!

I rushed right out with the hundreds of others.

He had a four-seat plane, one of them being for himself.

He had to fight to get to the crowd, shouting, "I'm the pilot! I'm the pilot, let me through!"

He got to the plane and realized he had made a huge mistake. People were thrusting cash in his face. Someone was holding up a brick of bills, bound in cellophane like he had been waylaid from a major purchase of drugs.

I'd like to say I fled, that I slipped away, left the crowd, and went somewhere safe. Not just to have the moral high ground, either; if I had managed to tear myself away, I might have found an opportunity to leave that the rabid mob wasn't aware of. But I shook a fistful of money right alongside all the others. Desperation makes you do things—this is not a new revelation. But with that level of brain function, god, it was like I had blinders on. I saw a plane, I saw a pilot, and for some reason, the hundreds of others ahead of me all clamoring to get on didn't factor into the equation.

The pilot picked three people out and thrust them inside his cab and locked the doors.

We tipped the plane over. We broke the windshield and pulled him out. We beat him to death. One of the passengers, too.

I say we, even though I wasn't at the front. I didn't throw any of those savage kicks to his head. But I yelled. I cried. I was part of the mob. I imagine there will be a lot of "last words" like this that are full of excuses and denial. Not me. If it meant I could have seen my kids again, I would have beat that man to death myself.

But I didn't, but we did.

And then it was back inside the terminal, like nothing had happened. Back to the terminal, where already invisible ways out were becoming increasingly scarce.

I went to use the washroom, and as I was drying my hands in the air drier, I remembered how my daughter Kate had been scared of it the first time she'd seen one. A little cry of fright, and then, brave Kate, tentative steps forwards. When it shut off automatically, she triggered it to start, and, while she flinched at the noise, she ran her hands in figure eights under the whooshing air and then giggled.

"Daddy, it's just the wind!" she'd said.

This simple memory came to me and destroyed me. I fell to my knees and was a sobbing mess. Kneeling on the floor of that washroom, gusts of air from the hand drier tugging at my dirty hair—that felt like the end. I couldn't see a way out.

"Someone waiting for you?" asked a man's soft voice in a highland Scottish accent. I didn't parse what was happening, so I only covered my face and nodded, fresh tears spilling out onto the cold bathroom tile below.

"Who?" asked the voice.

"My daughters. Kate and Becka," I managed. There was a pause. The air drier stopped.

"You trying to get over the Channel?" he asked, voice even quieter than before. I nodded fervently, eyes still squeezed shut. "Are you alone?" I nodded again.

I looked up at last and saw a tall, elderly man, who was looking fearfully at the bathroom entrance. He looked down at me and offered me a hand.

"Come with me," he said.

"What?"

"Hurry. I will take you, but you must say nothing," he said. He waited for my acknowledgment of his terms, which I did with a

serious nod and the stoic attention of waiting for further orders. He put a finger up to his lips to urge silence again, then led the way out of the bathroom.

He took me across the terminal, past a fire exit, at which he pointed discretely from his hip for me to see. He led us around the nearest corner, where we stopped, away from prying eyes. He peeked back around the corner the way we'd come, and ducked back towards me. He held up his hand to signal me to stay put, and I did, as he looked back around the corner, waiting for the way to be clear. Then, head still peeked around and watching the way, his hand gave me a countdown—3, 2, 1, go-go-go, and we rushed back the way we'd come. He opened the fire escape and shut it behind us as quietly as he could.

We followed a hallway to the behind-the-scenes of one of the conference ballrooms. There was a loading platform for catering, and he hopped off of it with surprising agility, beckoning me to follow him past several parked catering trucks. He came to a dumpster between two cube vans and looked around, behind me.

"Help me move it," he said in his soft Scottish drawl.

I did. He took me between the two cube vans and opened a sliding garage door. It was loud and he winced at our cover being compromised. I stared up in wonder at the contents of the large loading bay: a bus.

He beckoned me forward and he opened the door for me. I climbed the short steps and was met with an elderly woman pointing a gun at my chest.

"Wendy, it's all right," said the man. Wendy lowered the gun.

"But we haven't any more seats," she said sternly, in the same Scottish drawl. I looked down the length of the bus. It was one of those long-haul ones, with comfortable seats, and lights and air vents above them. Each one was occupied, faces staring at me with fearful eyes.

"He'll sit up here with me. He's got to get home," he said. I felt a hand on my shoulder, the elderly Scottish man, and he gave me a little push inside.

"We're away," he said. "Wendy, take your seat please," he said. They exchanged a brief look, silent council indecipherable to one not party to their ways. Wendy nodded, then sat down. The driver took his seat and pulled a lever to close the door.

"Sorry, but the floor is all we have," he said, looking up at me and gesturing for me to sit next to him. "You can use the steps, I don't mind."

I'd like to say that I cried tears of joy, or that I thanked him, or that I did anything other than sit down quietly, but the exhaustion was too great to have done anything else. All I can do is tell you is that there was a husband and his wife named Wendy, from somewhere in the Scottish highlands, that drove a bus full of dozens of people out of the Frankfurt airport, putting themselves in great danger, and that they asked me for nothing in return.

"Heads down!" shouted the driver as we got going. I heard gunshots. He sped us away and onto the Autobahn. From there it was pretty clear driving. Into Belgium was no problem, but when we hit the French border . . .

I will hate to be cursing the French with my last breath; it's too absurd. That rivalry was already absurd. But I suppose I have good reason; they were the only thing in the way of getting across the Channel.

When it became obvious that we were in a parking lot and not in a lineup, I left. Then I did offer a nod of thanks to my driver. He nodded back, grimly, and stayed with the bus as I made my way away from the parking lot of the highway.

I walked, skirting the French border, trying to find a way in.

One of many absurdities in these last days: thinking I could walk home from the border of France.

So you can see I tried. Oh god how I tried. But here I am, on the ass end of Belgium, staring out over the North Sea. I was planning on getting into France along the shore, and walking from there, but now, now I've spent every last reserve I had. Sometimes, the hallucinations make me think that I can see Bristol, just there, across the water. It's beautiful water now. I haven't seen a ship for days.

A kestrel floated above me for a whole afternoon once, and we watched the sea together. I imagined we were old friends, and that he hadn't a care in the world but for to visit me sometimes, and look out at the sea with me in silence. We looked together, watching the sun sparkle off of the gentle peaks, reveling in the warmth of the sun's rays on those clear and gorgeous days.

My sides hurt, and there was blood in my urine this morning. My head aches all the time, and sometimes it stabs with intense pain and it makes me nauseous. My body is shutting down, one system after another giving up on me. My armpits are swollen, and so is my neck; some malfunction of my lymph system perhaps.

So here I am, the mess that I am. I'm in a little cottage on the cliffs by the water. I can use binoculars and see that the French border is now unguarded. But I am dying. I know it. I can walk to the edge of the cliff to look out at the water, and the other direction to the well at the edge of the field, but no further. Yesterday, I collapsed in the field on the way back and spilled my water. It took nearly the last of my strength to get a fresh bucket and haul it inside.

And now I cannot stand.

I crawled to the loo this morning.

If I wanted, I could still crawl to the cliff.

But I think I'll rather here, in this bed, this stranger's bed.

I am afraid. And I am lonely. There is no one here. I will die sad and alone, in pain, ineffectually lying here in a place I shouldn't be. Oh god, I am alone.

No, no there's my old friend now. My kestrel friend, floating so peacefully in the air just there. If I angle myself in the bed a little, I will be able to see him better.

PART 5
WAKING

Even the most rational approach to ethics is defenseless if there isn't the will to do what is right.
—Graffiti on the Vladimir Central Prison, Vladimir, Russia

You must understand that before all this, I was assisting in some research for my post-doc. I wasn't the most qualified to be doing what I did, but my country called and I answered. Not at first. At first I thought that we could continue our research on the lab animals. But of all the creatures on the earth, only humans were unable to sleep. When my country called, I answered. I was co-opted into running highly experimental treatments and forced into violating the fundamental ethics of my profession, and my conscience.

They brought in somnologists who directed us. And because no other animal was being affected by the plague of insomnia, they brought in *people* to experiment on. I was told they were prisoners who had volunteered. Some of the test subjects themselves verified this, and maybe that was true for them, but others fought until they were drugged or beat into cooperation. They installed ape cages, crates that wouldn't even be fit to be called cells.

A man whose name I never learned oversaw the guards without a word. He was not tall, and he was not muscular, but somehow he seemed like he would win any fight. He watched everything, all the time. If ever he needed rest, he sat in a chair and rubbed his feet for a few minutes. If ever anyone pled for better conditions, this man would use sign language at them. I didn't speak ASL but I saw the sign enough times to translate the various parts of it: "Gorillas asked for this, too."

It was long, *long* into the nightmare, when we were brought a huge number of people. We had to put them three or four to a cage. We were told to, and I'm paraphrasing here, *Throw ethics out the window*, and try anything that could possibly be used to make people fall asleep.

I and the other researchers protested. They shot one of the subjects.

"They will be killed anyway. Use them. Make them sleep. Save them, save yourself, save the human race."

My country called, and I answered. Who better than I, at the forefront of research, new to the field, young and virulent, who better to find the cure and save the human race? We ran endless experiments but few tests. The only test we were told to care about was the ANA test: Asleep/Not Asleep. We had many of them hooked up to monitors to keep track of their brain function, but they may as well have been hooked up to a skipping record player for all it told us.

They had to kill a few more subjects—I think it was four in the end, before they got all of us doing what they wanted. I tried to lead the pack and set an example, but the others were more set in their ways and couldn't see that we were the only ones standing between the human race and certain extinction. As the shots destroyed the would-be test subjects, I found **acceptance** washing over me, and I embraced my role in what was to come. I urged the others to join me, and, though hesitantly at first, they did follow the example I set.

I threw myself into the work. I made the choice to see the subjects as nonhumans. This has been documented before, but never in these circumstances. I knew that if I, or someone like me in some other lab somewhere, didn't find the answer we were looking for, that humanity would perish. We were working to stave off the very real and very imminent threat of the extinction of the human race. And if all was at stake, anything became permissible. And if anything was permissible, then my subjects had to be nonhumans. I did terrible things to them, so they had to be nonhumans. The noises they made were just byproducts of some approximation of sentience, some cruel joke that the machines were playing on me to test my resolve. At some point they brought in a surgeon and all the subjects' vocal chords were removed. It was much more humane for all involved, subject, guard, and researcher alike.

They were biological machines meant to simulate humans so completely that it was almost impossible to tell the difference. The only way I knew how to separate the machines from the humans was that humans weren't confined to the cages. If they were in a cage, they were a machine to be experimented on. If they were not in a cage, they were a fellow human who I was trying to save.

Their encryption keys had been corrupted, and I was trying endless strings of combinations to unlock the function I sought. ANA became a pop-up window in their eyes. Even when some of them shut their eyes, I had to do a secondary ANA test: Alive/Not Alive. I had many ANA1s test positive, only to fail the ANA2.

Things became rather like some parody of science. Like a movie director who once saw a film that took place in a lab and was trying to approximate the look of the thing. Or like a prison director who wished he had been a scientist. Method was reprehensibly lacking. The most we could hope for was that everyone continued to update the test subjects' charts and kept their own experiments to their own subjects. There were several botched experiments, where drugs were administered to the wrong subject. Sometimes the drugs interacted spectacularly.

There were no proposals, no oversight. There was simply coming up with an idea and executing it. What a thing, to suddenly have the freedom and the opportunity to operate without limits.

We did learn many other things during that time.

It was several hours before I realized that one of my fellow researchers was not just resting on the floor near the break room.

I requested help from one of the guards, and together we hefted him into the body bin. It was not long before it was emptied. They did a good job at keeping our lab conditions clean and maintained like that; bodies were removed promptly, fluids were cleaned immediately, and we were kept stocked in delicious food and beverages throughout. Whatever we needed to keep going, we were granted anything . . . to an extent. I will say that when one of the researchers began his "Comparative Taste Analysis" study it was quickly stopped and he was removed from the premises. For some reason that one was stopped, but nothing else we did warranted intervention. Some of the more radical approaches were even encouraged, which in turn promoted more outlandish and even reckless experiments.

I was asked to continue on with administering a cocktail of drugs to a subject after another researcher collapsed on the floor of the lab. She was taken to the body bin. How many had that been? How long had it been since they'd brought any new people in to help, or to be subjects?

There were so few guards left. The silent man was still there, still watching.

I took a moment to walk the banks of cages, half of them empty, and in a lucid moment of awareness, grabbed another researcher by the arm.

"Are we the only ones left?" I asked her. She looked up from her tablet with wide eyes.

"Look at this, look at this bloodwork," she said. I took the tablet from her and promptly dropped it. The screen shattered. Of course I couldn't escape the effects of the insomnia; I'm sure I was very nearly dead by the end. I picked the shattered tablet up and read between the sunburst rays of cracks. It meant nothing to me but I nodded.

"Come see," she said. She led me to a cage where one of the machines lay, chest rising and falling rapidly, eyes shut. I looked at the monitor and it told me that it wasn't sleep we were seeing.

"It's not," I started, but then the delta waves dipped, rose, then dipped again.

"Delta wave achieved," she said.

"My god, what is it? What did you use?" I asked frantically, grabbing the man's chart to have a look. I had administered the last treatment. It was me. I let out a little cry of joy.

The silent guard rushed over to join us, but his knees went out from under him and he stumbled and crumpled to the ground. I went to him. His eyes fluttered, and he seemed shocked. He adjusted himself into a more comfortable position and grasped my arm.

"Hey, come over here," I called to the other researcher. But she was on the ground too, laying where she had fallen in front of the cage with the sleeping man.

I looked back to the guard. His eyes drooped, then shut completely, and he fell limp. I helped his head down to the ground carefully so it wouldn't strike the hard floor. I felt his pulse, which was steady. I rose but felt my head swill with clouds, and a curtain fell abruptly across the stage of my awareness. I barely had time to drop to the ground and put my head on the cold, hard floor.

When I awoke I knew it wasn't anything we had done. All the guards had fallen asleep, all the subjects. Everyone had slept. It was over, and nothing I had done had mattered.

It's mine it's mine, everything the light touches is mine! Here hangs King Kim, the last human being, and lord of the whole world!

—Signboard accompanying a hanging body on a bridge, Bakan, Cambodia

I had the town all to myself.

"Late fees be damned!" I shouted as I went past the library.

People had left to be with family out of town, or to try and be in the city, following where they thought there'd be power or military protection.

Once, a truck full of raider hooligans came through and ransacked a bunch of houses.

They spent a few hours in the two-lane bowling alley, having fun, while I hid in the attic of the church. A dangerous place to hide in retrospect, but then, how was I to know that churches were one of the most burned-down buildings of the whole shebang?

They were the last people I ever saw. Or, you know. Then.

Once they headed out, I had the place to myself.

Not that I didn't think there could be others. Fool me twice . . . I became a master of paranoia.

When I started in with the mirrors, well, that project occupied me for days at a time. I was still in the attic, waiting to be sure that the hooligans had indeed left the town. I was watching a car door mirror, which gave me a view down the main drag. It was small, but I could see their taillights in it. Until I couldn't. And that's what got me looking around, seeing how else the mirrors on cars let me observe the surroundings.

When I came down from the church attic, I spent hours gathering mirrors. Ripping them off of cars mostly, but also going into houses to pilfer the better, larger mirrors from walls. I got pretty good at stripping them out of bathrooms, even when they were affixed pretty well. They didn't need to have perfect edges. Even the shards of broken mirrors from my failures saw use.

I picked my Watch Spot. Okay, I know it's weird, and there might already be names for things I invented, but I didn't know that at the time, so I gave names to all these things. Like Watch Spot: a very specific place in the town that gave me access to the best view of my domain. All of my mirrors pointed at Watch Spot. I picked the top of the library. It was high up and it was central.

The elementary school had been setting up to have a bake sale when things got hairy, and their supply room had been left unlocked. I found their pavilion tent, the kind to keep a street-side vendor and their goods safe from the sun or rain, and made it my own. I got sandbags from the hardware store, not that they were for sale—they were in the display window, propping up the store mascot, a Bigfoot. I leaned the Bigfoot up against the wall and took his supports to use on the tent.

Watch Spot had big rubber bins all around it, for food, medical supplies, guns. I searched for the nicest chair I could find, which turned out to be a padded leather recliner from the mayor's house. I put it at the front of the library in my staging area. I tied ropes all around it and hauled it up to Watch Spot. I scraped it up a bit in the process, but it was still comfortable as hell.

Once safely in my throne, I had a view of my Mirror Lines.

Mirror Lines worked to send views of the things I wanted to keep an eye on right to the Watch Spot. I had six. Mirrors angled *just so* to give me an eye on a specific spot, but also anything in between, in their path. If the mirrors could see it, so could I. The longest one I made consisted of more than thirty mirrors. Hours spent extending the line out and out, checking back down the line between each adjustment to see that I'd got the angle exact.

I also took to keeping several mirrors on me, in pockets, so I could look around corners if I needed to. And then they became like a second set of eyes. If you could extend your vision out as far as you could reach, wouldn't you? The mirrors became my eyes. I started using them all the time, looking at the world only through mirrors. Wherever I walked, I would watch my step in two mirrors—a round one in my left hand to watch the ground, a slightly larger oval one in my right hand to watch the way ahead.

Two Mirror Lines were fixed on my house. I kept supplies hidden there and wanted to know if someone was snooping around it. So I had a Mirror Line on the back yard as well as the street. The whole street. So I would have time if someone drove up it in time for . . . who knows. I got guns and hid them around town so I could be all cool and jump for cover and come rolling back to a crouch with a shotgun in hand.

So the House Mirror Lines were viewable on the top two mirrors of my surveillance setup at Watch Spot. Sitting in that leather recliner I held my head just right to see all six Mirror Lines at once, each one like a monitor in an array of feeds from security cameras. The leftmost two were Mirror Lines that watched the east of town, one for the road in, and one for a side road that was mostly for logging but could also be a way in. The two on the right at Watch Spot were fixed on the west, one on the main road there, and one down the main drag, just in case I missed someone coming in. I made adjustments daily.

Once it was just me, I realized it might not *just* be me. All the animals left in town. I opened up houses and took stock of who I had left. I led the way with my mirrors, one angled down, one angled up and ahead, peeking around corners and into rooms, hands swiveling this way and that to give me the best scan.

All the dogs had been taken. People loved their dogs. I didn't find a single one.

I'm sure some cats got left behind, but I didn't find them. If ever I found a house with cat food still in it, I opened the bag and tipped it over on the floor, just in case there was still someone there that needed it. I had more than enough food for myself, so it was no skin off my back. I did see several ferals, but I was pretty sure they would get along just fine without people.

The feral cats actually were a blessing—not just for me, but everyone. They certainly rose to the occasion and fulfilled their purpose, the purpose we used them for originally anyway, and kept the vermin population down. Rats were good food, but not if it meant they brought back the bubonic plague or some other fresh hell like that.

People weren't big on birds, but I did find a lorikeet at the school. It had a huge pile of food in its cage, speckled with droppings.

I brought the bird, whose name I never did learn, up to Watch Spot and went back for its food, and a new bone beak-sharpening thing.

When I walked with something in hand, I had only the one mirror to watch my step, and I alternated it angling at the ground and the way ahead. I got pretty good at scanning things using my mirrors, but using just one while I carried something was beginning to stress me out.

I kept the lorikeet with fresh water and food, and in return I had a pretty bird to look at. I would have liked to set it free, but letting domesticated pets out into the wild was basically killing them, only it took longer. My new companion I simply called Bird.

The only time I went out of town was to check and see what the little farm nearby had to offer. I rounded up a lot of supplies from the house and went to do a scan of the barn. My mirrors swiveled all around letting me take in the whole interior of the barn. There were bales of hay, an old, unlit lantern, and—movement. I approached cautiously. When my mirrors caught his eyes just right and he looked back at me, his big brown horse eyes were rimmed with white—frightened I guessed.

I didn't know jack squat about horses, but I did know that if I left him there he would die. The farm was empty. I took my best guess at hitching him up to a wagon in the barn. I'm sure I didn't get it right, and maybe that's why he hated it so. Or maybe they left him behind because he was old and ornery and didn't like to be hitched, I'll never know. Maybe they forgot him. Maybe he had no one. Just like me.

So that's how I found Ham. I couldn't stand the thought of calling him Horse, but I wasn't very creative when it came to picking names for things (gosh, can you tell?) so Horse and Man became Ham. He *was* quite a ham though; though ornery and downright grumpy at times, he was very spirited and quite an attention suck, so the name ended up fitting.

Ham pulled that cart, with me walking beside him in solidarity, with all the supplies I could find at the farm, back into town for me. I rigged a tarp up against the back wall of the building and used a few pallets from the grocery store to make a fence and stacked the hay against it. It wasn't a pasture, and I'm sure I got a ton of things wrong about caring for him, but at least he wasn't starving and alone in a barn.

I made a new Mirror Line to watch over him, but it wasn't really a Line like the others—a single mirror, a huge wall mirror in an ornate guilt frame, at just the right angle over the lip of the roof, let me watch his pen from above without having to add any more pieces to the surveillance setup. He figured out how it worked and would sometimes watch the watcher, seeing how long he could stare at me before I caught him and made a silly face at him, which he'd sometimes answer with a knicker, or sometimes a huff, depending on his mood I think.

We did a patrol of the town twice a "day," that is to say, once every twelve hours. Ham took me around town at a languid pace.

I had guns strapped behind me on the saddle and a wicked hat I found in someone's closet—a wide-brimmed bison leather hat that made me feel like a champ. I didn't care that he was old and that the tack probably wasn't done up right, I felt like such a badass when I rode him. Sometimes I called him *pardner*.

Ham and I, making the rounds of the town, stopping at every intersection to listen. The world gets real quiet without people in it. No traffic, no planes, no nothin'. That was when I started to be able to hear the other things that maybe I'd been missing before. Birds. The way the wind rustled the weeping willow by the library. Crickets, frogs, the buzz of insects and beat of my heart. All became loud to me, the soundtrack of my existence as the last man on earth.

Somewhere in there I got really fed up of only using the one mirror when I had to carry something, so I began to attach mirrors to myself. When one hand was otherwise occupied, I could use the ones attached to my legs to see around. And even when I had both ones in my hands going, they were a lot more effective if I had a lot of angles to draw from on my body. I took a bunch of small mirrors out of left-behind makeup compacts, and used wood glue to stick them to a vest, and then to a pair of swim trunks I wore over my regular pants.

I wasn't at my best after so long without sleep, but I decided I'd keep trying to go on as long as I could. I kept a diary during that time, but, reading back on it, it was mostly gibberish. There's a lot of stuff about Mirror People, who I could sometimes see through mirrors. But they weren't real. There was a whole page that only contained the word "BOOM!" over and over again, but I have no recollection of what that could possibly have been about. Maybe it had something to do with the smoldering crater that used to be the mayor's house?

Ham became increasingly agitated at me, and I wonder if it was because I was losing track of things, forgetting when I'd fed him or leaving him saddled up after a patrol.

There was a hawk around and I'd seen it eyeing Bird. I put a towel around Bird's cage whenever I wasn't there, and I guess hawks don't have a theory of object permanence or whatever it is that lets us know when something is still there even when we can't see it. So the towel hid Bird from predation.

Ham had object permanence. I played hide-and-seek with him a few times. It's not like I hid in places that were hard, but he still found me every time. Once, we played in the entire town. I was hiding in an empty garbage can (no lid), waiting for him to saunter up and find me, when I heard something like a gunshot. I can't be sure it was a gunshot, because I could have hallucinated it, but it roused me from my game and I took Ham back to Watch Spot, where I went immediately to check the Mirror Lines, mirror in the left hand scanning, mirror in the right hand scanning.

One was showing the asphalt of the road instead of the straight-ahead stretch of the main street. My breath caught in my throat and I stared at the broken Mirror Line for a moment, hoping the mirror in my hand was just playing tricks on me. I angled it away and then back at the offending monitor-mirror, but it still showed me only the asphalt. I did a quick calculation, mentally tracing over the string of mirrors that led down to the main street, and decided it was one of two mirrors that had malfunctioned.

But why? They were all secure. What could have moved them? Enough to knock it askew? I took a gun with me and followed the line of mirrors, keeping my gaze mostly on the mirrors attached to my legs; they gave me a wide view of what I was coming up on, my two eyes turned into farther reaching compound eyes, like an insect.

I found the offending mirror and repositioned it; it had only been bumped slightly, and there were a few feathers on the ground around it. Perhaps a bird had been hunting here and knocked it? Perhaps Hawk? I stood and listened again, hoping it had been a bird, but prepared for more nefarious culprits.

I heard another crashing noise, back in the direction of Watch Spot.

I hurried back as fast as I could, relying again on my leg mirrors to show me the way. I saw a person in one of them and froze, abandoning one of my hand mirrors in favor of the gun on my hip; I drew it and hurried to find cover, while keeping the person in view on my legs. I ducked behind an electrical box, inactive and hopefully not a bomb. I peeked my one hand mirror around it and honed in on where the person stood. They were inside the movie rental store. I squinted and they stared at me, unmoving.

We watched each other for a long time like that. Their gaze was unsettling, and it took me a long time to realize that it was because they never blinked. There was another jostling sound, from nearby—something was happening at Watch Spot. I couldn't stay pinned on the side of the road, not while my hard work was being tampered with. There was a terrible screeching, and I steadied myself and took aim at the unblinking person. Their eyes didn't waver from me once. As I shot, the window shattered and fell, and once I had a clear view I could see that my bullet found its mark, right in their neck. They remained standing, staring. I admired their tenacity; had they even flinched? I knew they would be dead in a matter of moments; blood was pouring out of their neck and down their cardboard chest. I decided it was safe to go defend Watch Spot.

I hurried up to the roof, gun in one hand, mirror in the other.

Everything seemed normal; I stared at the Mirror Lines for quite a while, trying to glean any hint of movement, any cause of the ruckus I had heard.

I don't know how long it was before Bird's cage came into view in one of my hand mirrors, and I saw that it was knocked to the ground, the towel strewn nearby, the wires bent in a few places. The hawk hadn't been able to get at Bird, who was still inside the cage. But his chest was heaving and he lay on his back, eyes half shut, little feet up in the air. He died before I could right the cage, and I buried him in the flower planters at the front of the library.

Then it really *was* just horse and man.

I went back to where I had seen and shot the person. They were still there, standing, unblinking, blood running from the bullet hole in their neck. I decided to leave them like that. If they didn't cause me trouble again, they could stand there and bleed all they want. Though, they weren't bleeding at all. And it wasn't really a person; it was just cardboard. It was a pretty convincing illusion that my mind was creating though; when I touched his neck, my fingers came away bloody. He never blinked once.

I glued some extra mirrors to Ham's saddle. And I made him a sort of neck-sash, affixed to his bridal tack to stay up, so that I had even more angles of sight to draw on when I rode him. There wasn't a single makeup compact in the town left unpilfered by my mirror-hungry hands.

It felt like a long time of just horse and man. Our twice-a-day patrol, feeding him, brushing him, watching the Mirror Lines, listening to the sounds of the empty world around me. Hands flitting mirrors this way and that, scanning, always scanning. Sometimes I would see another person in the mirrors, but usually there was something off about them; their gait sort of loping or their head bent at an odd angle, enough to let me know that they were a figment of my imagination. I would ride Ham up to them and face him towards the apparition, and he never reacted as though anything was there. He became my litmus test; surely Ham would let me know if the person was real.

I never let my guard down. A strange paradox, thinking I was the last man on earth, and yet, watching the Mirror Lines for trouble, which I thought would come in the form of raiders. And if they had come, it would have shattered the notion I had built up that I was the last one. . . . But I could finally get to play with the elaborate defense system I'd set up, guns hidden in parked cars, guns taped on the inside of awnings of all the main street shops, guns even buried in the ground.

When you're the last person alive, you can do whatever you want.

I was laughably unadventurous I suppose. The list of my shenanigans includes: drawing a huge chalk mural of a chicken on the side of the town hall, dressing the hardware store Bigfoot up in ridiculous clothing, and making a pile of money and valuables. I knew they weren't worth anything, but it was still sort of neat to be able to stand over a pile of wealth—coins, bills, gold things, silver things, jewelry, gems. Sometimes I imagined I was a dragon, hoarding treasure. Sometimes, in that little scenario, I would kill any knight that came to slay me. Sometimes I would let him kill me.

More often than not, they would come and offer up a virgin to appease me.

It began to not matter that I was the last man on earth. Sitting in my leather recliner atop the library at Watch Spot, looking from one Mirror Line to the other, checking and rechecking that I was alone, alone, alone. Except for Ham. Ham, who I'm sure was starving to death near the end. The barn only had so much hay, and I could only find so many oats. And by then anyway I could hardly move, let alone think straight enough to formulate a plan to go find more food or let him out to graze. It was all I could do to get some nutrition into myself.

Who knows how long I was like that. Sitting in that chair, Mirror Lines silent and still, empty bird cage off to the side, ornate mirror over Ham showing me his drooping back. If I could remember how often I ate a granola bar or tin of fruit, I might be able to calculate the timeline, but as it is, I only know that, when I woke up, there was a pile of wrappers and cans strewn about me.

Miraculously, Ham was still alive. I don't remember doing it, but at some point I'd cut open a bag of feed and just left it open in his pen. The barrel I'd set up to catch rainwater from the gutters was very nearly empty, and I imagine it wasn't the most pleasant thing to drink. There was dung everywhere and he was supremely unhappy, but he was alive.

I brought him a jug of water I'd saved back at my house and let him drink it all. I opened a bag of oats and let him eat as much as he wanted.

Then Ham and I rode out of that town, because I knew that if I had woken up, that it might be over, and that I might not be the only one left. And I'd be damned if I was going to stay alone in that town, clinging to the notion that I was king of my domain, a dragon to be slain or to myself slay any that dared confront me. I took a lot of extra mirrors with me, and I set them up in a perimeter whenever I stopped for the night.

I took the road out of town, and I suppose the only thing left to say is that I did find people, and when they saw me they said I had madness in my eyes and that Ham was afraid of me, even as I rode him, afraid of me. They called me Disco Ball Man for a while, then Mirror Man.

Someone that knew about horses took care of Ham until he was back to better health, and when I was also back up to snuff and living in a world that had other people in it, I went to visit him. He nuzzled me, forgiving my past errors in his care, and we were friends again.

The effects of thinking you're the last man on earth stay with me though. I know it's a remnant of the madness I developed there on my own, but sometimes I feel like I'm still the only human left alive, and that other people I see in my mirrors are hallucinations. But Ham reacts to them as though they are there, so I will trust his judgement. I wonder if this will ever stop. And what will I do when I no longer have Ham to tell me if the people in the mirrors are real?

All your base are belong to us lol dickbutt.jpg #rekt
—United States Department of Defense website,
after it was hacked

This is one chapter a lot of you would skip over if you didn't know the full story. Gamers were skipped over all the time before, so it's nothing new to us. But before you do, know that this is the story of the workforce that rebuilt your world. To understand us, you're going to get a bit of how our lives were before the insomnia plague hit. I'll do my best to make it understandable; I think anyone who's lost themselves in a game, be it *World of Warcraft* or chess, can relate to the tale I have to tell. You might have to do some lateral translating. Think of your passion, and see if you can transpose yourself into my place. We're not so different, you and I.

With functionally unlimited time, it was a gamer's paradise. There were people doing all sorts of world-record attempts out in the real world, but for us, we suddenly had a level playing field on which to compete, and *god*, was it fun.

The speed runs were the first things to trend. To see how fast you could complete the main story quest in the new *Elder Scrolls* game, or even in some classic from your childhood, was the zeitgeist. Hah, we called it a zeitgeist; spirit of the times? *Times?* Like there was a god of speed runs, watching as we pushed those digital avatars of ourselves to complete games faster and faster.

To understand us, first understand one thing about the way neurology works. When you drive a car, your brain actually extends the boundaries of your body to envelope the whole vehicle. You *become* the car. It's the same with video games; when you are controlling a character on screen, you *are* the character. When people talk about playing games, they say, "I ran up to the door and picked the lock, and then this Skeleton Lord came out and attacked me!" Notice: "I" and "me"? When you're reading a book, you don't tell someone, "I decided to take the ring to Mordor," or whatever. Games make you feel like it is you, because, well, it *is*.

It's an external extension of yourself.

And that's perhaps why we fared so well. We existed both as biological creatures, suffering, but also as digital entities, and we managed to mesh the two together and get a sort of immunity from it all. I mean, we still were affected; some of us turned into Dreamers and Starers for sure, and some of us starved to death or died of dehydration, but we fared better than the general public. Because our minds were somewhere else, kept in a pseudo-stasis.

So knowing that, I'll tell you about my realm.

The Elder Scrolls one was the first to take off. A popular role-playing video game: you make a character and go through the world following a set of quests on different story arcs, according to your tastes. My Khajiit was a contender for the main quest, but I botched one of the missions near the end and it gave me extra NPC conversation that ate into my time. I was close, but some guy in Minnesota beat me by several minutes. Whatever, he didn't manage to complete his full set of Daedric armor, so I'll count it as a victory.

And then there was the *New Minecraft*, where we all agreed on a seed, a world generation code, so we were all playing an identical map. With that one, there were several goals, so it wasn't all or nothing. Everyone got a little something. I got the first to have a full enchantment setup, and a set of Protection IV/Unbreaking III diamond armor.

Someone else did an impressive run to a nether fortress and managed to collect three Wither heads, a rare drop from one of the formidable enemies that spawn in that hellish dimension. He assembled them to make the Wither Boss and defeated it to gain a nether star, with which he built a Beacon. His victory screenshot was beautiful: his avatar, in a skin he'd designed himself, looking like a marble statue, standing in front of the lit beacon beaming into the sky, a diamond sword in his hand, a chicken peeking cheekily into the frame near his feet.

There were other speed runs for *Grand Theft Auto*, *Super Mario*, *Zelda*—anything under the sun was an option. If you had a game, you played it. Every online community had its coordination hub, and we invented scores of quests to compete at, to try and best each other and prove our gaming prowess, how 1337 we were (oh come on, 1337? Using numbers as letters is *called* 1337speak, "leet-speak," from being an *elite* hacker or gamer or programmer or whatevs).

You get the picture. I know you might not care about it, but it mattered in several ways. First, as I said, the online worlds kept more people alive than any other medium. We were lost in our games, inside, unmoving; we were conserving energy, and we were safe. Surely if the world didn't end, we thought an army of neck-bearded man-boys and thirteen-year-old *Call of Duty* brats were going to inherit the earth. A chilling thought, especially for the women of earth.

(Side note: the gender disparity was much misjudged by the general public, as well as by gamers themselves. Before the plague, fully 45 percent of gamers were female. Perhaps it was their proclivity to create male characters, and mute their mics, so that they were treated as men and not called out for being "gamer chicks," worked to proliferate the stereotype of gamers being men. But Gender Issues in Gaming is a whole other book in itself. The main point is that we were almost as many women as we were men.)

All right, so what we had was a force of people staying inside, playing games, day in and day out. We were busying ourselves in the digital realms, keeping out of trouble and conserving our physical energy by focusing entirely on our games.

Psychologists were already understanding that such games were changing our brains. The reward-based systems were addicting. There was seemingly nothing gamers wouldn't do to fill up a little bar, to increase their stats, to level up. Across the board, humans like seeing their progress as tangible representations, and gaming is the first thing in the history of humanity to do it so efficiently, to pull in the human mind so greatly that people have died of dehydration while ensconced in their games.

We had engineered something brilliant. All those gaming quests, all that competition, it was preparing us for the greatest quest of our lives.

Sure, some of us weren't necessarily the most ept with real world situations. We had embraced our kingdoms of digital villains and leveling up and hoarding treasure and rare items, and the real world couldn't hope to compete with it, not when you did a cost-benefit analysis. For a $70 game on my already-bought console, I could eek out hundreds of hours of gameplay. And when I finished, I could make an entirely new character and come at it from a different angle. A righteous paladin one play-through, a sneaky assassin thief the next. What in the real world could compete with that?

And people were hungry to get things done. People would join together on servers (hubs that hosted games for people all around the world) and random strangers would ask, "What can I do?" We wanted to help, we wanted jobs. We wanted to push that level-up bar higher and higher, we wanted to see the fruits of our labor and share them with others who would understand our accomplishments.

So when the power finally went out, the gamers did one of two things. A swath of them killed themselves pretty much right away. You can't just become another person and have that level of community interaction, that level of quest-reward system pumped into your veins for weeks straight, and not feel such despair when you're unplugged, and thrust back into a world on fire, suddenly feeling the horrendous effects of the insomnia you'd been ignoring.

The rest of us, well, we had conditioned our brains to fit the questing model so perfectly that it wasn't really that surprising that we tried to transpose it into the real world. People had been taking about the *game layer* for a few years, and its time had finally come.

We had predesignated times and places picked out for meetings. We weren't so far removed from what was happening that we didn't understand that the world was ending. We were just watching from the sidelines, from the safety of our online boards, from livestreams, from the constant updates on our favorite news aggregators.

So when the power went out in any given city, we had anticipated it, and we already had plans.

We all had our frickin' zombie-apocalypse contingencies, you think we couldn't adapt and come up with something for an actual apocalypse as it was occurring? It was cake. Sure, having grand schemes on a message board online was one thing; enacting the plans in the real world was entirely another matter. But we came together.

I don't want to brag (Just kidding, I think I had a big part in organizing the rebuilding of the world? Hell yes, I'll brag.) but the Game Of Life Stat Sheet was my creation.

When we finally fell asleep, those of us that woke up emerged and found the world in shambles. We enacted Plan "Game of Life." My Game Of Life Stat Sheet (shortened to G.O.L.S. Sheet, eventually just GOLS, like "goals") was widely distributed at that point. I'm sure everyone thought it was a joke. And it sort of was. But when the despair hit, when we could have just laid down and died, instead we had stat bars to fill.

There were many places with success stories stemming from using GOLS, but I guess you wanted mine, so I'll give it to you. Keeping in mind, as of course I imagine you must for every entry into this collection, that I have a massive bias. I will try and be as truthful as I can be, but, well, there's no instant replay here. No screencasts, livestreams, no Twitch.

All the radio broadcasts, and any newscasters on TV before the power died, were drilling the same things into us. *If you fall asleep and wake up and all this is over, go to the town hall. Go to the town hall. There will be people at the town hall.* Those poor reporters, trying to keep themselves awake enough to deliver news until the bitter end. But at least they got it into our heads to go to our town halls when/if the plague was ever over.

So to the town hall we went. We were all young. We were pretty much all between the age of nineteen and fifty. Maybe we don't need as *much* sleep as we get older, but perhaps we need it more, to repair our bodies as we age. Being young and healthy and vital was no protection: the ones that need the most sleep, for their brains to develop, the under-nineteen crowd, needed drastically, *fatally* more sleep.

So as we assembled, we fell into a hierarchy of leadership sort of cobbled together on the fly. Mrs. Barsol, the principal of the high school, was there, and she was as solid and fierce as I remembered. Many of us had been to her office for a scolding or a pep talk or just for a person to listen to us.

We silently nominated her to lead us. There were others, but as the majority of us seemed to have been led by her before, or knew her as an important pillar of the community, we decided that she was best. The mayor's son didn't like that at all, but I loudly reminded him that we didn't elect leaders by primogeniture. I took Mrs. Barsol aside and told her, somewhat sheepishly, of the GOLS sheet. I pulled mine from my pocket and unfolded it.

She listened and nodded as I tried to explain to her, just as I did to you, how our brains had been trained, and how I thought we could use it to our advantage. If only we could be led. If only someone could give us quests. She listened and let me get to the end of my unpracticed explanation, then paused to formulate her response while I waited nervously.

“The world was full of quests before, but now I think they are much more apparent,” she said with a half smile. “Do you have copies?” she asked. I nodded, relief flooding over me to know that I’d made my point well enough for her to get it, and that she was open to the idea of actually giving it a try.

Our town had gone from roughly 6,500 down to 358, well below the global survival rate of just under 8 percent, mostly due to our average age being very skewed towards the retired and the very young, both demographics having a much lower survival rate.

We were a small enough group that we could know most everyone, or already did. Several of my friends were there. My piano teacher was there. One of the people from my street was there.

But I only had five copies of the GOLS. I handed one to Mrs. Barsol, and she looked it over, then nodded.

“Add something to it that gives a level up for every day. *Every single day* that someone has this sheet, they need to be able to tick something off on it or add to an XP bar.” My jaw dropped. She gave me that half smile again, though her eyes began to glisten with tears. “My son used to play games, and some of them he would only log onto to get the daily reward, even if he wasn’t playing it that day. Can you add it?”

“Can you help me copy the sheets? We need more.”

And that’s how I was introduced to Jeremy Pendragon, who became my right hand, my confidant, my friend. He managed to pump most of his levels into one of the five custom stat slots.

The GOLS were pretty all encompassing, general skills, but I knew everyone would want to have room to show off their particular niche talents, so I left five slots blank, as Personal Special Stats (PSSs). Jeremy's were Book Binding, Papercraft, Candle Dipping, Wick Weaving, and, his highest PSS, Penmanship.

Jeremy Pendragon and I set up in a conference room at the town hall and began copying GOLS. His hand was steady and practiced. Mine was okay, but not nearly so beautiful; after a few side-by-side comparisons, it became clear that I should let the artisan take over the work he was most suited to, and I helped Mrs. Barsol with some other things.

That night we had a meeting. There were many meetings all over the world in those days, those wonderful days when we had slept, those awful days when we had woken up to find how close we can come to extinction.

I had the floor to speak my piece, to pitch GOLS to them. I knew it was going to be hard to get non-gamers to understand it at first; I tried to come at it from the psychology of it, sort of like the explanation I offered you earlier. Seems reasonable, right?

I wasn't prepared for them to reject me outright.

"We need to be consolidating the food into a centralized location, clearing bodies; we don't have time for any of this," said an older man in the crowd. Older, as in, perhaps late forties. Not *old* old, not by a long shot. Well, not old *before*. Now he had a good forty or fifty years to be one of the oldest people on the planet.

"We'll only help organize things, and to build morale; don't you want to keep track of your accomplishments?"

"If we don't all die of some plague from the bodies, I'll count it as a morale booster. Now cut it out with this *game layer* crap and let's talk about real life problems," he said gruffly, earning some minor mutterings of approval from those around him. I sighed but didn't want to leave it so easily.

"We'll do the other stuff, too," I said, sweeping my gaze over everyone, "but if anyone wants to be in on this, it's going to be fun. We need fun still. It'll be motivational, it'll be good," I said, hoping my explanation from earlier would garner at least a few followers. "We'll stay and talk, after the other things have been discussed. Join us." Join *us*, even though it was just me and Jeremy, and maybe Mrs. Barsol. Trying to get the feeling of a group in there, welcoming, exciting.

I stepped off the stage and took up a spot against the wall. Someone was talking about clearing the roads when Jeremy whispered to me.

"Good job, we'll get there," he said. I nodded, and we waited out the other speakers, volunteering on road clearing and reconnaissance respectively. After Mrs. Barsol called the meeting to a close, she did me the honor of adding to it for my benefit.

"And now, party creation will begin for the Gibsons Rebuilding Committee. Anyone wishing to join us, please stay. The rest, we'll begin bright and early tomorrow." She banged something on the podium which signaled an end to her bit, and those in the town hall rose and filed out. Jeremy and I sauntered up to the stage, and I'll admit I was nervous to see just how many would be staying behind to join us. Mrs. Barsol perhaps saw this, and dropped down to sit on the end of the stage, where Jeremy and I pressed in, waiting, not daring to look back at the crowd to see who would be staying.

"Jeremy, Riley, how many people are usually in a *D&D* party?" she asked, perhaps to distract me from my nervousness. Jeremy and I glanced at each other in brief council.

"Five? Any more than six gets problematic," I explained, "but up to eight can work." I'd been in a group once, and we'd run two campaigns—one with five, and one with nine, and the DM (Dungeon Master, also sometimes called the GM [Game

Master]) had a heck of a time keeping the game going when we were nine.

"Looks like we're in luck then," she said, nodding over our shoulders. I turned then and was met with five others.

Two were girls, or I guess I should say young women. They were in their midtwenties, both blond, one tall, taller than me, and one about five eight. They were there as a team. I shook their hands.

"I'm Riley," I said.

"Laura," said the taller one.

"Betty," said her friend.

There were two boys, or I guess I should say young men. One was maybe just out of high school, perhaps one of the youngest in our town, and the other looked related to him, but older by perhaps half a decade.

"Riley," I said, extending my hand to the younger one first.

"Ashley," he said.

"Rick," said his . . . brother? I was certain they were related.

The fifth was a large man. Not large like overweight, but large like a lumberjack. He had a beard. He looked like he was in his late forties. I silently rejoiced that he in particular joined us—if "we" were all "kids," it'd be much harder to be taken seriously.

I shook his hand and he had a handshake to end handshakes.

"Al," he said. "I hope you know what you're doing here, I'm sticking my neck out. You seem like you're going to do something interesting here though. So let's hear it." Al didn't mess around.

"Right," I said.

"This is Jeremy," I said, introducing him so he wouldn't fade into the woodwork like so many gamers were used to doing.

"Jeremy, Riley, Laura, Betty, Ash, Rick, Al, and Mrs. Barsol," I said.

"Please, Mrs. Barsol was my slave name," she said. "Call me Jay."

"Yes," said Jeremy, pulling out the copied GOLS to distribute, "yes *this* is the time to choose a new name. Now because it's a *Real Life* Stat Sheet," he said with some bemusement, "we should keep it to something plausible. Nicknames, middle names, something fun, but rooted in our real life lives. I'm going to go by my last name, Pendragon," he said. I only got it just then—his handwriting skills were perhaps acquired and honed to make use of his fierce last name, a skilled scribe, a loquacious letterer.

"Riley hardly needs another name," said Laura. I hoped that hot feeling on my cheeks wasn't me blushing but I'm sure I was, though I couldn't yet tell if it was because I was being made fun of (my instinct) or because she was going somewhere with her observation.

"I mean," continued Laura, "I always thought Rye was what they called you, right?" she asked. "And it's like wry, like clever," she clarified. Her friend Betty elbowed her in the side.

"Or rye like the grain, rye bread," she said with a hiss.

"Either way, I like it," I said. They looked at me to gauge my sincerity. I nodded and held my hand out to Jeremy for a pencil. He plunked one in my palm and I slapped my sheet down on the stage.

"Ry, R, Y," I said. "Then no one will know which it is meant to be," I said.

"Cool beans," said Ashley. Jeremy handed him a pen. "I've been running from my name my whole life. It's flippin' bad enough having the last name Rash, and I don't care if it's ethnic. Ash Rash? Jesus man, I don't ever want to hear that name again. Bro?" he asked his (confirmed) older brother Rick, who nodded.

"Going with Fee?" he asked.

"How did . . . how did you know?" he answered.

"Like I've never seen your gravatar pop up online. A phoenix rising from the *ash*," said Rick, rolling his eyes. "A bit obvious, bro.

But go for it," he said. "I'm going to stay with just Rick though," he said. I nodded. Jeremy passed the pens out to everyone, and we lined up against the stage to use it as a desk.

"Yeah man, no pressure, that's cool," I said. Trying to let them know that it was up to them. No pressure, no judgement. That was the best part of being a nerd. Once you got to the point of being made fun of, that's when you knew someone was your friend. Until then, utter respect for one another's ideas was paramount. We didn't know the party dynamic yet.

"And I'll keep Al, but I might add a middle name later, I haven't decided."

"Laura stays Laura," she said.

"And Betty, stays, well, maybe just Bett."

It's amazing how just the simple act of taking charge of your name can be so empowering. Names define us from the day we're given them, and yet we have no control over them at all. As soon as you get a GOLS sheet and you fill in your name you make it your own. It gives you dominion over your life in a way you've never felt before (unless you were already a gamer—I'd had more names than I can remember). It was a good first taste of the control and order to come.

Jeremy, Riley, Laura, Betty, Ash, Rick, Al, and Mrs. Barsol became a party then, became Pendragon, Ry, Laura, Bett, Fee, Rick, Al, and Jay. I know it's hard to keep track of names, and you don't really need to. I just wanted to get that down, because those are the names of the people that helped me save our town, and that helped spread GOLS across the continent. *Early adopters* should be recognized for putting themselves out there against the majority. So while you might not remember them, I count this as a historical document, and I think it's important for them to be remembered, for them to go down in history.

Pendragon, Ry, Laura, Bett, Fee, Rick, Al, and Jay: the Gibsons Rebuilding Committee, the GRC.

We started filling in stats right away, and I explained to them more about the 5 PSS, the five Personal Special Stats, the custom skills that they had liberty to pick for their unique talents. We tried to keep them to skills we thought we'd still use. Those ranged from Photography to Gardening, Timber Falling to Watch Maintenance. Between the eight of us, we had forty different PSSs.

So that was the party-creation process. It feels a little weird to document, because it's hard for me to know if "outsiders" will find it interesting. But if you've never done it, just know that it can be a thrill. A hugely exciting thing to craft a new group, to think of what skills you have or what skills you *want* to have, and put pencil to paper, and you get a kind of exhilaration that binds the group together.

We had control over our lives, for what felt like the first time in a long time. Total power to direct ourselves.

"So," asked Rick, "who's the DM here?" A simple question that let me know that Rick had gamed before. Had it been *D&D*? Maybe *Call of Cthulhu*? Jeremy pointed at me. I wasn't one to decline; the group needed a leader, and since it was my idea it seemed obvious. But he was just calling attention to it for the others, to let them know that someone was sort of in charge.

"So what's first then, boss?" asked Jay.

"Our primary mission will be to draw other people in. Everyone is to have three GOLS sheets with them at all times, so that if someone (and two of their friends) wants to join, you can get them in right then and there. You walk them through what we just did; name, 5 PSSs, the whole deal.

"It'll be hard at first. I guess we just set an example; pull your GOLS sheets any chance you get. Anything you're doing is getting you XP (Experience Points), and you record it as soon as you can. Take pride in your work. When we pass one another, let's tell each other what we gained that day.

"Pendragon," I said in example, "you level up in Penmanship yet?"

"Sure did," he answered. We high-fived.

"Always positive, always lifting each other up. This is about support, this is about binding people together and acknowledging the good work that we do. Got it?"

"So our first mission is to use GOLS in public and to be there for anyone that wants to join us?" asked Laura. I nodded. She held out her hand and Jeremy gave her some blank GOLS, each one rolled up with a piece of twine tied 'round. GOLS scrolls, he called them.

Those early times were difficult, but we did what we set out to do. Each of us did it in our own ways, but always there was the interaction when we saw one another. High fives and claps on the back. The first time I saw Al out and about, he was so intimidating that I couldn't imagine high-fiving him. But he waltzed right up to me and asked in a booming voice (so that everyone could hear).

"Ry, you level up in Food Security yet?"

"This morning," I answered. I could see he meant to high-five me and I swung to meet him, resulting in a blow to our hands that left my whole arm stinging. I tried not to show it though, and continued on my way like it weren't no thang. As planned though, the exchange had not gone unnoticed.

It was frustrating for me to see *the others*. They toiled away, making progress yes, but it was easy for their efforts to go unnoticed. This was when we started adding visual shibboleths to our attire. ~~Jeremy~~ Pendragon got the first—a nice patch with a quill and a flourish of ink under its nib. He wore it subtly on his jacket breast, but when asked, he would tell them that he'd got his first Meta-Level in Penmanship.

Spirits waned in *the others*. As our GOLS party grew closer, the rest of the town seemed despondent and lethargic. The grief hit us all differently in that time; it was a brutal thing to face. So many dead, such despair. But where the GOLS brought us together, *the others* were alone. It made my heart ache for them, to know I could help them, but only if they wanted it.

I watched as order fell apart. The town fractured into two sides; one thought that we needed to focus on getting ready for the winter, and the other thought that establishing a communication network with neighboring towns was more important.

Organization was poor, and I agonized to see a duplication of efforts due to lack of coordination. As their spirits plummeted I wished I could just scream at them to fill in a fucking GOLS sheet and to see if it helped. But we weren't a dictatorship; this wasn't DC we're talking about here, we were still trying to function as a democracy.

After the first suicide, we met in the town hall.

~~Mrs. Barsol~~ Jay urged them to adopt the GOLS sheets. We were nearing a tipping point—what percent of a population needs to adopt something before it becomes the norm? I'm not sure what it was before the apocalypse, but after it, when we were rebuilding, I figured it was something like 10 percent. (It turned out that it was much lower—low single digits in most cases; the bigger factor was what *kind* of people were needed to proliferate the spread of the meme.)

At the time of the first suicide, there were fifteen people with GOLS sheets.

Jay's invitation got another three after that somber meeting, but it was a dark, dark time.

Over the following days, Al was able to pull some of the older people in slowly. I think he lured them with the idea that *it was good for the kids,* knowing that they'd see the benefit once they got going as well.

The twenty-somethings and thirty-somethings were easiest, but I'm not sure if that was just because of the age range of our core group. Like follows like, and we had a leg up with those ages to begin with.

I mean, it still wasn't easy. There were a lot of naysayers.

"Quit wasting time," they said as I pulled out my GOLS to fill in a point in Fuel Management. We'd been gathering firewood all day, and that was important.

"Just counting my XP in Fuel Management," I said. "Oh man, I'm going to level up tonight!" I said; my excitement was genuine. We had picked titles for the various level ranges, and I was about to cross the threshold from *Scribe* to *Acolyte*. "Hurrah for Fuel Management!" I said, cheering myself. Giving it such a serious name appealed to some, even if my antics were somewhat absurd, and that evening I managed to get two of "the older ones" to fill in GOLS.

Each night we met at the town hall and had a brief powwow. We'd announce any new members and they were encouraged to tell us their 5 Specials.

Always the day after, we made sure that the new recruits got asked about their GOLS. Always binding together, always propping each other up. It was of course all subjective—how do you decide how much XP to give yourself for any given task? Because it was left to us to be our own judges, sometimes adjustments had to be made. Don't misunderstand though: adjustments were always made to *increase* XP. We were hard on ourselves. If we saw someone had done a good job and had not really awarded themselves an appropriate amount of XP, we'd sort it out that evening, thus recognizing their efforts in front of the group.

The tipping point happened when a reconnaissance party arrived back from scouting—Vancouver was a short boat ride away, and we wanted to know how things were going down in the big city. The runners talked to us in the town hall, and they seemed chagrinned at their findings. They introduced someone from Vancouver, a forty-something with silver on his temples and a military jacket. Under several medals on his breast I saw a peculiar patch, one of a fist holding a hammer against a lightning bolt.

"I'm told," he said in an authoritative voice, "that someone once known as TreeBeardTopiary lived here." My heart leapt and I rose to my feet.

"That's my username on—" I started, but decided to keep it simple; "that's me," I finished simply.

"Well son, most of Vancouver is using GOLS sheets now, and I understand we have you to thank for it."

Pretty much everything he said after that was just his mouth moving and this crazy ringing in my ears; I could not fathom such success of GOLS as he was telling us about. He motioned for me to come up on stage and when I didn't respond right away, Pendragon had to give me a push forwards. All the sound came back into my world then and I heard him saying something about foresight and leadership.

I joined him up there and he pulled a patch from his pocket and pinned it to my jacket breast. It was an icon of two hands shaking against a target background.

"This young man's ideas are saving lives and helping rebuild the world. If y'all want to get with the program, you'll find that you're playing with the big kids. And now if you'll excuse me, I do believe I just leveled up in Diplomacy," he said. He held his hand up expectantly and I only hesitated for a minute before I high-fived him.

The town hall didn't know what to do at first.

Jay signaled to our party to get going though, and we circulated through the crowd with GOLS sheets.

Jeremy had been making copies diligently the whole time we had been struggling to make it happen, and they finally saw the light of day.

It was successful beyond my wildest dreams. I know it wasn't used everywhere, but it was widespread enough that most everyone at least *knew* about it.

Pendragon and I went back to Vancouver with the General, and from there we traveled the country.

Together we developed the GOLS achievement standardization. Certain cities had local variants. I couldn't have anticipated most of the ones that had to be created on the fly; how could I have known there'd be a need for a Wolf Defense patch, but goddamn if some of the northern locations didn't need one. They adapted, and, as we grew old in the world as we rebuilt it, I got to see so many wonderful level-ups.

There was an achievement patch for damn near everything, and the most prized were the ones that told everyone that you'd helped in a big way.

Not everyone used GOLS; in some cities, people used it as a secret religion, pumping up their stats in silence as they worked alongside people that didn't understand how their motivations had been honed and crafted, but who understood they were working with a seriously dedicated individual.

You know someone was a gamer from the Before Time because their GOLS sheet is likely framed on their wall. Or maybe it's still in use, tucked away in their pocket, still getting levels in Masonry, Salvage, or Barter.

By 2050, (there will be) more plastics (in the ocean) than fish (by weight).
—The Ellen MacArthur Foundation's
"The New Plastics Economy"

<Transcription excerpt begins.>

Blanche: We now convene the special meeting of Rebuilding World Government Special Think Tank, at Bibliothèque de Genève, Prom. des Bastions 1, 1211 Genève 4, Switzerland. Regular Presiding Officer, Anne Blanche, is present, as is the Secretary, Marta Levison.

We open the floor to the reading and discussion of the vision statement of one of the New World-Wide Population Control Act proposals, as read by Dr. Rose Betrand, head of Analytics, New Population Control Committee, PhD of Population Ecology.

Dr. Betrand: Thank you. I'll get right to it. The census takers have done their great work, and all over the world experts like myself have determined the best course of action. We have had to extrapolate for some parts of the world where data is not reported, but we are confident in our conclusions.

Before the pandemic, world population was approaching eight billion. Now our best estimates place us around seven hundred million. We are not in danger of going extinct. We have been given a great opportunity here, an opportunity to shape the human race with intention, with awareness to our numbers.

Two-thirds of the survivors are of reproductive age. The rest are too old. None are too young.

We are left with 200 million women to reproduce.

Of course this issue brings up the very contentious issue of eugenics, and I'm prepared to—

Dr. Rasmusen: Are any of us really prepared to—

Blanche: Please sir, the chair asks that you keep your comments until after the—

Dr. Betrand: No it's all right, let's hear it.

Blanche: The chair recognizes Chloe Rasmusen, "Reverse Eugenics and the Split of Homo Sapiens Sapiens" paper co-author, PhD of Population Ethics.

Dr. Rasmusen: It doesn't have to be evil, we have a real shot at doing something great for the future of humanity here.

Dr. Betrand: Doctor, tell us then, who would you propose we, as you put it in your paper, bail out of the gene pool, remove from the breeding population?

Dr. Rasmusen: Breeding as a human right is utter nonsense—look where it got us! The numbers don't lie! If this insomnia hadn't taken us down as much as it did we would have continued to destroy ourselves. Eight billion people! 1.6 billion cows, over a billion sheep and even more pigs! We ate the oceans dry, we fucked the planet for future generations of people, all of who would have the right to pop out as many babies as they wanted, without regard for if they could afford them, if society could afford them, if the earth could support them.

Blanche: Doctor, please calm yourself or I'll have to ask you to leave. Get to your point.

Dr. Rasmusen: My point is that our worst were outbreeding our best, that we were practicing eugenics in reverse, where the brightest, most capable people were choosing not to have children. We have seen what that does, and we know it's unsustainable.

Getting us to agree on just how many humans the earth can support is damn near impossible. It was *the* issue of our time, bigger than climate change, and yet, we couldn't talk about it. Because telling people they can't have a baby is a *human rights violation!* Pft, please. Motherfuckers, *having* a baby should have been a human rights violation!

Blanche: Doctor, you'll have to sit down now please. We will hear more from Rose Betrand, on the New World-Wide Population Control Act.

Dr. Betrand: Thank you. Dr. Rasmusen has some very good points, and I do not disagree with anything she is saying. You can imagine it was very frustrating to be in our field when humanity was headed that direction. Every person exists solely to make more people. We'll have to ascend to a higher level of being, have to overcome millions of years of primal, base programming to make this work. We're going to have to be masters of our fate now.

The human race has a second chance. If we use our heads, if we are careful about this, we can get ourselves under control.

This all supposes that everyone is going to play along . . . Which they won't, I know. There will be war again. There will be noncompliance. My hope is that we get enough of humanity on board with The Act that they can effectively police the rest.

So my proposed core of The Act is this: reproduction is no longer a human right. We do not get to decide that we can have a baby as an individual any more.

How do we accomplish this without a travesty of corruption? I know, right? It's not going to be perfect, but we have to try, damn it we have to try.

At first, it's going to be easy. The survivors will hardly be curbed at all. It's the future generations that will be affected, but they won't know any other way, will they? We have to set a good example. We have *such* an opportunity here.

I have laid out The Act in three phases, and they are as follows:

Phase 1: Every female survivor who wants to have babies can have up to four babies. If there are women who cannot have a baby, they may enlist the help of one who can. If any woman gives up her child in this manner, they are permitted to have more than the allotted four children, to a maximum of eight. The children they give up are not their own—they are considered the children of their adopted parents in every way, but the children will be openly told of their parentage, their genetic heritage, and made aware of any such siblings they have. This first wave of babies are part of Generation 0, the rebooting of the human race.

Efforts are to be made to inform them of their fathers. If in doubt, multiple people must be included in the family tree.

Phase 1, Subsection A: Keeping family trees is compulsory. We must be careful here; we cannot inbreed. People must travel around and spread genetic diversity. Moving cities every few generations perhaps. Something to get the human race spread around, something to homogenize us and prevent some repetition of inbred small-town population problems from the past. It might not be a problem with millions and millions of us still living in urban areas, but many small towns have been reduced to only a few dozen, and it's for them and their future generations that the Family Tree must make a comeback. Iceland showed us the way in the Before, perhaps we can use their app.

We don't need to figure that out just yet though. Right now it's all about the numbers.

If we account for some women not wanting babies, and other women receiving babies from Giving Mothers, as we're calling them, we go from two hundred million women, having four babies each, to the first generation, the first actual distinct generation in human history, having eight hundred million children. This brings our population up from 750 million, to, let's round some more, double that—1.6 billion.

Phase 2: Generation One, as we are calling it, may have as many as *three* children. Rules from the Survivor Generation apply: any that cannot have babies and desire them, may work with another woman to have children.

So 1.6 billion x 1.5 = 2.4 billion people.

Then we move into Phase 3: Maintenance Mode, the true test to see whether humanity is ready to grow up and take responsibility. Generation Two is permitted to have two children, and *only* two children. Same rules apply for people wanting children but who are unable to reproduce. Womb max occupancy limit is set at eight.

If we're lucky, we'll be 2.4 billion people.

Look, it's not like we're saying who can have the babies and who can't. We could try and eliminate a host of genetic diseases. Now's the best time to try. I'd love to try. Shall we play that game for a minute? Dr. Rasmusen, would you join in the discussion again for a moment please?

Dr. Rasmusen: Thank you, Doctor. I have a wish list ready, of course, but hear me out before you drag me away. What would the perfect human race be? What rules would we have to enforce? People with congenital heart defects may not reproduce. People with family history of severe mental illness may not reproduce. People with autism-spectrum disorders in their family, people with diabetes, blind people, deaf people, people whose families have a history of dying earlier than age seventy. Any condition we know to be genetically inherited can be weeded out in a single glorious generation.

Would there be anyone left to reproduce at all?

We can't do it.

In an ideal world, we'd leave the breeding up to the best and brightest of us. The paragon of human genetics, those with the smartest brains and fewest genetic defects, would sire the future of human kind.

Some places, this is happening. Some places are perhaps a braver, newer world than the rest of us.

But the plan the world over, to avoid too big a rights-shock, is the one Dr. Betrand just gave you.

Babies for everyone. Anyone who wants them.

Blanche: Thank you Dr. Rasmusen. Dr. Betrand, please continue.

Dr. Betrand: Indeed, at first, babies for everyone. Anyone who wants them. And then *by god* we will curb our reproduction. We will not destroy ourselves this time. We will make this plan as a species and we will *follow* it, and we will grin and bear it.

Every child born in the After will have it taught to them how it was in the Before. The problems of overpopulation. The way we wrecked the earth in ways that they will still be able to see and feel.

Maybe they'll have a restored version of earth to grow up in—all the wild stocks of fish that were going extinct because of us can bounce back. In twenty years, in forty years, maybe the animal systems we were collapsing will be able to recover.

They might grow up and see that everything's fine. *Look at all the goddamn cod, there's enough to support more.*

No. No there isn't. We thought that before. Don't be us, Generation One, and Generation Two, don't you *dare* think that you're better than your grandparents. The Survivor Generation has survived the insomnia, yes, but they are also the survivors of humanity's previous life. You don't know what it was like. Seeing species after species wink out of existence because we wanted to eat them. Because they lived in places where other things we wanted to eat could make themselves fat for us. Because we liked some part of their anatomy either to look at or to consume. Because we thought the ocean was an inexhaustible cornucopia of fish and shellfish and crustaceans. We wiped out whole systems without even batting an eye. This is simply what happened. Just, *oh well, the white rhino went extinct today*—if we even noticed at all. Did any of you even notice?

Dr. Rasmusen: Do you know where our oxygen comes from, for fuck's sake?!

Dr. Betrand: The ocean is our life and we need to drill these facts into the heads of every child born in the After.

The biologists need to get on it, get on documenting how things bounce back. Our food strategies need to be planned by scientists that know about interactions within food chains. We must not go back to the old food model either, but that's not my area of expertise. Insects will be the new protein, and I don't mind—I enjoy cricket tacos every now and then, and they're quite tasty.

And in that same time, the technology around reproduction will be a major focus; the reversible vasectomy and reversible tubal ligation are a top priority, and may very well be ready for when Generation One reaches the age of reproduction. Maybe by then, we can come to an agreement on if reversible sterilization should be mandatory.

By the time you get The Act published, I may well be dead, killed in a better-executed car bomb (I had a scare with one last week), or lamely shot through the head by someone upset that I'm trying to tell them what to do in their bedroom.

Dr. Rasmusen: This notion of privacy has got to go, too. On the plus side, now that it's okay to let your opinions about having children out and made heard, people are doing so. Anyone that is on the side of The Act is loud about it, just as loud as the moronic idiots that think they should be allowed to have a dozen mewling larva to make them happy.

Blanche: Please Doctor, let her finish.

Dr. Rasmusen: We're going to see war, the breeders and I.

Nations' armies will split in half, just as the public is doing. And the rest of the world will annihilate the breeders before they let you spread your idiot seed beyond what you're allotted.

Think of your children. Think of the future of the human race!

Blanche: Doctor, that's quite enough. Please be seated.

Dr. Betrand: Because we're set on this. Maybe it won't be my plan that gets enacted, but one of them will be. One way or another, now is the time to take charge of our future, as a species, as a united human race.

Dr. Rasmusen: If you want to live on this planet, you will get in line, and you will have your four babies, and then you will stop, or one day you will find yourself with a rope around your neck, a hood over your head, thrown in the back of a van. And when you wake up, you will not have ovaries any more. If you are very, *very* lucky, you will have a bottle of pain killers in your pocket to help you with the recovery.

Blanche: Dr. Rasmusen, any further interruptions from you will result in your ejection from this conference.

Dr. Betrand: We are all in this together. Look here, how fun it will be to have a defined generation. All the parents working with children who are all the same age. What a marvelous opportunity to study childhood development in such segmented generations. Will the oldest siblings become the leaders by default?

The first children born in the After are going to be spoiled little brats, no doubt about it.

As long as they get it into their head about just how many children they're allowed to have. They are the lucky ones. The last generation of people born who will be allowed to increase the population. After them, with Generation Two, Maintenance Mode only. Two per.

That's all that matters now.

It's a numbers game, and we have numbers enough to destroy ourselves again. We can't let it happen.

We have to try.

Blanche: The Rebuilding World Government Special Think Tank thanks Dr. Betrand for her reading of the vision statement of her proposal for the New World-Wide Population Control Act. Further proposals will follow a one-hour lunch. Meeting adjourned.

<Transcription excerpt provided by Bibliothèque de Genève.>

Loners don't have a chance! Party up, join a group, help your neighbors. Together, we can get through this!
—Propaganda fliers plastered all over Seoul, South Korea

I don't know why you asked for my story. We didn't see any of the riots. We weren't part of any of the brave things that happened during The Longest Day. We didn't do anything special, except survive. If that's why, as in, you need a tale of people simply *surviving*, then things are worse than I thought. Anyways, here we go.

I know it's a huge coincidence, but when you think of all the crazy shit that happens at university, and all the silly, insane things friends do together, it's not actually that farfetched that my friends and I had made a bet to see who could stay awake the longest, beginning on the very night that the insomnia plague began.

There were five of us, and we were the kind of friends that everyone in the world wishes they could have. When we showed up at parties, we had the attention of everyone there. Not because we looked (or were) cool, but because we had each other and loved each other so fiercely, that we were these lighthouses showing the way for anyone brave enough to stare at the beam and see the land.

Haha, when they read this they're going to laugh at me. But you know it guys, we were all that, and more. Everyone wanted us, wanted to be us or be near us. I'm glad we were able to keep it just us five though. Any more and it would have upset the balance.

Alec, Taikla, Jim, Zoey, and I—going to concerts, museums, camping, on all sorts of adventures together. The perfect team. Also the perfect survival group.

So it was five of us.

They all had their areas of interest which they shared with the group, and I was sort of the wild card. A jack-of-all-trades. I was the one phoning them up just as they were getting ready for bed, asking if they knew where we could find a shop that rented costumes at such an hour, and if they'd ever seen the movie *Eyes Wide Shut*. Sometimes they followed me on wild adventures, sometimes I was off on my own. Which was all right by me. I loved them, but I think I was keen to do way more than they were prepared to. Once you settle down, you're not so quick to put yourself out there all the time. Jim and Taikla were together, and Alec and Zoey got together not long into starting school. I was still looking for the right person, so I kept on heading to strange social functions, meeting new people, searching out that one that would turn our group of five into an even half dozen.

It was exhausting.

After a few years and several failed relationships, it was getting me down.

After a week containing not one but *three* dates that failed in spectacular fashion, Taikla saw me waning first. It was board games day, and she saw that I was one step behind in the build cue, my galactic domination strategy taking a severe hit due to my ineptitude. She noticed, yes, but took no mercy, sending a formidable fleet into my home sector and squashing my resource production.

It was like she used it as a diagnostic. My reactions to her invasion told her my mood, and my retreat into a neighboring quadrant told her that things were perhaps more dire than she had guessed. As the glue that bound the group together, she dove headfirst into my mood and how to help me.

"All right then," she said out of nowhere, after the game, "I propose a group adventure. We've got reading break coming up, and I think we need to do something epic. Not epic like, climb a mountain," she said, silencing Alec before he had a chance to suggest just such an adventure, "I mean epic like, like something cool, as a group."

"Crash the masquerade party in the English Properties," suggested Zoey.

"Sneak into the art gallery and tape googley eyes to every piece in that boring statue exhibit," suggested Jim.

"Stay awake as long as we can," said Alec. We had no answer to that; no further suggestions were meted out, while we mulled it over.

"The longest anyone's ever gone is eleven days," he continued, leaving a strategic length of silence before he spoke next. He'd thought about this before. "I bet we could do it."

"I'd miss the first class of my Paleobotany 304 class, but that's the only one. Friday, Saturday, Sunday, Monday," said Taikla, counting on her fingers. When she got to the second Monday, she had ten fingers up, plus one, provided by Alec. "We could do it."

"Is everyone cool to take the Monday off?" I asked.

"This is preposterous," said Zoey. "There's no way we can do it. Eleven days? You know how frickin' long that is?"

Oh Jesus, Zoey, we did not.

But the idea had been planted, and the more we thought about it, the more we talked about it, the more insane it seemed, but also the more fun.

"Even if we don't manage to go all eleven days, let's just see how far we get," said Zoey, hoping to reign in our insane plan.

"We could all put a twenty into a jar; last one awake gets it," suggested Taikla.

"Eleven days or bust," countered Alec, defiance and determination writ large across his face.

Hah! Can you imagine if we'd started earlier? What if we had been awake for eleven days and then finally gave in to go to sleep, and found that we couldn't, that no one could. Maybe that happened to someone. But not us, *thank gods* not us.

We added an extra layer to the challenge: Taik and Jim were going to make the apartment a *cold spot*, as in, disconnect us from the outside world. No internet. And their place was already shit for cell reception. We decided that we would withdraw from the world, and only reemerge when we had slept, like some sort of monkish retreat, a vow of internet silence. I was almost more impressed that we managed *this* portion of the plan as long as we did. We were all pretty connected, pretty used to being plugged in and having our feeds constantly updated with everything we put in them.

So we had to become an island. Or maybe just shipwrecked on one. With a huge store of food and things to entertain us. Yeah right, a shipwreck, roughing it, sure.

Taikla was in charge of movies. We gave her requests, and she mustered them for us. TV shows too. All on her laptop, rented from iTunes or borrowed from people's Blu-ray collections, or downloaded, when neither of those options worked. We had two hundred and sixty-four hours to fill, and we wanted to have a library of viewing choices to keep us soothed while we embarked upon our insane idea. We decided collectively on a few series to burn through. Can eat up a lot of time with a back catalog of TV shows like we had.

I was in charge of field trips. Outings at regular intervals, which I arranged in order of ones we'd need our wits about us for, to ones we could bumble through without a brain in our head. Each night there was something to go to. Of course after the plague hit, a wrench was thrown into many of my planned outings, but ah well.

Alec was in charge of walks. We figured a great way to stay awake was going to be to walk. He planned tours all over the city for us. He also put them in order of most challenging to least, so when we were at our most enthusiastic at the beginning, we'd be able to tackle the harder ones, and as we waned, we'd have easier and easier routes.

Zoey was in charge of food. She had meals all planned out for us, and snacks and drinks and everything. We figured we could be trusted to operate a stove for the first three or maybe four days, but then after that, we knew we'd be pretty poorly off, and so she planned cold meals. Thank Christ she was such a good cook; if it had been me, I'd've lobbied for more order-in stuff. But that would have got us nowhere fast, after it hit. As it stood, we had at least eleven days' worth of meals, and when we figured out how dire everything was, we made it last.

Jim was in charge of music. We were going to force ourselves to get up and move if we felt the sleep taking us, and dance music was key. He spent a while loading up an iPod with playlists that would keep us awake. Or, that was the plan anyway.

So the day before it hit, our Day One, everyone else's normal day, we mustered. Taikla and Jim were hosting us. They had a small apartment, but their couch was comfortable and their kitchen table was good for board games. I sat on the couch, Zoey and Alec on either side of me, and Jim lay on the floor on a throw pillow. Taikla's laptop was hooked into their big TV, and she knelt in front of it like a holy relic, scrolling down an extensive list of scheduled movies and shows.

I handed out the list of the field trips. Alec gave out eleven sheets of paper to each of us, each with a different route in red snaking through the city. Zoey handed us our meal schedule, with a list of "any time" snacks and beverages. And Jim waggled his iPod at us.

Taikla made a blog post announcing our epic plan. We took a single group photo to kick it off, with a mountain of pop, juice, chips, and other such junk behind us, taking up the entire space in front of Jim and Taik's wall of bookshelves. After she made the post, she disconnected the router and put it in the closet.

Eleven days. Five best friends. Games, movies, music, activities, fun, and each other.

Boy oh boy, were we in for it.

That night, we didn't sleep. We felt pretty energized, actually. We went out to a Bike Rave, sometimes standing on the sidelines and watching the colorful show, sometimes joining in when the music got just too good. We went on one of Alec's walks, which took us through China Town, under that beautiful old-style dragon arch, and wove our way east, alongside the industrial corridor that led us back to Taikla and Jim's. There, we put on the first episode of *Deadwood*. After it was through, we constructed the most epic personal pizzas that have ever been made.

Alec's was a tower of meat.

Mine had neat concentric rings of three kinds of mushrooms. (Zoey, you shut your face; mushrooms on pizza are the best) (that's just how we roll; we picked up a lot of phrases from the cartoons we watched, the shows and comedians we all loved; if it seems mean, it isn't. Like I said: it's just how we roll. You know I love you, dollface.)

Jim had pretty much a smattering of every single ingredient available.

Taik had a pretty standard Hawaiian-Canadian (which, for those of you not in the know, is ham, pineapple, bacon, and mushrooms, with a drizzle of maple syrup).

Zoey did a pretty mean Mediterranean.

The pizzas were for that meal and the next, and we each swapped a few slices to try each other's. Another episode of *Deadwood*, and another.

We played some Battleblock Theatre, passing off the controller when it was time to switch players. Then we decided to get old school, and Taik set up Jim's old Super Nintendo. *Super Mario Kart* lasted a couple of hours.

More pizza. More *Deadwood*.

We didn't really start to feel tired until that evening.

And because we were off in our own little world, we didn't know what was going on. We didn't realize that we weren't the only ones that hadn't slept last night. Haha, we felt so accomplished.

It was the middle of the second night when we hit The Wall. Well, not all of us, and not all at once. I hit it first. My energy plummeted. The world seemed dull and stupid. I wanted nothing to do with it. I dragged my feet as we walked home along a route that Alec had planned for us, away from an admittedly fun free concert in the city's largest park.

"Come on Rug-Doug, let's get the lead out here. No moping. Night number two is no time to let your head hang down." Ah, Zoey. She didn't hit *her* wall until the third night, also on the walk home. But by then I had picked back up, and managed to retort with "Slowy-Zoey, what's the down low-ey. Come on come on, no time to be dragging your heels here."

So we managed to hit our strides and our lows at different times, helping each other through those first days, those days when we were just friends embarking upon a silly but epic undertaking.

"How is it possible that we need sleep this badly?" said Jim, after another episode of *Deadwood*. "My god. I mean, I never really thought about it before." His eyes sort of bugged out of his head as he stared at the wall, focusing on nothing, the edges of his world starting to get rough. "Like," he continued, "everyone that has a shitty night's sleep thinks, *Oh man, sleep is super important*. But I mean, *this* important? We're dying here—" (it's ok Jim, you didn't know, you didn't know) "—and after only four nights? I don't really see us making it, guys."

We'd been living in a bubble. Games, movies, anonymous outings, and walks. That night, we'd walked past a pretty major car crash, and it had shaken us up, but we had no idea that it was one of the many that were happening all over the globe due to the sudden saturation of tired, inept drivers, making errors, killing themselves and anyone in their path when they made their mistake. We were Shaun in *Shaun of the Dead*, at the beginning of the film, when he's just out to get milk or whatever, and oblivious to zombies that are all around him, mayhem on every street corner.

We watched an *X-Files* episode called "Sleepless," and cued up another. When the opening credit music hit, Taikla snatched the remote from my hand and paused it on the final shot of the opening credits sequence.

"You guys," she said with dire seriousness, "*The X-Files* slogan is 'The Truth is Out There,' right?" said Taikla. It plainly was, paused on the big screen for us all to see. We looked at her, puzzled at her non sequitur, but curious as to where it was going.

"Guys, it doesn't just mean that it's out there, like it exists and they'll *find* it, it means that the truth is out there, like farfetched. *Out there.*" We stared at Taikla for a moment.

"Daaaayyyyuuuuummmmmm," was Jim's first reaction.

"Sheeit," said Alec.

"Someone has literally been waiting, like, twenty years for us to get that," said Zoey, laughing.

"We sound like a bunch of frickin' stoners," I said.

"Hold up," said Taikla, looking at the window, where the blinds were drawn for a better TV-watching experience.

"You hearing things already?" asked Jim.

He'd made us a little timeline, of what symptoms we might expect at what points in our endeavor to stay awake. He'd put it on the fridge. We had our own colors of magnets to move around on it when we started experiencing things on the timeline; so far, the only magnets on it were each of the five colors, stuck to "way tired." Auditory hallucinations were not blocked in until after five nights, and this was the morning of our third night without sleep, so it *was* early for Taik to be hearing things.

By then though, sound was different. Their fridge was driving me mad. The hum of their lights got louder. When the bathroom fan was on it was like a jet engine next to my ear. Our filters were crumbling, and sound was one of the first things to get to us. We sort of lost selective hearing, so every sound started to be as loud as every other sound. During that last *X-Files* episode, I found myself squinting at the TV, as though it would help me focus on listening better, and hear it past the madness that the fridge was driving me to.

But that's not what was going on with Taikla. She threw open the blinds and opened the window, and then we heard it too.

The riots around the world started at different times, but for us, it was that morning after the third night. We saw a few small pillars of smoke rising in the distance, cars on fire, probably.

"Get the router plugged in," said Jim urgently. We went into a sudden panic; we had been unplugged for a mere four days and suddenly we felt like we had been blinded.

We waited impatiently for the green lights of the router to signal that we had a connection. We jumped on our devices; Jim, myself, Zoey, and Alec on laptops, Taikla on her and Jim's iPad. We surfed for five minutes and it became apparent that the shit was going down. We spread out, covering different news sources, and called out headlines and important facts as we found them.

Taikla delved into what could be causing it. Alec covered news overseas, Zoey and Jim covered Canada and the US, and I went local.

"There's still air traffic," said Alec with disbelief. "No one in the world has slept for three nights, and they're flying planes full of people," he said, his hands shooting up to his head and grasping fistfuls of hair in frustration.

"Anything on the Texas power grid has gone dark. Jesus, how long until we lose power?" asked Zoey.

"I'm on it," I said.

We chopped away at our keyboards. Hours went by. We hunched lower and lower down, the weight of the disaster settling onto us with each headline, each YouTube video, each news segment.

"Shit, we have to eat. And shower. And we need to do other stuff after; we need to prepare better," said Taikla.

"We'll need more water," said Zoey.

"No Zo, it'll rain, we'll have water," said Alec. "What we'll need is food. And meds; it looks like people with ADD spectrum disorders are faring much better, because they have meds. Doug, you still know a guy?"

"I do."

"Stop stop," said Zoey. "I mean yes you're right, but *right now* we need food and water and to shower. We need to keep it together. Pace ourselves. Taik, go have a shower. Jim, come help me make some food. Doug, Alec, drink a liter of water, and then wash out that big Rubbermaid bin that's in the hall, and the lid, and fill it with water like your life depends on it. Add a cap full of bleach from under the sink."

We didn't argue. It felt good to have direction. I wanted to keep going on the net, but she was right: we had to take care of ourselves.

In the end, that's what saved us. We had regular times for bathing, eating, drinking, resting. We kept to a pretty rigid schedule, because we'd had one drawn up before it all went down. Instead of the concerts and outings that I had planned, instead there were blocked-in scouting missions and supply runs.

It was deadly serious, but it was something we'd spent time talking about before. Well, sort of. In the zombie apocalypse, which of these mid-rise apartments would have the most food to pilfer? Which of them would be the most dangerous to us if they were on fire? Which of them would make a good fallback position? What if alien invaders could hear but not see? What if gravity suddenly inverted? What if, what if. We had talked about a ton of apocalypse scenarios; now that we were living one, we knew what we were doing. Theoretically. Sort of.

Well of course there were no zombies, but a lot of the things were the same.

It's not like we didn't believe it at first; we all tried to go to sleep that evening, just to see. Until we did that, it wasn't quite real. Even when we turned our phones back on and they called their moms and dads (cell service was still available then; thank god we caught it before it went out or they wouldn't have been able to say—).

I had no one to call. Everyone I loved and cared about was with me, or rather just below me, out on the sidewalk at the intersection to get cell reception.

I leaned on the windowsill and watched my friends talk to their loved ones. Hands covering mouths. Tears being brushed away. Heads nodding as they listened to the advice of the ones who cared about them more than anything. Being watched over by the one who had only them.

When they came back inside, it still didn't seem quite plausible. It was preposterous, it was unbelievable. Of course, we only had to experience a single night to make it real.

As we lay awake in Jim and Taikla's apartment, trying to fall asleep, waiting the whole night to be sure, *then* we knew it was real. When we convened and had breakfast the next morning, we knew, and we carried on with our survival plan.

Jim and I set out to the supermarket near the train station.

Yeah right, us and the whole of East Vancouver. Jesus. It wasn't like it was all ghetto to begin with, with like, those metal things that slide down over doors and windows. It was unprotected, and the whole front entrance was smashed. It was mostly quiet, but I'd guessed the bulk of the looting had already happened there. The lights were out. Aisles were strewn with things. Flashlight beams scanned all around. The occasional whispering could be heard. There were a few people inside, taking whatever they wanted.

Jim looked at me and shrugged.

"Gotta do what you gotta do," he said.

We went in and took what we could, filling the backpacks we'd brought.

Back at the apartment, as soon as we got in, Zoey bared the way and handed me a towel.

She pointed at the shower.

"Yes'm," I said cheekily, but glad to have a bit of quiet after the stress of being out in the world, looting. Looting? Jesus. It's not like we were taking electronics; just whatever food we could find. I think that's different. I hope it's different.

It was a full three days of that. Supply runs, gathering information, preparing.

Alec set up containers on the roof of the apartment to catch rain water.

Jim and Taik's bedroom was converted: we tipped the bed up on its side and shoved it against the wall. The room became a walk-in closet, full of supplies and food.

So yes, three days of coming to the realization that the world was in a heap of trouble.

But then, then we needed a break. After a run one night, Jim and I came back to the apartment, exhausted, to the smell of roasting turkey.

Taikla, Zoey, and Alec were sitting at a beautifully set table. There were candles. There was a pretty good spread; mashed potatoes, cranberry sauce, roasted veggies, gravy, and a huge turkey.

That's when I cried.

Everyone had their own highs and lows. This was strange; for me, it was both a high and a low at the same time. Everything felt awful; my ears were being assaulted by that damn fridge, and the hum of the lights, my eyes were scratchy and raw, and I'd had a headache for two days. But there were my best friends, sitting at this beautiful table, which was full of food.

It was a different sort of wall to hit, and I hit it hard. By the time Taikla got me into a chair at the table, I was wracking with sobs. Taikla rubbed my back, a soothing palm traveling up and down and back and forth. My head was in my hands, my fingers pressed into my eyes as though they could stem the flow of tears. When I finally wiped them I saw a plate of steaming turkey before me, that Alec had put together for me, with a little pat of butter on the mashed potatoes just the way I like, and I lost it again.

When I say everything was raw, this was part of it. All the layers of facade and defenses had been stripped away with each sleepless night. There was no filter for external things, smells, sounds, but also no filter for emotions. Once the dam burst, I was pretty wrecked.

"Taik," I managed to finally get out, "eat. Eat. I'll be fine. This looks amazing," I said. "You all look amazing," I said, bringing a fresh wave of raw emotion bubbling out of me.

We all broke that way, at some point or other.

And we helped each other through it.

So did the drugs.

We did get meds like we had talked about. I still knew a guy. He was busier than ever. Cost us a pretty penny. But we got 'em. Got 'em before they were all gone.

And once we knew what to look for, we started checking medicine cabinets for all the things that would keep us awake, that would energize us. We were careful with those though; we'd seen the video of what happens when someone takes too many uppers. Seen videos of people running through the streets with mortal wounds, as though they couldn't feel them. We didn't want to be them. We wanted to hole up in Jim and Taikla's apartment and weather the storm.

At first, we took uppers all together, so we could all be a sort of pretend version of our normal selves, and have the energy to do things together. But as the crisis wore on and *on*, we decided, in one of these lucid, drug-induced waking times, that we should ration them even more. Only *one* of us had to be competent, and could care for the other four. We drew up a schedule of who would take what meds when, and indeed, the system worked. There was always one of us firing on most cylinders, leading the group. And we rotated who it was. Slipping in and out of lucidity near the end was only made bearable by whoever was "on watch" and helping us through it. Feeding us. Guiding us around, sitting us in front of the TV. Rubbing our backs soothingly.

When the energy got low, and I mean low, like *zero* motivation to do anything, we worried that it might be the precursor to becoming Starers. So we tried to do more things together. The supply runs had all but ceased, so we stayed in and stayed together.

We watched more TV, seemingly endless TV. We burned through *Deadwood* like it was nothing. That Swedgin guy was just about the best character I've ever seen. Until we started watching *Battlestar Galactica*, and then by god I wished Admiral Adama was there with us to tell us what to do.

That's when Jim hit his wall. I guess Adama reminded him of his dad. He actually fell forwards off of the couch and onto the floor, arms curling around his head, and cried. We paused the show and weren't sure what to do. We put our hands on his back and said soft things to comfort him. Taikla took him into the bedroom and held him until he calmed down. The Wall affected us each differently, but mostly it was a private thing to get through. Once we got through it, though, I knew I was somehow stronger after my turkey-dinner-cry, and Jim, well, Jim seemed at least more stoic, more solid somehow. His eyes had a sort of determination in them after he rejoined us on the couch.

We switched back to *The X-Files* for a while after that. And then *Sons of Anarchy*. Days of television. Days and days. Weeks.

Thank god for BC Hydro. They're the real heroes in all of this; those people that went into work to make sure the power stayed on. How on earth did they manage it? I know hydro lasted way longer, because it didn't really need human intervention, but those poor people who relied on coal: god damn, I don't think we could have lasted without power. *Lights off, power on.* We watched TV, but the five of us were careful not to use what we felt was more than our fair share.

But we had power, and last we did.

And when it did finally go out, we'd stored enough candles and Coleman lanterns to last us.

We played board games by candlelight. Although it wasn't so much playing them as it was *pretending* to play them. We moved through a fog, our brains turning to mush in our heads as we tried merely to exist, make it to the time when it would be our turn to take a pill and feel awake, feel alive. Those times were hard as well though; when it was my turn, I nearly lost it when I became lucid enough to see my friends and how bad they looked.

You probably have a ton of description of what people's faces looked like near the end, when we hadn't slept for weeks and weeks, and it felt like we were dying because we probably were. But all that cosmetic stuff aside, my friends' faces were actually different. Not just the way they looked tired, but something deeper than that. They weren't themselves any more. They were almost blank. Not Staring, thank god, but like, on the teetering verge of not being there anymore. I think that's how a lot of people died; just sort of . . . left. I almost couldn't take seeing them that way, but I tried my best to soldier through it and brought them each out of it for a few moments while the drugs coursed through me and kept me functional.

I held Zoey's face in my hands and looked her right square in the eyes.

"Zoey, I know it's hard but you have to fight it. You have the next turn to take a pill, and then you'll be fine and dandy like me."

"Rug Doug, you look awful," she said.

"I know. But hey, I feel almost human. Hang in there." She nodded.

Taikla had seen the exchange and was waiting to catch my eye. She blinked into existence, her face animating into a dead-tired but lucid impishness.

"Doug," she said seriously. She held up a box, some box of our meagre rations left in the supplies. It was a box of bread crumbs.

"Doug," she said again. "Mother. Fuckin'. Bread crumbs."

"Aw yis," I said. She put the box down and started stacking gaming pieces on the table.

I found Jim and Taikla in the living room, standing face to face with their foreheads pressed together, staring at each other.

"Jim," said Taikla.

"Taik," said Jim.

"Jim."

"Taik."

Over and over again. Back and forth. Saying each other's names. There was no end in sight. I sighed, left them to it, and made food. When it was made, I brought them some and had to interrupt them, pulling them apart and sitting them down on the couch.

"Eat," I said. It's not like it had been months. We weren't gaunt or anything. But their faces were starting to show it, though how much of it was hunger and how much was exhaustion and a deep-rooted terror, I'll never know.

Our walk-in closet of food and supplies was running low, but by then we were nearly dead anyway. We were still trying to stop becoming Starers (though we didn't know what caused that symptom of the plague to manifest, we stuck to our theory that being too inactive could be bad).

But always, we were with each other. We shared meals, what little meals we could cobble together as things ran low and we were just glad we still had Taik's spices to help season whatever meagre grub we could rustle up. At some point or other, some of us, and I won't say who because it could have been any of us, and was *all* of us even if we didn't say it out loud, wanted to end it.

Society was gone. Everything had fallen apart. Fire had taken out part of the east side. Our food stores were nearly depleted, and we had barely enough energy to walk, and no cognitive ability left with which to function as anything other than mindless robots, going through the motions of the schedule we had set out at the beginning, set on repeat when we got to another end of the eleven-day cycle. Whenever we had a pill in our system to pep us up, it was awful to see what was happening. All it would have taken was one of us to not give the next pill to the next person on watch, and we would have sat there and rotted.

But as one of us voiced thoughts of suicide, another was there to reassure, to show the face of love. Even in our state, so far gone that we were no longer ourselves, we could snap out of it for long enough to quell that terrible path.

Other groups killed themselves.

We weren't other groups.

We were in the living room. Taikla and Jim and I were on the couch, Zoey and Alec were on the floor, on a big throw pillow in front of the long-dark television. I think Taik was the one on watch, but I'm not sure.

We had tea-light candles lit, safely in big holders so they could burn down harmlessly.

To avoid staring, we were playing flashlight tag. I had a laser pointer, and the others had LED flashlights from camping, except for Taikla, who had the other laser pointer, a green one that was so bright it almost hurt to look at the dot it made.

The red dot on my laser pointer was holding its own in the corner of the room to the left of the TV. Taikla's green laser was "it," and she was after one of the LED beams, keeping to the roof and walls in the rules we had come to make. No going on posters. No going on bookshelves. Bare walls and ceiling only.

I was watching the green laser dot corner one of those LED spots when I fell asleep.

No warning, no nothing, I just, that was it.

I fell asleep.

I woke up to Jim shaking my shoulder gently.

Taikla, Zoey, Alec, and Jim stood above me. All smiling.

"Hey bud," said Jim, offering me a hand to help me up. "We did it."

"Did, did I just sleep?" I said. My head felt like it had been freed of a great fog, the terrible weight of ineptitude and deplorable mental degradation finally lifted, and I knew that it was over. "You slept, too? We're all, we all—" I stammered. Jim hugged me. And then we were all hugging, one big group hug, at the end of it.

It was a long road ahead of us, but breaking free of it, that feeling of coming out the other side of that terrible, terrible time, was such a high. We went up on the roof together to have a look, and that first sunrise was the most glorious thing any of us had ever seen.

We all cried then, but it wasn't a wall. It was a door.

An afterword from the editor

This is, and will be for a long time, the greatest shared tragedy in human history. No other event has touched the lives of every person on earth, and no disaster has come as close to wiping mankind out of existence as the Insomnia Plague.

I've spent most of the last four years compiling these stories. Not all I collected made it to this book, and there are others which I wish I could have found but are irksomely absent. We've heard whispers of things which no one will talk about. Certainly many more events will come to light; the optimist in me thinks there are more tales of heroism than there are of barbarism, but who can say. Not I; my mental health has taken too great a toll in collecting these stories, and I shall have to leave further archival work to others with a greater fortitude for this gruesome task.

But enough about my weak tolerance for dealing with history. After all, this is not a collection of facts. It was not myself for which I undertook this task.

These tales serve not as a reminder to us—for we will never be able to forget that time, as much as we'd like to. No, not for us who survived. It is for the future generations that this history is written. It seems just absurd enough to slip into myth and legend, to become a story instead of a warning. And we must not let that happen.

So it is for Generations One and Two, and their children and all the children after that, that we must be very clear about this.

We do not yet know what caused it.

We do not yet know if it could happen again.

We were brought so near our extinction completely without warning.

Never forget, and never let the future forget. And for god's sake, don't ever cut the funding into sleep research until we know which beast it was who brought us to the edge of oblivion. Better still, until we know which beast it was who pulled us back *from the brink. Because I'm fairly certain it wasn't any of us here.*

Sleep, and sleep well.

ACKNOWLEDGEMENTS

What a wonderful support I've found in my agent, Beth Campbell, over at Bookends. Beth, your guidance and help throughout this process has been invaluable, and I will forever be grateful to you for adding me to your roster, for making Sleep Over a better novel, and for finding a home for it.

A huge thank you to Cory Allyn, my editor at Skyhorse. Cory, the transformation that Sleep Over went through between when it got to you and when it went to print has been enormous, and I know your influence has made it a better novel.

Thanks to the innumerable people who've talked to me about sleep, and the myriad of specialty topics I needed to know about to get it right. I've informally interviewed so many people for this project; your collective wisdom, experience, and anecdotes helped me form what I hope is a not-too-inaccurate tale of the insomnia apocalypse.

Love to Nerd HQ and the La Fontana crew. What a wonderful place, full of wonderful people. Gian & Co., you helped more than you'll ever know.

When I was struggling to find the right name for this manuscript and playing around with different titles, I have to thank Matthew Sun for having the insight to let me know I'd already found it. The magic may have been inside me all along, but sometimes it takes a good friend to point out the obvious. Thanks Matt.

I have so many good friends who have helped me hone my craft in general, and this novel in particular. Chats we've had about sleep, insomnia, how the world works, and speculative science-fiction digressions have all helped make this book happen.

And before *Sleep Over*, your thoughts on my previous works helped lay the foundation upon which I slowly built a road that let me finally achieve my goal. Thanks for indulging an author, and for being my friend.

And lastly, to Aaron. Our paths may have diverged, but having you walk beside me as I went on this journey was tremendously wonderful. Thank you for all your help along the way.

H. G. Bells's blood type is Maple Syrup, swimming with the microcosm of bits and pieces of projects-on-the-go. She's spent most of her life writing in Vancouver, Canada, but is feeling the call of the wild more and more. She's maxed out her GOLS sheet in "Hot Bath Enjoyment," "Games, subsection: All Sorts," "Tinkering With Entertainment Systems," and "Film Projection." Find her at hgbells.com.